Pra

Aliyah

Temporary Home was so good and entertaining to read;
the characters were full-bodied and I found that I could
identify with them…an excellent read and one that this
reader would recommend without a doubt.
~ Whipped Cream

# Books by Aliyah Burke

*Code of Honour*

A Marriage of Convenience
The Lieutenant's Ex Wife
A Man Like No Other
When Stars Collide

*Kemet Uncovered*

Talios
Devi
Linc
Saffron
Taber
Ashia

*In Aeternum*

Casanova in Training
Harbour of Refuge
Protected by Shadows
Polar Opposites

*Interludes*

Temporary Home
Alone With You
Till We Ain't Strangers Anymore

*McKingley*

All the Wright Moves
The Best Thing Yet

Risky Pleasures
Pure Harmony
Irresistible Forces
Seduction's Dance

*Astral Guardians*

Chasing the Storm
Highlands at Dawn
Fields of Thunder
Branded by Frost
Driven by Night
Moon of Fire

*Keeper of the Stars*

Keeper of the Stars: Part One
Keeper of the Stars: Part Two
Keeper of the Stars: Part Three
Keeper of the Stars: Part Four
Keeper of the Stars: Part Five

*What's Her Secret?*

Preconception

*Single Titles*

Through the Fire
Seducing Damian
Unbreakable Bonds

Temporary Home

ISBN # 978-1-78651-914-6

©Copyright Aliyah Burke 2016

Cover Art by Posh Gosh ©Copyright 2016

Interior text design by Claire Siemaszkiewicz

Totally Bound Publishing

This is a work of fiction. All characters, places and events are from the author's imagination and should not be confused with fact. Any resemblance to persons, living or dead, events or places is purely coincidental.

All rights reserved. No part of this publication may be reproduced in any material form, whether by printing, photocopying, scanning or otherwise without the written permission of the publisher, Totally Bound Publishing.

Applications should be addressed in the first instance, in writing, to Totally Bound Publishing. Unauthorised or restricted acts in relation to this publication may result in civil proceedings and/or criminal prosecution.

The author and illustrator have asserted their respective rights under the Copyright Designs and Patents Acts 1988 (as amended) to be identified as the author of this book and illustrator of the artwork.

Published in 2016 by Totally Bound Publishing, Newland House, The Point, Weaver Road, Lincoln, LN6 3QN, United Kingdom.

No part of this book may be reproduced, scanned, or distributed in any printed or electronic form without permission. Please do not participate in or encourage piracy of copyrighted materials in violation of the authors' rights. Purchase only authorised copies.

Totally Bound Publishing is a subsidiary of Totally Entwined Group Limited.

If you purchased this book without a cover you should be aware that this book is stolen property. It was reported as "unsold and destroyed" to the publisher and neither the author nor the publisher has received any payment for this "stripped book".

Printed and bound in Great Britain by Clays Ltd, St Ives plc

1

# Interludes

# TEMPORARY HOME

# ALIYAH BURKE

# Dedication

To the real life inspiration for Sam. I know you will persevere no matter the obstacles. My life is better for having met you. No matter what anyone says, you are incredible. Thank you for allowing me to be part of your life. I love you. Many thanks to Nancy who encouraged me to write this story, your friendship means the world to me. And to my husband who has always been supportive of my writing. Last and never least, my heartfelt thanks go out to the men and women who serve this country and protect us.
God Bless you!

# Chapter One

"Get the hell out of here, you mangy, good-for-nothing kid! Don't let me catch you around here again."

Samuel Hoch went flying through the air only to land in a partially frozen puddle. Seconds later a splash sprayed his face with icy pellets.

"You do and you'll wish you were dead."

He already did. Sam scrambled towards his bag as the heavy door slammed behind him. The wintery wind swirled around, biting into his skin with vicious tenacity. Fighting back his tears, he tried to get up only to slip and fall again, this time wetting the rest of his thin and worn clothes.

*It isn't fair. Why am I out here?*

"Easy there, son."

Sam stared up in shock to find a tall black man standing there looking down at him. He took in the white hat with the black brim, the blue pants with a blood-red stripe on them—visible from beneath the dark coat—and the shiny shoes. He knew what he'd found. Or rather who had found him. A Marine.

The man extended his hand and it seemed that even the leather of his gloves was spotless.

"I'm fine," he snapped, embarrassed and a bit frustrated.

"No harm in accepting some help." The man's tone never changed. His deep bass rumbled, reminding him of thunder.

Sam reached out slowly, half expecting the hand to jerk away or hit him in the face. Neither happened, and the man lifted him clear of the freezing water with ease. Sam's teeth began to chatter as more of Minnesota's winter wind slammed into him.

"You have anywhere to stay tonight, son?"

Mute, he shook his head as the large man began shrugging out of his coat. Sam was in awe of the uniform and never even moved when the heavy coat was placed on his too-thin shoulders. Immediately he warmed as the wind was blocked. The sleeves were too long and they fell to drag on the snowy ground. All he could think about was how nice it was to no longer be freezing.

"Come on, son. Let's get you to some shelter for the night. Going to get right cold tonight."

He lifted his head and stared up at the imposing figure. If the wind or cold affected him, Sam couldn't tell. The man seemed unbothered by it all. He still hesitated — he'd seen what happened when boys went off with adult men. Those images and screams gave him nightmares.

"I have your things, come along."

He walked beside the now-silent Marine. His smaller steps were weighed down by the heaviness of the wool coat. He didn't mind the heat but he was exhausted and so hungry. At the end of the alley, the man paused and glanced down.

"Name's Dean Richardson."

"Sa...Sam Hoch." The words were painful sliding through cracked lips.

Dean turned left and walked again. "Nice to meet you, Sam."

That was it, all the man called Dean Richardson said as they walked along the snowy streets. It didn't take too long before they were walking up the steps to a large stone church. They didn't go in the front but headed around to the back. There Dean knocked.

Warmth and bright yellow light spilled out when the door was opened. An older man with silvered hair stood there.

"Dean. Good to see you."

"Thank you, Father. I brought someone who needs some help" — a pause — "at least for the night."

Kind blue eyes found him and soon Sam was welcomed

inside. There were about fifteen other boys running around. They all halted in what they were doing and stared at him. He stepped closer to the tall Marine.

"We should have some dry clothes which will fit you. I'm Father Michaels, by the way."

"S...Sam." His teeth still chattered but he was not as cold as he'd been before.

Another gentle smile. "Come along, Sam. You'll feel better dry and with some food in you."

He peered up at Dean who gave an encouraging nod. "Go on, son."

He went and when he returned, Dean was still waiting. His coat, with its muddy and snowy hem, rested beside him on a second chair. His hat sat next to him on the table. Sam couldn't explain his relief at seeing him there. The man spoke to Father Michaels. The light gleamed off his shaved head, creating an even more imposing figure. Still, the brown eyes, which met his were soothing.

Dean approached, gestured him into a chair at the table then sat across from him. "You're going to be okay, son." He reached out his hand, a card extended from his fingers.

Sam took it and read the printed words. Staff Sergeant, Dean Richardson, United States Marine Corps. He didn't know what it all meant but he was glad to have it in his grip. There were also phone numbers on it.

"Work and home. You can call me any time, Sam."

He didn't know what to say and so just blurted something out. "I'm sorry about your coat."

Father Michaels set a plate of food in front of him before disappearing again.

A wide, brilliant grin. "Not to worry. A little dirt never hurt a coat." He got to his feet. "You're safe here, son. Father Michaels is a good man."

After stabbing some of the ham from his plate, he shoved it in his mouth. "Why did you —"

"Don't talk with your mouth full." Dean's reprimand was delivered in an authoritative yet calm voice.

9

He swallowed and tried again. "Why did you help me?"

"Everyone needs help at some point, Sam. Remember that." Dean walked off, slipping on his coat and holding his hat.

Sam watched the man speak with Father Michaels then open the door and step though, simultaneously placing his hat on his head. Then Dean Richardson was gone. And Sam again felt alone.

For the first night in over a month, Sam crawled into a bed, which wasn't made of collapsed cardboard boxes or on a heating grate. His bag of personal belongings was beside him as he snuggled beneath the warm blankets. In his hand he held Dean's card. Too exhausted to remain awake, and confident he was safe, at least for the moment, he succumbed to the sandman's irresistible lure.

"Sam!" a voice called. "Sam!"

*Twenty-seven years later, Washington State*

"Sam!"

He jerked and looked around. A dream, it had only been a daydream. Sam Hoch glanced down at the boy who'd fallen to the deck of the ferry. His mother — at least he assumed it was his mother — pregnant and with a harried expression on her chubby face, hastened to them as fast as she could.

"You okay, son?" he asked, reaching out to help the child up.

He nodded, accepting the assistance. "I was hiding from my mother. What's your name?"

His heart clenched at the innocence the boy had. What would a childhood like that have been like?

"I told you not to run on this ferry, Sam." The mother was out of breath and her expression was concerned.

"I was bored," the child whined.

Sam stood so the woman could have his seat. She accepted and sank heavily beside her now-pouting child. "Thank you," she said. "For helping him and for giving up your seat."

"Everyone needs help at some point." Sam walked away as Dean's words slid from his lips.

Dean. His mentor. His friend. And the man he'd thought of as his father. The reason he was on the ferry from Seattle to Bremerton. Dean was in hospital. He'd been diagnosed with bone cancer and had been undergoing chemo. It hadn't been going well lately and they'd had to stop the chemo and admit him, just to see if they could put some weight back on him and get him strong enough to endure the treatment again. It didn't look promising, though. Nausea churned in his gut at the thought of losing him.

Aside from the Corps, Dean Richardson and Dean's niece had been his only family.

"It is so like the commercial. This man is wearing the same thing."

Sam heard the not-so-hushed whispers behind him and continued to face forward. The boy he'd helped before. The one with the same name.

"You talked to him once, ask him." Another child spoke. "Or are you chicken?"

He knew what was coming. Sure enough, the little boy and his friend popped around him, both bundled up against the winter air off the water. One boy white and one Asian.

"Sir?"

"Can I help you boys?"

They shared a glance before a nudge was exchanged.

"Do you do like the commercial?"

He peered down, knowing that in his dress blues with blood stripes he looked the same as the Toys for Tots Marines on the television advertisement.

"Christmas is almost here," he said. "There's not much time left."

"I know. It's why we need to know."

Their expressions were so hopeful he was hard pressed not to smile. Beyond them he saw the pregnant woman again, her expression even more drawn and full of apology.

11

He gave her a small nod before returning his attention to the boys.

They spoke of the toys they wanted, games and clothes. When the ferry docked at Bremerton, he stared at the boys before going down on one knee. "I'll see what I can do, but remember the most important thing is being with family and those who love you. Help your mom out."

He regained his feet and headed for his truck to disembark.

\* \* \* \*

It wasn't long until he was striding through the Christmas-decorated halls of the hospital. On his desired floor, he strode briskly to the room, cover tucked between left arm and side.

Sam gave a sharp knock before swinging the door open. Four faces turned to meet his entrance and his heart leapt. He recognised only Laila, Dean's youngest niece. She was about his age.

She immediately rose and came to him. There was a smile on her face despite the tears in her eyes. "Sam."

Laila was such a tiny thing, she barely reached his chest. Still, she smelt familiar, like her mother had, like fresh-baked goods. He wrapped his arms around her.

"I'm so sorry, Laila," he murmured just loud enough for her to hear.

"Who are you?" a deep voice demanded.

"Dean, be nice," Laila admonished. "This is Sam."

Although in no rush to let Laila go, he looked until he found the scowling Dean. He appeared a great deal like his father, except for the expression. Dean Jr had anger all over his face.

"The stray?"

Laila's arms tightened around him. Old memories of being unwanted flashed before his eyes and almost dragged him back to being that small scared child.

"That's the one." His response fell casually, as if it didn't

12

bother him to be called a stray.

"And why are you here?" Dean again.

"Enough, Dean." A faint, rasped voice drifted from the bed. "He's here because I asked him to come. Come closer, Sam."

The frailty in the voice made him sad but he obeyed the command. Gently, he placed Laila away from him and approached the bed. He didn't know the others' names but it was something to deal with later. Their faces showed their displeasure, only Laila's was welcoming.

Gone was the large, strapping man who had befriended him that cold night all those years ago. In his place lay a thin man who appeared as if a sneeze would break him. Tears threatened to choke Sam and he furiously fought them off.

Brown eyes, still sharp, met his and a smile filled the wizened face.

"Come."

He walked around the bed until he could see the door, Laila and the other three.

"Yes, sir?"

Dean took his hand and Sam hated how weak the once-powerful grip had become.

"Leave us."

Sam noticed the anger on the faces, aside from Laila's, and with much grumbling to themselves they finally vacated the room as Dean had ordered.

"Thank you for coming," Dean began.

"You know I will always come when you call."

"I...I left some things to you, Sam. Laila has them."

He didn't want to hear talk of things that would happen once death arrived. "I don't need anything. You've given me so much already."

This time Dean's smile was tired. "I'm very proud of you and the man you've become, Sam. I've always thought of you as my son."

Tears burned his eyes but he refused to shed any. He knew Dean wasn't too much into public emotional displays.

"Thank you, sir."

"I need you to do something for me."

"Anything." He would move mountains for this man if he asked him to do so. And if he couldn't find a way to do that, he'd blow the shit out of them to get them out of the way.

"It's almost Christmas." A series of coughs passed. "I have been volunteering at a local children's home. Second Chances. I need you to fill in."

"Consider it done."

"I also want you to find someone and settle down. Be the parent I know you can be."

All Sam could do was stare as shock filled him. Dean knew he'd tried the fiancée thing before, and they both knew how poorly it had turned out. Why the hell would he do it again?

"Bring them back in." The order came around more coughing and he hurried to follow it.

Soon, he stood alongside Laila and the others surrounding the bed. Dean stared at each of them. "Look around this bed. This is your family. Never forget that. This is *our* family. Go now, I need to rest."

They all left together and rode the elevator down in silence. At the door, Sam paused, feeling dazed until Laila touched his arm. He shook off his thoughts of where the rest of Dean's family was. The man had a few more nieces and nephews but aside from Laila, they kind of kept to themselves. It bothered Sam they wouldn't be there while Dean was going through what he was. The three who *had* shown up had acted as if they wanted to be anywhere else.

"I'll ride with you and show you where the house is." Laila slipped her arm through his.

He nodded and led her to his truck, ignoring the hateful glares from Dean Jr. Laila gave directions and they arrived at a duplex. He parked behind the vehicle carrying the others.

"Come on in, Sam." She got out and he followed at a

much slower pace, holding his bag over one shoulder.

The tension in the house ratcheted up once everyone was inside. He set his bag down by the door and took in Laila's nice house on his way to the kitchen. Angry voices filtered back to him and he steeled himself for something unpleasant.

"Stop being an ass, Dean. He's family and of course he will stay here."

"I don't consider him *my* family, Laila, and if *you* put him up, I'll disown you."

Laila's gasp raked like talons through his chest. When her parents had died, Dean had welcomed her easily into his home, treating her as a daughter, not as a niece.

The other two—Chris and Tom, according to Laila—backed Dean. Furious on her behalf, Sam began to enter the kitchen. However, a new, unknown voice broke in. "Oh, for fuck's sake, Dean. Don't be such an ass. This isn't even your house."

Feminine and slightly raspy, the sound skated along his skin, making him hyperaware.

"Nor is it yours, Roxi, so keep it shut. Or else."

Sam stepped through the doorway, unwilling to let a woman be threatened.

"Or else what, Dean? Or else what?" Her voice grew darker and he recognised the warning in it, even if Dean didn't. She obviously didn't need his protection. She gave a disgusted snort. "That's what I thought. Laila, he can stay at my house, so your cousin doesn't flip."

Everyone fell silent and he glanced at the woman again. She was taller than Laila but still shorter than him. Her hair was pulled back and piled up, showing off a slender neck and making him unable to tell how long her hair was. Skin the hue of dark cocoa covered her lush figure. She wasn't fat, she had the curves of a real woman, not a half-starved model.

She—Roxi—had silver piercings all along the ear he could see. Well-worn, medium-blue jeans and a hot-pink, tight

T-shirt moulded beautifully to her body.

"Such a whore, Roxi. Don't even know the man and you're ready for him to be with you in your house."

He ignored the young boy in him who had been thrown away and was still searching for something he knew would always be his. It wasn't rational. Still, it was something he had to face. He focused on Dean and the hate spewing from him.

Roxi, however, only laughed. Her amusement flowed like warm velvet over his skin. "Don't be jealous, I don't want your STD, Dean. Or is that *STDs* now? I have discerning tastes, you know, ones that don't include you. And while everyone here knows I'd never let you in, I have no problem with this man staying with me."

"You don't even know him!" Dean thundered. "None of us do aside from Laila, and I think she's enamoured with him."

Roxi touched Laila's arm softly. "Doesn't matter," she said. "He can stay with me."

"Why?" Dean sounded strangled.

Roxi lifted her head and stared directly at Sam, unsurprised, as if she had known he'd been there the entire time. Her gaze went over him and he noticed the gleam of appreciation. Her eyes were coffee brown and steadfast.

"Because, Dean. Just because. It's not anything you'd understand."

But Sam did. Around her neck sat the eagle, anchor and globe, emblem for the United States Marine Corps.

"Semper Fi," he said.

Everyone but Roxi jumped. She gave him a slight smile along with her nod.

Roxanne 'Roxi' Mammon had never been one of those women who found themselves light-headed at a single glance from a man. But then, she'd never met the famed Sam Hoch. Until now. And so here she stood, staring at the man across from her in Laila's kitchen realising her 'never' had just been erased.

*Not to mention it makes me glad it's harder to see my blush because he's making my skin feel oh so hot and flushed.*

This was him? *The* Sam Laila spoke so highly of? Holy hell.

If the Marines she'd worked with had been like this, perhaps she would have fought harder to stay longer. The man standing there, Sam, was quite simply a work of art.

He had his cover stowed under his left arm and he wore blood stripes. Although his matching midnight-blue coat sat hidden behind a black jacket and she couldn't read his rank, his broad shoulders and lean hips weren't obscured.

Short, dark hair — a Marine high and tight — tanned skin and vivid eyes. She couldn't tell the exact colour from across the room. Chiselled features gave him a harsh appearance. He obviously wasn't a man who smiled often.

Laila recovered first and hurried to Sam's side. He put his attention on her and immediately his countenance softened. It was all over his face how much he loved Laila.

Blowing out a short puff of air, Roxi headed towards the duo, disliking the jealousy she experienced at their affection for one another. A mental reprimand and she was again focused.

Sam lifted his head and speared her with dark, sapphire-blue eyes. Not just any blue, but one that reminded her of the deep blue of the evening sky. Pure and intense, containing an extremely subtle violet undertone all combined with a silky shine.

A quiver rocked her and she thanked Boot for teaching her to keep her emotions hidden. Her best friend faced her and Roxi's anger grew again at the stress and pain evident in her expression.

"Roxi, this is Sam. Sam, my best friend, Roxi."

"Nice to meet you, ma'am." He punctuated his statement with a sharp nod.

*Manners. Another point in his favour.*

She smiled easily, ignoring the serious pounding of her

heart. "Roxi, please."

"Thank you, Roxi." Laila squeezed her hand.

"Anytime, darlin'. I'll tell you what. Let me get him settled and dinner will be ready in about an hour from now." She turned her head. "And you three, it's my house we'll be eating in so if you're rude, I'll kick your asses out. Nice and quick with no fuss or muss. Come on, Marine. Let's go get you set up in the guest room."

"Go on, Sam. I'll see you in an hour."

Roxi moved by Sam and bit the inside of her cheek to keep her moan contained. He smelt masculine and it made her think of long winter nights, or days, on a thick rug before a fire where he would…

*Whoa there.* She slammed the brakes on that train of thought right quick. At the door, his arm moved beside her as he hefted his bag. The heat emanating from him nearly distracted her.

*Oh, perhaps this wasn't such a good idea – he's here because Dean is hospitalised.*

Outside, she paused to glance behind her. Sure enough, there he stood. The setting sun cast its golden glow upon his face. He'd donned his cover and her heart skipped a few beats. Sam had barely said five words to her, yet she couldn't help her immediate and intense attraction to him.

She caught a brief glimpse of sorrow on his face before it was wiped clear. Something more than worry over Dean's situation. *What makes you so sad?* His gaze shifted to her and she gave him a smile.

"Don't worry, I'm just next door to her."

She pointed to the ranch house that neighboured the duplex. She and Laila lived in a subdivision and had about a quarter acre of land each. So while their houses weren't right on one another, they were not far apart. Heading for the door with him on her heels, she gave herself another mental pep talk—this wasn't about getting some. She pushed the door open and was instantly hit by a combination of warmth and the smells of cooking food.

"This way."

She led him through the living room and down to the hallway. After pushing open the guestroom door, she flicked on the light and moved to the side. He stepped by her and set his bag down beside the bed. He'd removed his cover when entering her home and held it now as he faced her.

"Make yourself at home. There is a bathroom is across the hall, towels and whatnot are in the tall cabinet in there for you to use."

All she could see was them in that bed, naked limbs entwined.

"Thank you."

So many responses almost fell from her lips, but she kept them to herself. Before she left the room she paused at the door and turned back. "I'm sorry."

"For what?"

*For the way they talked about you as if you weren't even there. Nope, can't say that.* "The reason you came. Master Guns being in the hospital."

His expression flickered yet never changed. "Thank you."

She had an overwhelming urge to gather him and hold him close. An urge to do other things as well, but for all she knew she wasn't his type.

"Holler if you need anything." She walked out and left him to his own devices.

Back in the kitchen, she began setting the large table. As she placed the last glass, lost in her own thoughts and the music playing, she glanced up to see him standing in the doorway. Watching her.

*Shit!*

Her heart pounded thunderously. And she'd thought he'd looked fine in his Marine blues. He now wore light blue jeans—a worn pair—which made her curl her fingers into the flesh of her palms to keep from touching. Exploring. And did she say touching? Definitely, lots and *lots* of touching.

19

His shirt was black with 'Marines' in gold lettering across the middle, followed by the eagle, anchor and globe.

A man simply shouldn't look that damn good. She cleared her throat and gave him a smile. He'd showered, she could tell by the remaining dampness on his short hair.

"Can I get you anything?" *Me perhaps? Naked? Stilettos only?*

Sam shook his head. "Smells great."

"Thank you. There are sodas in the fridge, tea, beer, just... help yourself." She tore her gaze from him, refocusing on the table instead of the hard masculine Marine body in her kitchen.

"Can I help?"

His voice was right by her ear as she stood before the dishes cabinet. The scent of pure man teased her senses. Okay, so it was more of a torture because she couldn't touch. Her nipples tightened and her clit pulsed with need.

*Damn, it's been so long.*

"You can g-grab the plates."

He didn't wait for her to move. Instead, he shifted his physique immediately behind her and reached up, effectively trapping her between him and the countertop. Oh, dear God, she was going to melt. It felt like mini-Tasers were being applied to her wherever he touched, catapulting her body into a state of hypersensitivity. Firm thighs, taut abs — and let's not forget the large cock, which she could feel against her ass.

Damn near panting like a bitch in heat, she had to fight not to press back into him or whimper when he stepped back. The separation helped to clear her mind. Helped. A wee bit. As she went for napkins, she watched him surreptitiously. He moved with a leonine grace and coiled power.

*Imagine all that in bed.*

A flood of wetness made her bite back yet *another* groan. She really needed to go out and get laid.

"What do you do for the Corps?" She hoped her question would keep her mind off the things she'd love to do with him. Or to him.

"Recon."

Hot and dangerous. Her body throbbed. *So much for keeping my mind off sexual things.*

"How long have you been in?"

"Almost twenty." A pause. "Seventeen."

Wow. He was close to retirement. "And that's where you met Master Guns?"

"No."

She waited for an embellishment on the single-word answer but got nothing. Swallowing her sigh of frustration, she grabbed a sheet of breadsticks and placed them in the oven. The rich, hearty scent of the cooking lasagne spilled out and she sighed in pleasure. One of her specialities and a favourite dish of Laila's, so it coincided wonderfully.

The remaining time she and Sam worked together in silence—she didn't pry anymore and he seemed content to say nothing. She thought about him in recon.

She'd just pulled out the lasagne and set it on the table as he placed the breadsticks in a basket when his head snapped up and every muscle in his body tensed.

"What?" she asked softly, recognising his look as one who hadn't decided if the noise was friend or foe.

"We're here!" Laila called out.

For a brief moment his entire body softened and again that unpleasant feeling of jealousy filled her. Roxi didn't understand it—he wasn't hers to be jealous over.

"Right on time," she hollered back. "Just putting it on the table."

Laila and her cousins entered and the tension increased. She rolled her eyes as Dean took a seat at the end. Sharing a look with Laila, they each took one beside the other end and Laila tugged Sam into that seat.

There wasn't a lot of chatter over the meal and when she got up to remove dishes and bring out dessert, Sam was right there with her. Again he helped.

After they'd finished eating, Sam and Laila went to speak

privately. The other cousins had left and she was wiping off the table the moment her friend tracked her down.

"Thank you so much, Roxi."

"You never have to thank me, you know that."

Laila pushed in chairs. "Thank you anyway. And for Sam too."

"You know I haven't a problem with him staying. I know he means a lot to you." She wanted to ask so many questions about him yet somehow managed to keep her mouth shut.

"He does. What about Eric?"

"He doesn't come 'til next week. And he'll be fine with it."

"Thank you again." Laila hugged her and pressed a kiss to her cheek. "G'nite."

"Night, hon. Keep me posted. I'll swing by the day after tomorrow and see him."

"I will. Love you, Roxi."

"Likewise, Laila. Go home and get some sleep."

Soon she was alone in the kitchen. She headed for her kettle to heat some water then she felt him behind her. Everything changed when he was in the room. Without turning, she licked her lips.

"I'm making tea. Would you like a cup? I can also offer coffee or hot chocolate."

No response and she peered over her shoulder.

He stared at her. Was it her imagination or was there possessiveness in his gaze? "Who's Eric?"

# Chapter Two

Sam had experienced jealousy before. Quite a lot actually, growing up. At how the other children had parents and siblings as well as a home and perhaps a room of their own. Special holidays with the family. Yes, the feeling wasn't anything he didn't recognise.

It was the situation.

Ever since Roxi had stood up for him, without having even met him, and said he could stay with her, he'd been in a bit of wonderment. So this time when jealousy revealed its ugly head, he'd known it was different. He didn't like another male name causing her to be so happy.

*You just met her, for all you know she's married*, his brain chimed in.

He refused to believe it. She stood there watching him alertly, her rich coffee-coloured eyes never wavering. He stepped closer, trying to ignore the pounding in his blood that told him she was his and he should grab her. Kiss her.

*I don't want to just kiss her.* Another realisation rocked him. He didn't sleep with women just *because*. He had no wish to form attachments that wouldn't…couldn't last. But if Roxi crooked her finger at him, he would follow without a second's hesitation. He wanted to feel her body against his, touch her skin, run his tongue along the pulse in her neck. Taste her. Fill her. Hear her cry his name. *His.* No one else's.

He moved towards her, almost out of control. Her eyes widened a bit before her tongue sneaked out and dampened her lips. It was a direct line from her tongue to his cock.

"Eric is my nephew."

God, her voice. That alone could be a fantasy. Wresting

his raging libido back until he regained the upper hand, he gazed over her face, taking in her full, kissable lips, thick and curved lashes and her flawless skin.

"And he lives with you?"

Her smile was immediate, illuminating her entire face. "Not permanently, no. He's enrolled at the military school nearby. He stays with me on breaks."

"Not his parents?"

"My brother, Ritchie, is overseas right now, and Eric's mom" — a fierce scowl — "let's just say she's not fit to pick up dog shit." A shrug. "It's a long story, but basically when she flipped out he — Ritchie, I mean — was still overseas. I was home on a leave and brought him to stay with me. This is the arrangement we've ended up with. If Ritchie is home, Eric goes there and stays with him. If not, he's here."

Sam was amazed. "And his mother?"

"Who knows. Stoned somewhere, high on something, drunk in a ditch, who knows. Maybe rehab. I just want her far from Eric." Her tone had no sympathy in it.

"How do you deal with deployments with him, then?"

She turned back to the whistling kettle and poured the water into mugs. He realised he'd not told her he wanted anything, but she was still making him something.

"I don't have to. I'm out."

He heard the wistfulness in her tone. She added tea bags and sugar before peeking back at him.

"Enough about Eric. Tell me about you, Sam. I've heard a few things but to hear Laila speak, you're Superman."

He took their mugs and led the way to her living room, before placing them on the coffee table. Then he sat on the sofa, the other end from Roxi.

"I've known Laila since before her parents died. She's wonderful."

Roxi's eyes hardened, but the emotion was so fleeting he wondered if he'd imagined it. Then she nodded.

"She is. But you're still not telling me about you."

No, he wasn't. He tried avoiding talking about his past.

"You heard Dean Jr. I'm a stray."

"Bullshit." Her answer came instantly and with force. "Dean is a jackass who doesn't know his ass from a hole in the ground. You are *not* a stray." Her eyes burned with determined fire.

Her defence of him struck deep and he had to gather himself to focus back on the conversation they were having. "How do you know Dean?"

A snort of derision. "He showed up about two years ago. His mom had been some rich thing who apparently never told Master Guns she was pregnant when she left him. I guess it was some kind of confession from her. So this spoilt brat shows up with his two brothers, Chris and Tom, more assholes. I still haven't figured out why they're here. Not entirely sure it's for a good reason. Laila is so desperate for family she will put up with anything, almost."

He would rip Dean's arms from his body and beat him with them if he hurt Laila. "You really don't like him."

"Hell no. He's an ass and a bully. The other two with him are the same, and Laila, well, she's Laila."

He nodded and reached for his tea. Mint. He felt her watching him and lifted his gaze to hers. She didn't blush and duck away. Instead, she held his stare and allowed him to see the appreciation in her eyes.

"Still haven't said anything about you."

Roxi was right again, he'd managed to steer the conversation away from himself. "Not a lot to say. I'm sure Laila has told you all about me."

"Nope. She hasn't. I asked her and she said it was something I would have to ask you when I finally met you."

"She said that?"

"Yes. So I know very little about you aside of how proud Laila and Master Guns are of you." She drank some more tea, curling her legs beneath her. "But I can see you don't talk much, so it's okay if you don't want to tell me anything. I won't pry."

Roxi curved her hands around the mug and closed her

eyes. Sam couldn't tear his gaze from her. He wasn't ready to open up but he wanted to hear her talk more.

"Tell me about you."

She opened her eyes and they twinkled. "All right, but it's gonna need some food, so I'll be right back."

True to her word, she soon returned with a plate of petit fours. She placed it on the cushion between them. His cock pulsed as she reached for one and bit into it with a lusty groan. A very vivid mental image of those full lips around his shaft slammed into him. His fingers tightened around the handle of the mug.

*Shit!*

"Me," she said on a purr of pleasure, which only seemed to encase his length in steel. "Well, I have the one brother I told you about earlier, Ritchie. And my nephew, Eric. Our parents are living in Georgia, which is where we grew up. No sisters. I was in the Corps for ten years. Now I'm here in Bremerton where I work with Laila at a bank. See, not very exciting."

"What do you do at the bank?"

"Security. Laila's a teller, but I'm sure you knew that." She shifted and sat cross-legged. "I was going to be a cop but I couldn't. Not with Eric."

He ate one of the fours. Lemon this time — it went perfectly with the tea. "Why not?"

"Ritchie's job is dangerous. Eric needs to have at least one person as a constant in his life."

"What branch does your brother serve in?"

A slight shake of her head. "None, he's with a construction company over in the Middle East."

He understood. Having done a few tours over there, it wasn't the safest area. But it was good money if you went as a civilian. He flicked his gaze around her place and couldn't help but feel comfortable. She was waiting for him when he returned his questing look to her.

They talked some more. It was late, he noticed after a while. The petit fours were gone, as was the tea in their mugs. For the first time in a long time, since before he'd got the news on Dean, he felt his body relaxing.

Roxi gave him a warm smile as she rose from the couch. She swiped the mugs and plate. He closed his eyes, only to open them when he inferred her presence.

"Come on, Marine. You look like you could get some use out of a bit of shut-eye."

He saw her in his arms. Limbs entwined. And a bolt of electricity rocketed through him. He rose and again noticed how well she'd fit in his arms. Against him. On him. Under him. Sam walked behind her after she'd locked up the house, down the hall to where the bedrooms were.

Roxi faced him at the room he was in. "Good night, Marine."

He struggled with his need to touch her. "Good night, Roxi." He'd tried calling her ma'am before and she'd nipped that right away, telling him Roxi was just fine.

Another soft smile and she left him there, heading into her own room. Sam got ready for bed and when he padded across the hall for the last time, he glanced down towards where light spilled from the crack at Roxi's room.

He rubbed his bare chest as he entered his room and closed the door. Climbing into bed in his boxers, he sighed heavily then drifted off to sleep.

\* \* \* \*

He was being grabbed! Sam reacted on the instincts he'd learnt in the Corps as well as his childhood. He refused to be hurt anymore. But when he rolled on his assailant it wasn't a man's body he felt. No, it was one with curves.

"Easy there, Marine. It's okay. You're safe. It's me, Roxi."

Safe. Bremerton. The intoxicating scent of autumn. Roxi.

He opened his eyes to find her beneath him. Light from the hall illuminated her face and the arm he had hard across her neck. There was no fear in her gaze, merely understanding.

*Fuck.*

27

"I'm so sorry," he said, removing his arm so she could breathe easier. He touched his fingertips to the skin at her neck. Embarrassment stung his cheeks. Christ! He could have seriously hurt her, or hell, even killed her. "So sorry."

Her hands settled softly along the sides of his face. "It's okay, Sam."

"No, I hurt you, Christ, I—"

She placed two fingers over his mouth. "I'm fine. It was my fault, Sam. Not yours." Her other hand slid around to the back of his head, fingers constantly moving, offering soothing caresses.

"I—"

"You were having a nightmare. I forgot I can't just shake you awake as I would Eric. You're Recon."

Not an excuse in his mind. She should be protected at all times. "I should go."

Her eyes narrowed. "No. You should stay. Sleep. There's no reason to run, Sam. I'm fine. I swear."

She shifted, reminding him he was nearly naked and she lay beneath him. Tearing his gaze from her face and neck, he rose a bit and peered down at her.

A buckskin, spaghetti-strap camisole barely hid her full breasts. He could imagine her heated core touching his hardening cock. Yes, he was right, she fit perfectly against him.

"Do you want to talk about it?" she asked. The fingers covering his lips disappeared and she encircled his neck.

His gaze drifted to her full lips, lingering there before continuing on to her eyes. Concern was foremost but there was no disguising the desire that smouldered behind it.

"Sam?"

Lord, it was hard to think straight when her touch appeared hell-bent on driving him to distraction.

"No," he murmured, closing the distance between their mouths. Part of him waited for her to tense, scream, or demand he get off and the hell out of her house. It never came. "I'm so sorry," he whispered, brushing his lips against hers.

They were soft as velvet and smooth as silk. She arched into him with a faint groan. Fire exploded in his blood and he wanted nothing more than to press closer and learn everything about her. But he didn't. He rolled off her and reached for the light.

"Let me look at your neck," he said over his shoulder. There was no answer so he peered at her.

She still lay where he'd rolled them. Her hair billowed around her like a black silken cloud. One strap of her camisole had slid from her shoulder. He swallowed hard. Roxi's black shorts were moulded to her firm, toned legs.

*Fuck me.* His cock went harder, if possible. Closing his eyes, he prayed for strength and reached for his jeans. Keeping his back to her, he jerked them on, hiding his erection.

He froze at the light touch along the small of his back.

"Sam."

It was nearly his undoing. The toe-curling voice she had and the simple act of her fingers upon his skin. He ground his jaw and swallowed hard.

"Let me check your neck, Roxi." He faced her. "Please."

She climbed off the bed, looking like a woodland sprite, all cute and tousled. He led her across to the bathroom and under the bright light had her sit on the counter and stood between her legs to inspect her neck. No signs of bruising — that relieved him greatly. Through it all, Roxi sat silently, allowing him to do his thing. Still her gaze never left his face.

"I told you I was fine," she commented when he'd finished.

"I needed to check."

"I know."

He stepped back and she slid off the counter, eyes transfixed on him. Before he knew what had happened she'd pressed a kiss to his cheek then was walking out. "Get some sleep, Sam."

Back in his bed, he burrowed his face to where Roxi had

lain—although not for long—the sheets smelt slightly like her. Autumn. That was the only way he could explain it. Subtle, soft, warm and with a slight hint of spice. The scent wrapped around him like a comforting cloak and accompanied him to sleep.

\* \* \* \*

Roxi stood in her kitchen and stared out of the sliding glass door, which led to the backyard. Unconsciously she rubbed her throat. Damn it! How could she have been so stupid? The sound had woken her and as she would have with her nephew, she'd gone in to wake him. One problem, she'd tried to shake awake a Recon Marine in the same way she would her ten-year-old nephew.

Sam's reaction had been swift and precise. She'd been lucky to get out her words at all. Despite that, she wasn't scared of him. Quite the opposite.

Then add how it felt to be captured beneath his muscled body. His cock pressing against the apex of her thighs. Admittedly, she'd only exhibited hot desire for him then. And that brush of his lips along hers. No other had affected her so and it had hardly been a kiss at all.

*Sigh.* Okay, so Laila wasn't the only one who had it bad. Some of his stories were legendary and she'd fallen for him through myth. Sure, she knew Laila thought of him as a brother but to hear her talk about him, he could do no wrong. So they both had strong feelings for the man, Roxi's just weren't along the brotherly vein.

*Only, he's not a myth anymore.*

A heated flush skated along her skin and she knew he'd entered the kitchen. Readjusting her gaze so she no longer stared out past the glass, she watched him.

Grace. Power. And sexuality off-the-charts.

Wanting to see him without using a reflection, she turned. He stood by the table.

Staring at him was something akin to suddenly being

30

starving and knowing no matter how long you ate or drank it would never, *could* never be enough. It was still early — the first rays of morning had just begun to splinter through the dark.

He peered at her with those incredible blue eyes and her heart's cadence kicked up a few notches. She smiled and couldn't begin to say how relieved she was to see some of his uncertainty fade away.

"Morning," she said.

"Morning," he replied.

His deep voice dragged along her skin much like thick velvet. He kept dropping his gaze to her neck. She stared at him in his jeans and another snug shirt, grey this time.

"I'm fine, Sam."

"I could have —"

"You didn't." She cut him off as she closed the distance between them.

Lord, he was big. All over. And hot. Her nipples beaded as she imagined his hands on her breasts. Cupping, kneading, tugging. A flash of heat poured over her and she took a deep breath to get herself under some semblance of control.

Toe-to-toe, she stopped. She had to tip her head back in order to maintain eye contact. He swallowed and she felt this incredible urge to lick him. Over each hard, muscled inch.

*Okay, I'm losing it. He's a guest. Not my play-toy.* Oh, but what a play-toy he'd be.

"I'll have some breakfast ready in just a few. You can move your truck into the drive, on the left side. Never mind. You can park in the garage too, I'll open the door."

She hurried off to do that before she forgot herself and did something insane like jump at him, wrap her legs around him and see where that led. Couch. Bed. Wall. Hell, she wasn't picky.

*I really need to go out and get some.*

She opened the garage then turned, only to smack into his rock-hard chest. Crap. She'd been so into her fantasy of where to do him that she hadn't realised he'd followed her.

His arms snaked out and he caught her by the upper arms as she wobbled.

"Thanks." Her word was breathy and she gave herself a mental reprimand for it.

His response wasn't verbal, just a nod of his head. She missed his touch when he removed it but she kept her mouth shut as well. He passed by her and she inhaled deeply, allowing his scent to infuse into her skin. Then she watched him walk away, admiring the view before she went back in the house.

She worked on breakfast and when the garage door closed a tingle rippled through her. Not much later, he reappeared in the kitchen.

"Almost ready," she said, pulling a piping-hot waffle off the iron and placing it on a plate. Once she'd added some sausage, she paused. "Do you like eggs and sausage?"

"Yes."

The response was directly behind her and rocked her with her another wave of lust. "I'll let you dish up what you want, then. Take as much as you like."

Their fingertips brushed as the plate exchanged hands. Licking her lips, she went back to the waffle iron and poured batter for her own.

"Hey." Laila spoke, breaking in to the small world they'd created.

"Hey, yourself. Come on in and grab a plate," she called back.

"Morning, Sam," Laila said, stepping into the kitchen.

"Good morning, Laila."

Roxi watched them embrace and ignored the reappearance of the green-eyed monster. She placed the next waffle on a plate and Laila took it from her. After grabbing another plate, Roxi made one for herself.

She normally didn't mind Laila coming by. It wasn't uncommon for her to pop over for a meal, but for some reason this morning, all Roxi wanted to do was snarl,

"Mine!" and kick Laila out.

She could hear them talking behind her. Laila apologising for yesterday and Sam forgiving her. Roxi sat down with her waffle, eggs and the sole remaining sausage link. *I forgot how much Laila loves them.* She sat on the other side of Laila, leaving a seat between her and Sam, and began to eat.

Throughout the meal, Sam glanced at her several times, only to be dragged back into a discussion with Laila. Did she mind? No. Not at all. As long as she could continue to ignore the minor desire to snarl and lunge for her, there was no problem at all.

*Maybe I need professional help.*

"I have to get to work," Laila announced. "I'll see you this afternoon." She hurried and gave Roxi a hug. "Thank you again."

Past Laila's shoulder, she saw Sam watching her. Eyes intense. "Not a problem. Sam's a great guest. Go on."

Laila did, leaving after one final kiss to Sam's cheek, which had Roxi envisioning slashing Laila across the face with her nails. *Oh yeah, not a problem in the least. Definitely need some professional help here. Get a grip!* she admonished herself.

Sam left with Laila and she cleaned up from breakfast. She did her best not to go to the living room and peer out any of the windows to see what, if anything, they were doing.

*Have I mentioned how much I need to get a grip?*

She had and she did.

*Okay, it's official. I am seriously pathetic. Mooning over this man.*

After the kitchen was straightened, she turned and headed for her bedroom. She stopped on the way at Eric's room. She flipped on the light and propped herself against the doorjamb.

She loved her nephew more than anything. Her gaze travelled around the room, taking in the few posters. He had some pictures of the Marines, Transformers, and a few cars. His toys weren't numerous but the ones he had were nicely put away.

There was an ache in her heart and she sighed heavily only to stiffen when Sam's masculine scent converged around her.

"Very squared-away room." He spoke from behind her.

"Yes."

"When is he coming?"

Shoving her hands in her pockets, she paused. "Next Monday." She smiled at the revelation, imagining him back with her.

"I would have liked to have met him."

"You will." As soon as the words fell from her mouth she realised how presumptuous her words had sounded. She felt his gaze on her but continued to focus on Eric's bedroom.

"I'd like that."

The tension between them shot up. Her skin tingled with the insane urge to both touch and be touched by him. Licking her lips, she reached for the handle and slowly pivoted towards him while drawing it shut.

His large physique blocked her in and when he placed a hand on the door, halting her, she arched a brow in the process. Her belly did flips the closer he leaned. His scent washed over her, making her light-headed.

"Forgot the light." He leaned past her and flicked it off.

So close. He was so damn close.

"Thanks." Her single word fell on a whisper.

Seconds drifted by, their eyes locked on one another, until he finally stepped back. Grateful as well as disappointed, Roxi drew the door until it clicked. She ran her tongue over her teeth, all the while wanting to kiss him.

"I'm home all day," she said, moving by him. "So feel free to come and go as you please. I'll just go by the hospital later in the afternoon."

Roxi headed for her room only to be stopped by his touch on her arm. Praying for the strength not to do anything stupid, she manoeuvred to face him, caught off guard by the raw emotions in his eyes.

"Thank you."

"No problem," she said, trying to sound like it wasn't a big deal after all. Prove to herself she could do this without panting over him like a lovesick fool. Or a horny one. Perhaps that was what she was, both horny and lovesick. With a heavy emphasis on horny.

"Do you know where Second Chances is?"

"Yes. I can give you directions. You filling in for Master Guns?"

He nodded and she smiled. *This is going to be interesting.*

# Chapter Three

She was smiling again. Sam could feel the effect of her smile everywhere. It lit her face up. Correction, it lit *her* up, making her even more beautiful.

Roxi stood before him in a pair of silver-grey pants and a black, long-sleeved Marine shirt. Her hair was pulled back into a ponytail exposing her numerous earrings. They ran up both ears and he'd noticed they were all different.

Back to her smile. It did things to him. He'd been unsure and embarrassed about attacking her last night, but she didn't appear to have given it another thought. And she hadn't told Laila.

This woman amazed him. He knew she had Marine pride. A Marine flag flew on her porch, slightly lower than her American flag. Then there was her necklace and a few photos of her around her living room he'd checked out. She was a hot-ass Marine. She'd been a sergeant. Her love for the Corps was obvious — it made her sacrifice of getting out for her nephew all the more touching in his estimation.

"I'm doing some laundry today. If you'd like anything done I'd be happy to throw it in."

"I'm good, thank you."

"Okay. If you need to do some, feel free. It's the room without a door. Right down there."

"Can I fix the door for you?" There had to be some way he could repay her for all this hospitality.

Another smile and his heart kicked into a higher gear.

"I took it off because of how it opened. Into the room and it was just too hard with the space being so small. I'll add one on a track at some point." She shrugged. "Not high on my to-do list."

He could do that for her.

"Let me stop rambling and give you directions."

He kind of liked her rambling. He liked a lot about her. When she'd given him directions he went to his room and grabbed what he needed. Roxi was on the phone when he strode through the living room. She tossed him a wave before laughter erupted from her. Ignoring his desire to kiss her, he walked out to the garage.

He paused by his truck. Propped up on the handle sat a garage door opener. Roxi had given him access to her house—he shook his head in wonderment, pressing it. Washington's morning light penetrated the garage.

After climbing into his truck, he backed out and touched the button to close the door. To the left he spied Dean Jr, out smoking on Laila's porch, glaring in his direction. He growled low in his throat. There was something about that man he just plain didn't like. After ensuring the garage door had completely shut, he drove off to do what he needed to.

\* \* \* \*

Second Chances had caused a knot in his chest even before he'd hopped out in front of the two-storey building. There was a fenced area off to the side and he could see boys and girls out there despite the cold, windy weather. With a deep breath, he clenched his hands into fists. Beneath the leather of his gloves he could feel the sweat on his palms.

*Damn it. I have no reason to be afraid.* Yet he couldn't control the memories.

He strode up the steps then knocked briskly on the front door. An older man opened it, a smile on his lips.

"Can I help you?"

In a flash, he was transported back to being a little boy, terrified and unsure as to why he had been separated from his family. Would they ever come for him? Would he make it if they didn't?

"Are you okay, son?"

Sam blinked and cleared his throat. The man before him had pale skin and a head of bright red hair.

"Yes, sir. I'm Gunnery Sergeant Sam Hoch. Here to help out for Master Gunnery Sergeant Dean Richardson."

The smile broadened. "Of course. I thought you looked familiar. Come on in. I'm Father Dylan O'Toole. How is Dean doing? We are all praying for him."

They stepped inside and Sam gazed about the warm room. "He was awake yesterday. I'm going back this afternoon."

Children played here as well, the ones too young to be out in the cold for very long. He heard some cries from even younger ones coming from nearby.

"What was he doing? I'll pick up where he left off." Sam knew it wasn't the nicest behaviour but being here had hit him harder than he'd expected it to.

Father O'Toole nodded, understanding in his gaze. "Right this way. Do you know anything about plumbing? Painting?"

Sam remained silent as they went towards the back. Father O'Toole opened a door, which led to another room. Lights were powered on and illuminated the partially painted walls of the large space.

"He was finishing this up to be the playroom once winter gets here full force. There are two bathrooms in the back which also need some work. Forgive me for asking, son, but how long are you here?"

"At least until Christmas."

Father O'Toole smiled. "Wonderful. We'll get the Santa suit out and alter it a bit for you. You're a bit broader than Dean."

"Santa suit?" His heart stopped for a few beats.

"Dean is our Santa Claus. I assumed you'd be taking his place in that as well. I mean, he can't have kids climbing all over him when he gets out. We even have a Mrs Claus to help. And some elves." Father O'Toole reached towards him, stopping shy of actual contact. "Can we count on

38

you?"

"Yes, Father."

A huge grin and the man left him. Alone. Sam sighed heavily and went to the paint. He also checked the bathroom and made a mental list of what he'd need. What did he know about being Santa? Didn't matter, he'd do it. Letting down Master Guns was not even an option.

Mrs Claus. A slight lift of his lips as he envisioned Roxi in a tight, short, red dress—even though he doubted that would be the costume—and her at his side. Another sigh and he got himself to work.

Father O'Toole came for him at lunch when Sam was cleaning up, having finished for the day. "Come get some food, son." He glanced around. "You've made some great strides."

Sam had only part of one wall left. And the bathrooms. "Thank you, Father, for the offer, but I can't stay. I have some errands to run. I'll be back first thing in the morning and finish this stuff up then move onto whatever else you need."

"Thank you, son. For doing this."

Together they walked out to where the children were eating. Their eyes tracked him and while he nodded at them all, he still kept quiet. At the door, Father O'Toole put a hand on his arm. He glanced down at the pale hand resting on the black of his jacket, then the man's face.

"I can tell you are a quiet man and we'll try to keep the questions to a minimum."

Sam opened his mouth, only to close it when Father O'Toole continued.

"It's okay, son. We'll see you tomorrow. God be with you."

Sam headed for his truck then swung up into it. He stopped off at Wal-Mart and grabbed some clothes along with the items needed for the bathroom. Then he returned to Roxi's.

It wasn't Dean Jr on the porch at Laila's this time, it was

the other two. Smoking and laughing while they drank beer. More dislike swarmed him and he activated the garage door button. He couldn't explain his relief at seeing Roxi's SUV in there. He parked next to her Tribeca and got out. Bags in hand, he went to the door and entered the house after the garage had been secured.

Music filled the air, alternative with a nice pulsing beat to it. He made his way to his room—funny how easy it was to think of it that way—and set his purchases on the bed. Stepping back in the hall, he headed for the living room then on to the kitchen, where he froze as if he'd run smack into a wall.

Roxi was mopping. She wore another pair of those thigh-hugging shorts, white ones, and a sweatshirt. Her hair hung free and he itched to sink his fingers in it and tug her head back, where all he had to do was lower his own and...

His cock pressed insistently against his jeans. He loved staring at her and would have no problems continuing to do so—however, he also had no wish to freak her out.

"Roxi," he called, loud enough to be heard over the music.

She screamed and jumped. So much for not scaring her. With a hand on her chest she stared up at him, eyes twinkling as much as the silver in her ears.

"Well, shit, you scared me."

"I'm—"

"No need to apologise. I thought I'd be done with the floor before you got back." She reached for a remote and turned the music down. "I don't normally have it set that high."

He knew she'd spoken but damned if he could follow the conversation. Her sweatshirt, medium grey, was another Marine one with four succinct words printed on it—'The Few. The Proud'. His eyes drifted lower back to where the white of her shorts ended and the mouth-watering, hot cocoa hue of her legs began. Long and toned. He knew it would be some sort of heaven to have them wrapped around his waist as he stroked deep into her.

The tension thickened as he watched her socked feet move closer.

"See something you like, Marine?"

He jerked his gaze up to find her eyes, a blended mixture of desire and amusement dancing in them, as she watched his face. The gentlemanly thing would be for him to apologise. Ask for her forgiveness for his behaviour.

"Hell yeah." His response was deep and guttural.

*What do you know, I'm not that much of a gentleman after all.*

"Good."

Their eyes remained locked as she put herself right before him. He was surrounded by the subtle scent of autumn. He watched her hands slide up over his chest until they rested on his shoulders, nails biting slightly into his skin. He didn't mind.

*More.* His body sang the command.

More of her touch.

He forced himself to allow her to continue setting the pace, to stroke her fingers along his shoulders and neck. When she applied pressure for him to lower his head, he followed the silent directive.

Her eyes fluttered and began to close as his lips made contact with hers. Soft yet firm, they parted beneath his touch. Last night hadn't even begun to be enough. He gathered her up tightly in his arms. Then he reached for her ponytail and jerked out the tie holding it. Her thick hair cascaded down in cool silken waves and he secured his hand in it, anchoring her where he wanted her.

He swiped his tongue along her lower lip before sliding it into her mouth. Her taste swarmed him, sweet yet not overly so. And there was a hint of cinnamon and sugar. Raw sugar.

Her tongue rubbed his, breaking his control. A rumble left his chest and he plunged in. Her answering moan spurred him on. He delved deep, licking the sides and roof of her mouth. Wanting more. Needing more. She made his blood sing as she met him thrust for thrust. Stroke for stroke.

41

She held him tighter and hoisted a leg, wrapping it around him. She ground against his rock-hard erection. He lowered the hand at her waist to her ass and squeezed as he rubbed his length along her core in response.

One thing was on his mind, to be buried balls-deep inside her — as soon as humanly possible. Having her wet slit around him. And spill his release so far into her, she would never forget what it was like to be with him.

She whimpered and pressed harder into him. Lifting her with one arm, he nearly growled at the feel of her legs locking about his waist. She never stopped kissing him. He carried her until a wall rested at her back, then ended the kiss and stared at her. Her lips were swollen and slightly parted as she emitted sharp breaths. Holding her gaze, he manoeuvred one hand down the front of her shorts to find her panties.

"Wet." His single word sounded gravelly.

Her eyes were almost glazed over as he stroked her through the damp material.

"Sam," she said on a breathy sigh, undulating against his touch.

He needed to get her naked. He needed to sink inside her so completely she cried his name. Dipping his fingers beneath the elastic band, he ran two of them over wet lips and drove them deep inside her heated walls.

Tight, she was so damn tight. Her head thumped back on the wall, plump bottom lip caught in straight white teeth as a hiss left her.

"Sam."

He pumped his wrist, sending his fingers in and out. Her pussy held him so snugly he nearly came just imagining it around his cock. He brushed her clit and she came apart, gasping his name until he silenced her with his mouth. With his tongue, he matched the pace of his fingers and she orgasmed around them.

"Inside...me...you..." she demanded once she'd caught her breath.

Nothing sounded better. He withdrew his cream-covered digits and brought them to his mouth to clean them. She tasted like spices. His cock pulsed, echoing his impatience.

"Yes," he said, shifting to put her on the floor in order to remove her tight shorts and for him to free his straining erection.

"Roxi?" Laila's call shattered the moment, breaking the spell around them as effectively as taking a baseball bat to a window. "Sam? Anyone here?"

They froze and Roxi moved away from him in the space of a heartbeat. He could see the regret and frustration in her gaze before she spun and left him alone with a dick hard enough to break rocks and the heady scent of her on his fingers. *Oh yeah, and a shitload of sexual frustration.*

By the time the women came into view he'd managed to rein in his lust. He'd picked up the mop and stood on the newly cleaned floor, drying off washed hands.

"Hi, Laila."

"Hey, Sam. I came to see if you wanted to come to the hospital with me?"

He flicked his gaze between them. "Yes. Of course." Laila, still in her work clothes and Roxi, well, he wanted her out of everything. Naked. Writhing beneath him. On top of him worked, too.

"Coming, Roxi?" Laila asked.

"Not yet." Roxi held his gaze. "I'll swing by later. I have some things to finish first."

"Okay. Come on, Sam."

He went, pausing by Roxi. Gone was any trace of passion and he wanted it back on her face. He almost spoke but Laila came back and dragged him away to the door leading from the house to the garage.

"You drive, Sam."

"Okay."

As they left the house, he peered over his shoulder to spy Roxi leaning against the wall, watching him. The hunger was back. When he met her gaze she turned away. They got in his truck and headed to the hospital.

*We're far from finished, Roxanne Mammon.*

Laila was talking and he reluctantly left thoughts of Roxi and how amazing it had been being in her wetness, to focus on the woman in the truck with him.

* * * *

Life really sucked. Roxi had come to that decision the second Laila's voice had ended the most intense sex-against-the-wall she'd ever had. *And only his fingers were deep inside me. Imagine what it would be like once his cock is there.*

She swiped her card, picked the gasoline needed for her vehicle, and, shaking off thoughts of Sam, filled the tank. There was a bite in the afternoon's air but that couldn't even begin to cool down the fire in her blood Sam had started.

True to her word, she'd gone by the hospital to see Master Guns. Sam and Laila had still been there. Dean and his two half-brothers had been nowhere to be seen. Laila had been in Sam's arms, crying against his chest.

Roxi had only stayed a short time. She could feel the intensity of Sam's gaze even though she'd left the hospital. Hell, her body remained primed and ready.

Her nipples were beaded and so tight they almost hurt. Her clit was hypersensitive to the point where walking seemed only to arouse her more. She would be giving herself an orgasm just from the memory of Sam's touch if she wasn't careful.

Laila and Sam were going out to dinner, so Roxi would eat alone after she got home. She didn't mind — she could stand calming down. First through, she had another stop to make. Once the car was filled, she grabbed her receipt and headed on her way. There was no rush and she listened to some Gladys Knight & The Pips as the drive continued. Turning off on a side street, she parked behind her destination building. She waited until Gladys finished singing *Best Thing That Ever Happened to Me* before she exited the car and strode around to the front door.

"Hey, Roxi!" a few called out as she walked through the tables.

"Good evening," she replied with a smile.

"Roxi, I didn't expect to see you here today."

She glanced to her left and saw Juan Vargas standing there. He was a good-looking man who'd served in Vietnam and he ran this soup kitchen.

She smiled at him. "I said I'd be in today. Sorry I missed most of the serving. I'll just get started on the dishes."

Juan appeared like he wanted to say something but he didn't. He nodded before going to talk to a few of the regulars. When he'd sat in a chair, she migrated to the kitchen, drew on an apron and tackled the stack of dishes heaped by the triple sink.

It took her longer than she'd anticipated, so she was extremely hungry as she drove home. Sam's truck was in the garage and she wondered if he was here or over at Laila's, where the lights had shone brightly through the dark.

She made her way slowly to the door and pushed into the house. The only light was the one she'd left on in the hall. Closing the door behind her, she then went to her room, readying her things for tomorrow. When she stepped from her master bathroom after washing up she froze.

Sam stood there in a pair of workout pants—black with white piping—that hung low on lean hips. That was it. Nothing else existed to keep her gaze from ogling the specimen that was his body. Tautly muscled, tanned and mouth-watering.

*Don't forget panty-wetting.*

He stood in her bedroom doorway, a white shirt hanging from his fist. His eyes held her prisoner—that intense blue pinned her to the spot, it was as if she'd grown roots.

*Hunger.* That was the only word she could think of to explain what she saw in his face. Raw, animalistic hunger.

Then he moved. Flowed towards her with intent and

single-minded purpose. He tossed his shirt to the side with a flick of his wrist and never slowed as he bore down on her. He grabbed her upper arms and jerked her so her breasts brushed his naked torso. She felt no fear, only arousal.

"One chance to say no," he rumbled.

That was the furthest word from her mind. *Hell yes, now,* and *take me* were much closer to slipping free.

She had wanted him since she'd first seen him at Laila's house. And, true, it wasn't that far back, but she knew sometimes a person just had to follow their gut.

For an answer, she pulled free from his hands, reached up and wound her arms around his neck. "Yes," she whispered.

He cupped her face then kissed her. Man, did he kiss her. His lips covered hers and his tongue delved into her mouth. She moaned at the invasion, arching closer. He stroked her tongue, coaxing it to tangle with his. He tasted like *man*, she didn't know to put it any other way.

He took control of the kiss and increased its intensity. Her legs shook and she dug her fingers into the back of his head and one shoulder. Sam broke the kiss and reached for the hem of her shirt. She stood still as he pulled it off. Her skin felt on fire from the heated way he stared at her. Clad in her black bra and the jeans she'd worn in the afternoon — and a pair of socks — she still felt naked.

"Beautiful," he said, reaching out to trail his index finger over the exposed swells of her breasts.

He traced both of his hands down her sides, the tuck of her waist and joined them at the button of her jeans. She wanted to rush him, but she held still and tried to wait. He pulled her jeans down her legs and she lifted each foot when he tapped the ankles. His warm breath fanned her belly button and lower. Her stomach clenched with her anticipation.

"So beautiful."

He trailed his hands up her legs until he regained his feet and held her hips. Sam watched her from behind hooded eyes. He freed her breasts and swiped his thumbs over her taut tips.

"Ohh," she said with a shudder.

Those damn eyes flashed from her breasts up to her face. And he did it again. And again. Wetness soaked her panties as he continued to knead her breasts.

When he lowered his head and drew a nipple into his mouth, she arched her back, crying his name. He suckled hard and she pressed his head closer as with each lave of his tongue or nip of teeth, she felt a corresponding tug on her clit. She didn't know how much more she could take. And they both still had clothes on. Not many, but some.

"Sam," she gasped, rocking against him, needing something else.

He stood up and raked his burning gaze over her again. A bit light-headed, she licked her lips and reached for his waistband. She captured her lower lip in her teeth while she slid his pants down and he stepped free of them, leaving him exposed in his navy blue boxers. They couldn't hide his erection.

Her pussy contracted. She anticipated having him deep inside her. She reached out and cupped him—his hips bucked, pushing more of his length into her palm.

*Shit. He is large. Not to mention thick.* She nearly had her tongue hanging out of her mouth as she panted. Going slow was no longer an option for her.

"Strip, Marine."

He wasted no time and removed his boxers. She was transfixed on his cock rising from a thatch of black hair. Her eyes fluttered with her increased heartbeat. He gripped himself and slowly stroked his shaft during the time he stared at her.

"Lose them."

His voice was gravelly and trailed along her skin like warmed crushed velvets and silk. Goose bumps popped as she hooked her thumbs in the band of her panties and shimmied free.

Approval and increased hunger spread across his face.

She blinked and he was there. Holding her. Kissing her. Laying her back upon the bed.

His hard, muscled body covered hers, the mattress cushioning them. She widened her legs, allowing him to settle more firmly between her thighs. Good Lord, he felt perfect there.

In and out his tongue moved as he positioned the head of his cock at her entrance. She whimpered and wriggled beneath him, desperate for him to be in her.

Finally. He slowly filled her. Electricity spiked throughout her and she gasped. It had been so long and he felt *so* damn good.

He drew back and stared down at her, holding still. She knew he wanted to make sure she was okay, the question in his eyes in place of words on his lips. She slid her arms up under his and gripped his shoulders.

"Move, Sam."

A low rumble left him as he began to thrust. She undulated with him, legs aiding in her motions. Back and forth. In and out. Faster and faster he powered, only to slow—pulling her back from the cusp only to begin all over again. He never spoke and she didn't mind.

Her mewls and groans danced around them along with the sounds of their bodies coming together in the age-old dance. He nibbled her collarbone and stimulated her tight nipples. Flames burst throughout her.

"Oh...Sam...I...so..." She tossed her head on the sheet, back arching to take him deeper.

He shifted an arm under her left leg, hitching it higher. The added angle allowed him even more penetration. His face was set in a mask, jaw clenched and sweat upon his brow.

Thrust after thrust sent her catapulting towards the cliff. Closer and closer it raced. Bearing down on her. She tightened her internal muscles and watched pleasure ripple across his features.

She closed her eyes and embraced the rush. Jumped

headlong into the euphoria awaiting her. He powered into her three more times before his low roar filled the air. His seed erupted from his cock, bathing her pussy. His release triggered another of her own and she came again, milking his cock and screaming his name as he continued to piston his hips.

Sam slowed and pressed a kiss to her temple. If she had the energy, she would have stretched and purred like a cat. She didn't. Their slick bodies lay intertwined. She closed her eyes while he rose up from her and withdrew from her heat. Instantly cooler, Roxi refrained from reaching for him.

He got up and she bit back any words and her hurt of his leaving. There had been no promises. No words of love. Hell, there'd been barely any words at all.

*Grow up, Roxi*. With slitted eyes, she watched Sam draw on his boxers and walk from the room. She didn't know how to explain the emotions racing through her. Her tongue sneaked out and licked her lips as she fought back her shock at the realisation they'd not used a condom. *Shit. What the hell do I do or say now?* She wasn't ready to think about carrying a child.

The hall light went dark and she released a sigh. Tomorrow was time enough to deal with the possibility of being pregnant. She wriggled her way under the covers, feeling chilled without Sam's added body heat and the lingering sweat on his body pressed to hers. The click of her bedroom door had her lowering lids snapping open – she'd thought he'd left her for the night. No sound and yet she *knew* he was there. Sure enough, a bit later the bed dipped beneath his weight and he joined her below the blankets.

He trailed one hand up her arm and over her lips. Her body prepared for more.

"Where'd you go?" she asked, reaching for him, thrilled to find him hard and naked in her bed once again. "I thought you were leaving."

His lips found hers and he kissed her as he slipped one hand between her thighs and teased her clit. She widened her legs, inviting more. Craving more.

Moments later the broad head of his sheathed cock filled her and she moaned in pure bliss. Once he sat fully embedded in her, he nuzzled her ear.

"Locked up. I'm not finished with you yet, not even close. I also grabbed some condoms. I should have had one last time, I'm sorry."

Damned if it wasn't the longest sentence she'd ever got from him. Her reply turned into a groan once he began to move. It didn't matter. All that did was he was here with her. Condom, no condom, she didn't give a damn right about now. He flexed his hips again and she gave herself over to all that he could give her.

\* \* \* \*

Roxi stirred slightly, her internal clock going off. In seconds she realised a few things. Sam was still in her bed with her, he was asleep, and she was sore. In a very good way.

Sam lay pressed against her, his face in the crook of her neck and one arm draped across her midsection. Opening her eyes, she listened to his deep, even breathing during the time she adjusted to the dark. Content, she had to remind herself a few times to move.

She extracted herself slowly and carefully, not wanting to wake him. He didn't strike her as a man who got a lot of sleep. Swiping the clothing she'd set out last night to wear, she slipped from the room and shut the door behind her.

After a quick shower in the other bathroom, she was dressed and in the kitchen by the time Laila walked over to join her for their morning walk.

# Chapter Four

Sam went from dead to the world to wide awake in the space of a single heartbeat. His heart pounded and he struggled not to panic. It had been so long since he'd slept so deeply. He calmed as it came to him.

Roxi's house. But more than that, *better*. Roxi's bed. Where he'd spent the night. Blissfully.

He reached for her, only came up empty. Sitting in bed, he glanced around for her. She wasn't even in the room, not just not in bed. Late autumn morning sun streamed in, lighting the area. Resting back against the wall at the head of her bed, he took in her personal space. Honestly, he'd not thought about looking around when he'd entered last night.

Her walls were done in a mint green with chocolate trim. The colour scheme matched the furniture and bedding. Not a lot of clutter. He smiled as another memory of last night and early this morning travelled through his mind.

His cock tented the sheet and, groaning, he reached down, wrapping his fingers around it. She'd been so wet and so damn tight, he'd barely managed to withhold from erupting the very instant he'd pushed into her. He moved his hand up and down as he closed his eyes and relived the ecstasy of being deep in her.

Roxi had taken what he'd given and had asked for more. There had been no hesitation on her part—she'd not been shy about telling him what she liked or wanted.

He stroked his hand faster, tightening his grip until he came with a low grunt. He didn't move until he'd finished, then he padded to her bathroom and cleaned up. For a brief moment, he dwelled on the thought he'd not used a condom that first time. Then he shoved it aside—it had happened, couldn't change it now. It had been a mistake and not one he'd be making again. The lack of a condom, not the sleeping with Roxi. That he *definitely* planned on doing again.

Finished dressing, he opened her door only to freeze as he heard Laila's voice.

"Where's Sam, Roxi?"

He closed the door almost completely, not sure Roxi would want Laila to know he'd been in her room with her all night.

"In bed? I don't know, Laila, I was walking with you, remember?"

Swivelling, he repositioned himself to see up the hallway. Roxi stood at the end, leaning there. He felt himself stir and took his time digesting what she wore. Low-riding grey sweats and a white shirt.

"He doesn't sleep much and is usually up by now."

Laila was right. He could see her now, by Roxi. There was no way he'd make it to his room without being spied. Not with where Laila stood.

"So perhaps he's allowing himself to sleep in."

Laila scowled and crossed her arms. Roxi huffed and shrugged.

"You got me, Laila," she said in a dry tone. "Sam spent the night with me, in my bed. We fucked like bunnies all night long. I wore him out and left him sleeping in my bed."

Roxi told her? Sam wasn't sure he believed it. Laughter made him realise Laila didn't believe it either.

"You and Sam? Oh, Roxi, that's a good one. Why didn't you just say you hadn't any clue?"

Sam caught the slight tensing of Roxi's body, even from this distance. Apparently Laila didn't. Her laughter bothered Roxi. Why?

"I did tell you, Laila."

Laila's smile grew. "So you did. I just..." More laughter.

"… Oh, God, you and Sam?"

"This is funny to you?"

Laila sobered. "That's a good one. I don't mean to laugh, Roxi, but…"

"But you are. I get it, Laila. I get it." Roxi walked towards the kitchen, each step breaking his heart a little more.

He'd never seen Laila so callous before.

Laila peered down the hall again as if unsure, then she headed in the direction Roxi had gone. He sneaked to his room and grabbed his shoes, only to creep out and do a short jog. The house was quiet when he got back. He paused in the entryway and listened for any voices. Nothing. Alert, he cautiously made his way in. Peering in the kitchen, he noticed a figure at the table.

He had to be honest. Seeing Laila wasn't what he'd expected. She sat there, leafing through a magazine as she drank coffee — judging by the smell.

"Laila?"

Her head snapped up and a grin crossed her pretty face. "Hey. Where have you been?"

"Running." He lowered his head and looked over his sweaty body.

Her fingers flexed around the mug as if she waited for him to say more. Or had the wish to say something herself. When she didn't speak, he turned and headed to his room. He was aware she followed him but didn't stop until she touched him. The feel of her fingers upon him did nothing sexually for him, however he did halt. Silent, he rotated to see her with worry in her expression.

"Everything okay, Sam?"

He'd detected honest concern in her tone. "Yes."

"I know this hospitalisation isn't easy on you."

"Not easy on anyone."

"I know that, but it's harder on us than many." She squeezed his arm then released him. "I'm sorry I didn't stand up to Dean and the others for you to stay with me."

"It's fine."

She wrung her hands and when her lower lip trembled, he knew he was screwed. He'd always hated seeing her cry. He drew her close and hugged her. She easily returned the hug, despite him being sweaty from his run.

"You're coming for Thanksgiving dinner."

"Of course."

"I don't know what I'd do if I didn't have you to fall back on, Sam."

He brushed his lips along her forehead. "You'll never have to worry about that, Laila, we're family."

She nodded against his chest and held him tighter.

To his right, movement caught his eye and he saw Roxi step from her room, her hair drawn back and loosely captured at the base of her neck. She'd dressed in jeans and a long-sleeved Seattle Sounders shirt. The smile she gave him almost had him stepping from Laila's embrace to her own. As she walked by and up the hall, he was mesmerised by the sway of her ass and the booted heels she wore.

"Roxi?" Laila said from his embrace.

"Yeah?" She peered back.

"Want to do dinner tonight? For all?"

Sam caught the tensing of Roxi's jaw. "Sure, we can do it. Your house, just let me know what time. Preferably by lunch, so I have time to make something."

"Great." She stepped away from Sam and reached up on tiptoes to give him a quick kiss. Nothing new for Laila to do, yet this time he never took his gaze off Roxi. "I'll see you later, then. Both of you."

When Laila captured his face in her hands, he glanced at her.

"Have a good day, Sam."

Then she was gone. He took a quick shower and came out to find Roxi measuring the doorway to her laundry area. He watched her in silence, waiting for her to notice him. She stared at him before shrugging.

"Measuring. I have to run to the building supply store anyway and figured I may as well get a door while I'm there." She answered his non-verbalised question.

"Door won't fit in your Tribeca."

"I know. I'll have it delivered." She wrote the measurements down on paper then shoved it in her pocket.

"I'll do it."

She blinked and shook her head in confusion. "Do what?"

"Bring it for you. I have a truck."

"No, I can't ask you to do that."

"You're not. I have to finish up at Second Chances then I can go."

Roxi looked at him a short time before she walked to him. She slid her hands up his arms. Their gazes locked. "Okay, you want to help me. I'll help you. Let's go to Second Chances and we'll stop at the store on the way home."

*Home.*

There was that word again. He swallowed, unused to the emotions bombarding him.

Her fingers danced along the back of his neck. "Unless you don't want me in your truck."

Lust hit him. "I want you." The words were deep and raspy. Didn't make them any less true.

Her eyes heated with passion. "Good." She stepped back and walked off, crooking her finger at him.

He willingly followed.

\* \* \* \*

Three hours later, he was under one of the sinks at Second Chances. Roxi was busy finishing up the painting. She'd been all smiles when the children arrived. The staff had got some as well. While Roxi never forced him into any conversation, she always made him feel included.

"How's it going?"

His entire body stiffened at the sound of her voice. Willing his hard cock to give him a break, he replied, "Okay."

"Wonderful. I'm going to get the paint cleaned up and I'll be back to help you."

55

She left and he craned his neck to watch her walk away. She never seemed to mind that his answers were so short and succinct. His body thrummed at the prospect of having her close again.

True to her word, she returned shortly. He ogled her long, firm, jean-encased legs before she crouched and he could see her face.

"What can I do?"

He wriggled his way out from beneath the sink and sat. A grin tipped up the corner of his mouth. She had splatters of paint on her smooth skin as well as in her hair.

"You're smiling," she said with feigned shock. "What's so funny?"

He was so pleased she didn't seem offended that he may have been laughing at her.

"You…" He circled a finger around his face.

Dawning grew in her expression. "Paint on my face?"

"And hair."

She sighed then shrugged. "I'm surprised I'm not wearing more, honestly."

"Like little freckles," he said. Sam gave into his urge to touch her and played a short version of connect the dots with the paint splatters on her face.

In half a heartbeat, his world narrowed to just the two of them. He stared in her eyes, the colour of rich coffee, and startled himself with what he saw. His future.

Roxi crouched there on her haunches, watching him right back. Her hair, mostly pulled back, aside from the few wisps which curled around her face, gentled her appearance. Soft. Alluring. Heart-stopping. She was all of that and more to him.

His shaft pulsed when he skimmed her lower lip with his thumb and she nipped it with her teeth. The blaze in her stare told him she, too, was more than aware of the increasing sexual draw between them.

It was just as strong as it had been the previous night. He lowered his gaze and stared at the rest of her. She'd pushed up the sleeves on her shirt and the way she sat manipulated her jeans tight over her thighs and – he knew – her firm ass.

Lust pounded through him. He longed to lift her and impale her on his cock. Her back against the wall, head tossing as she screamed his name. Right here. Right now.

"Come on, Marine, we have a bathroom to fix."

He moved his hand around to the back of her neck and pressed, encouraging her to shift closer. She followed his silent directive without hesitation. He lightly licked along the edges of her lips before capturing her mouth with his own. Light swipes along the seam and she opened for him.

Their groans were combined as tongues met and duelled. His cock swelled even more while her taste rejuvenated him. Soul included. Roxi had this way of banishing ghosts from his past without doing anything.

The sounds of a door opening and footsteps snapped him out of the 'Roxi zone' he'd been in. Ending the kiss, he reluctantly removed his hand from her. He almost lost his newly gained control when her tongue sneaked out and swiped along her lips like she wanted another taste.

"Sam?" Father O'Toole called out. "Roxi?"

Gaze locked with Roxi's, he didn't move when she replied to the call. "In the far left bathroom. We're fixing the sink."

A keen sense of loss filled him as she stood and broke their visual connection. He lay back and returned to work with the wrench, listening to Roxi and Father O'Toole talking in the doorway. It was a good thing he didn't have to concentrate too hard for his mind couldn't – or wouldn't – let go of the time he'd spent in Roxi's arms.

* * * *

Roxi waited at the Seattle bus station. A mocha latte in her hand, she worried her lower lip. Her mind was a jumbled mess. She and Sam had settled into an easy routine over these past few days and she had no problem with him staying at her place. Granted, the nights in his arms didn't

57

up the sleeves of her shirt and they wa—

No, it was the not telling Laila that constantly ate at her. She wasn't blind, she saw the way Laila looked at Sam. And she knew her friend was possessive over him.

*You've fallen for him,* her brain announced.

After a sigh, she drank some of her latte. No point in arguing—she had. Fallen fast and fallen hard.

"Aunt Roxi!"

Eric's voice pierced her bubble and she blinked as her eyes threatened to well up with tears. He strode through the station in his uniform, cover under one arm and bag in the other. Beside him walked Sandra, the mother of another cadet, Roy, who'd escorted them here.

"Eric," she said fondly, setting her drink down and accepting his hug with pleasure.

"I've missed you," he whispered in her ear.

"Missed you, too." She squeezed tighter before releasing him. "Thank you, Sandra. Hello, Roy."

"Ms Roxi."

The women shared a smile and walked out to Roxi's SUV. With the boys in the back, she chatted with Sandra as she took them home. Soon it was just her and Eric on the ferry to Bremerton.

"Ready for Thanksgiving?" she asked her nephew.

He nodded. She reached in her purse and withdrew his Game Boy. His eyes lit up the instant he saw it. He wasn't allowed electronics at the academy.

"I have to tell you something, Eric."

He stared at her, his large brown eyes focused directly on her. "What's wrong?"

"Nothing, sweetie. I just want you to know there is a guest at the house."

"Who?"

"A man named Sam Hoch."

Eric was silent for a moment, the electronic device she'd handed him ignored in his lap. "Why?"

"He is a very good friend to Master Guns and came out to

see him while he's in the hospital."

"He's military?"

She nodded. "Marine."

"Cool. Can I play now?"

She fought the urge to haul him close and kiss him. "Of course."

Eric played the remainder of the ferry ride. She sat beside him and read a book. It was routine for them. Once he'd settled down a bit more he'd tell her about how things were going at the academy. His game play continued even after they got back into the vehicle.

The garage door sat wide open as they pulled in the drive. She could see Sam working by his truck but he stopped when he noticed them.

"That's him?" Eric asked.

She parked outside so he'd continue to have room to work in the garage. "That's him."

All six feet three inches of hard-bodied Marine Recon hotness. He wore dark blue jeans that made her mouth water. A navy blue sweatshirt covered his impressive upper body—his defined, rock-solid muscles, powerful arms, warm skin that smelt like...

"Aunt Roxi?"

She blinked repeatedly as she attempted to pretend she'd not lost track of what Eric had been saying. Unfortunately she had.

"Sorry, Eric. What did you say?" She glanced at him.

"You seemed lost. I wanted to see if you were okay?"

Shutting off the engine, she gave him a smile. "I'm fine. Let's go so you can change then play."

The joy on his face warmed her. Together they climbed out. Tears stung her eyes as she watched him replace his cover then grab his bag. Sam walked towards them, his gaze lingering over her before moving to the young man who'd joined her at the front of her SUV.

"Eric, this is Sam Hoch. Sam, my nephew, Eric."

"Very nice to meet you, sir," Eric said, offering his hand.

"And you." Sam shook his hand and glanced back to her. "Go on, Eric. I'll be in shortly."

He said farewell and hurried inside. She was again alone with Sam Hoch.

"How are you?" she asked, not really expecting an in-depth explanation.

"You left early this morning." His gravelly voice made her panties wet.

"I did. Caught an early ferry and ran some errands in Seattle before gathering Eric. How are you?"

They walked into the garage and the second they stepped around the shelf and couldn't be seen from the outside, she was in his arms, pressed flush to his muscular physique. Her groan of pleasure was captured by his mouth as he kissed her. His tongue swept dominatingly through the heated recess of her mouth. Stroking. Surging. Thrusting. She nearly sank boneless to the floor. Sam held her up. Body aflame, she had one thought — getting him inside her as fast as possible. He ended the kiss, dragged a knuckle down the side of her face, and gave her a passionate look, one which only reaffirmed her desire for him.

"I'm fine." His deep voice rasped over her.

Yes. *Yes*, he was. Sam rotated and opened the door into the house.

"I just need to put my things away."

Sam stared at her, not saying a word. Her nipples tightened and that insistent pulse in her sex began again. She made her way to her room only to stop outside the laundry room. The door they'd got no longer occupied a space in her garage but hung here. That's what he'd been doing.

Glancing from the door to Sam, she touched two fingers to her heart and mouthed, "Thank you." His gaze warmed and he gave a sharp nod before he vanished back out into the garage.

She skimmed her lips before sighing and entering her room. Sinking against the closed door, she breathed heavily. Sam Hoch was dangerous. Especially to her. The feel of him against her, *in* her, all of it risked her heart more every second.

While she didn't know the nitty-gritty details about how he'd grown up, Laila had said it hadn't been easy. Her friend hadn't said much more than that, but she got the gist of it. Sam had had it really rough. She wanted to cry for the little boy he'd been as well as the pain he'd endured, and she loved the man he'd become.

*Loved.*

Well, shit, she'd gone and fallen in love. *No. It's not been that long. I can't possibly be in love with him. Could I?*

Taking a bit of time to compose herself, she went to the kitchen to bake some cookies. Ingredients gathered, she began, her gaze on the backyard. After a bit, she frowned and walked to the door. No Eric. She checked his room. Not there either. Wiping a hand on her jeans, she opened the door to the garage and looked there.

Eric was with Sam. They were by his Dodge 2500, which Sam had pulled out and had lifted the hood on. Her nephew stood on a step ladder, watching whatever Sam did.

Her heart clenched with emotion as she observed them together. Sam nodded every so often and, smiling, she stepped back into the house. She felt safe knowing Sam was with Eric. Quite safe.

After the cookies were finished, she started work on supper and was lost in her own world when she glanced up to see Laila standing there. After a small jump, she smiled.

"Hey."

Laila gave her a tired smile. "Hey, yourself. Sam said you were in here. I see Eric's bonded well with him. He's out there chatting away while Sam works on his truck."

"I saw them earlier. It's nice to see." She gave a nudge with her chin. "What's up with you? You look exhausted."

"I am." Laila sat at the table, a groan escaping.

"Everything okay at work?"

"Yeah, that's not it. It's…well, Dean Jr."

Roxi clenched her fingers around the spoon handle she was using on the spaghetti sauce. She was making a dish Eric had asked for.

"What'd he do?" No response prompted her to glance at her friend. "Laila? Answer me."

"They're not good house guests. Chris was smoking inside when I got home. They're demanding and just rude."

Tamping down her immediate desire to rush over there and kick their asses, Roxi remained where she was. "Tell them to stay at a hotel, then."

Another peek at her friend and she witnessed Laila chewing on her lower lip with a bunch of indecision in her expression. When she sighed heavily, Roxi tasted the sauce and placed the spoon on the dish before giving Laila all her attention.

"What's the problem?"

"I don't want to lose him, he's family. They all are."

She narrowed her eyes. "Bullshit."

Laila jerked like she'd been shot. "What?"

"Sam is more family to you than Junior Fuck over there or his two useless brothers. You know it, yet you continually take Dean's side when you know damn well that excuse of a human wouldn't cross the street to piss on you if you were on fire."

"Language, Roxi."

She scoffed. "Don't have time to be delicate, Laila. Sam would move mountains for you. It's time for you to make a decision on who is more important."

Laila's eyes flashed fire. "You don't know what it's like to lose your family, Roxi. So kindly keep your damn advice to yourself. Dean's in a tough spot."

Ignoring the stab of pain, she lifted her chin. "Just because I haven't lost my parents doesn't mean I can't recognise an asshole when I meet one."

The sound of the door opening reached them and she knew there was little time before either Sam or Eric arrived. Perhaps both.

"However, if you need to believe Dean's above reproach, then go deal with him."

"Hi, Aunt Roxi," Eric said, bounding in. The seriousness which had surrounded him while he'd been dressed in his academy uniform had vanished. "Hi again, Miss Laila, are you staying for dinner?"

"No, she can't," Roxi spoke up before Laila could. "She has company at her house she wants to spend time with. Her *family*."

Laila met her gaze, anger and hurt in her eyes, then she looked away. "Maybe some other time, Eric."

Sam appeared in the doorway and Roxi knew he recognised the tension. Turning back to the stove, she picked up the spoon and stirred the sauce. "Bye, Laila."

The chair scraped back and she heard Laila's farewells to Eric and Sam before her voice faded. Roxi chewed her lower lip. Maybe she *had* overstepped but damn it, it was about time Laila stood up for herself.

Eric popped up beside her. "Almost ready?"

His eager question made her smile. "Will you please set the table?"

"Yes, ma'am."

When she drained the spaghetti, she watched Sam assisting Eric. He nodded occasionally as he'd done near the truck, but still rarely spoke. Eric, if he noticed, didn't seem to care his companion was mostly silent. He chatted along happily.

Pasta in a bowl, she placed it on the table beside the pot of sauce. Spinning back to grab the salad and bread sticks, she ran into Sam.

"Oh!"

He steadied her and she struggled not to press closer. "Everything okay?"

She glanced around for Eric.

"He's washing up. Answer me."

"Fine," she managed to mutter before extracting herself from his grasp.

63

He didn't believe her, she could see that. Still, he didn't press the issue. Which was good, because Eric soon returned. They ate, with Eric telling them about school.

Throughout the meal, she felt Sam's intense gaze upon her. After dessert, Eric went to play a video game while she cleaned up. Sam stayed with her. She kept waiting for him to ask her again what was wrong, but he didn't. She huffed and Sam glanced at her.

"Just ask already."

One black eyebrow arched in silent question.

"About me and Laila and what happened."

"Not my business, but if you want to tell me" — a shrug — "I'll listen."

She wanted to shake him. His gaze never wavered from hers. The epitome of patience. So unlike her.

"Never mind."

He blinked and went back to wrapping up the leftover breadsticks. She watched him for a few moments. He was wearing a nondescript black T-shirt and jeans, and they affected her in so many ways. The way the sleeve cuffs hugged his muscles only emphasised the strength in his arms. She knew how delicious it was to be held by him. The flat abdominals with the ridges that she loved tracing with both her fingers and tongue. Powerful legs and lean hips she loved having between her…

"Roxi?"

"Huh?" *Shit. Got caught staring and fantasising. Damn near drooling, and I wouldn't be the least bit surprised to be standing in a puddle. Or lake.*

Those damnable evening-blue eyes darkened with understanding and more than a hint of desire. Lord help her, she wanted to touch him.

"Are you okay?"

She forced a smile. Was she? *Most assuredly not.* She was horny as hell and pissed off that she'd fought with Laila. "Fine." Even to her ears the word sounded like it had been pushed through gritted teeth.

He came closer and crowded her back 'til the edge of a counter met her spine. "You're lying." His hard cock pressed definitely and defiantly against her and he moved until there was no light between them. His warm, masculine scent surrounded her in a blanket of security.

Yes, she was. Instead of responding, she merely shrugged. Another flex of his hips had her swallowing hard as her clit pulsed and nipples pebbled. Sam dragged two knuckles down her cheek before he stepped away. She missed his closeness immediately but held her tongue, for Eric walked in.

"Mr Sam, will you play a video game with me?"

Blue eyes met hers with a question in them. She gave a brief nod and basically held her breath until Sam and Eric left. Once she'd completed the last bit of clean up, she propped her shoulder against the archway between the kitchen and living room.

The guys were on the couch, faces intent on the game. She shoved her hands in her pockets and just watched their interaction. Eric looked up and gave her a heart-melting smile.

"Ready, Aunt Roxi?"

"Whenever you two finish."

"We're done now. Are you coming on our walk, Mr Sam?"

Again those blue eyes found her.

"Come if you like, Sam."

"Please, Mr Sam. I would love to hear more about being in the Marines. Aunt Roxi doesn't talk about it much."

"Okay," he said, still holding her gaze.

The television was shut off and they grabbed coats before walking out the front door. Night had fallen and so the street and porch lights lit their way. They walked with Eric between them.

"So what's it like being a Marine for you, Mr Sam?"

She watched from her periphery for his reaction to Eric's question.

# Chapter Five

Sam stared at the boy who walked with him and the lovely Roxi. Her nephew was an inquisitive lad. Smart too.

"It is an honour for me," he replied honestly. "With the Marine Corps you have a family." He paused. "Or another family."

He sliced his gaze to Roxi. She wore her hair loose and it fluttered with the breeze. The overwhelming urge to grab her and kiss her hit him. Hard. It wasn't like the feeling ever truly left him, though. She seemed a bit more relaxed now than she had back at the house, after whatever had occurred between her and Laila. He'd wanted to have her share but he didn't want to intrude on her business.

*Pathetic man. A Marine. A Recon Marine and feelings scare you.*

"Do you have a family, Mr Sam?"

"Eric, I don't think Sam wants to talk about that," Roxi admonished. Her eyes met his and were full of apology.

"It's okay," he said, surprising himself. Focusing back on Eric, he smiled. "The Corps is my family, aside from Laila and Master Gunnery Sergeant Richardson."

"What happened to your parents?"

"I don't know. I grew up in…in foster care."

There was no way he was telling a boy that his parents had put him in the car and had driven him to a city in Minnesota — a different state than he had lived in — and had left him. Alone. No money, no friends, no anything. He avoided looking at Roxi, not wanting to witness the sympathy in her eyes. Eric touched his arm briefly and he glanced at the boy.

"Aunt Roxi and I are your family too."

He was humbled. "Thank you, Eric." This time he did chance a look at Roxi and he swore there were tears in her eyes. He'd just had his defences breached by a boy he'd known less than a day.

Roxi steered the conversation back to a less emotional topic for him. He found himself amazed at the difference between the boy walking with him and the one he'd met in uniform. Eric knew how to have fun and relax when he wasn't in uniform. Something Sam had not managed to do.

Back at the house—he'd waved to Laila on the porch but hadn't swung off to talk to her, unwilling to leave Eric and Roxi—he was surprised to see the boy grab a board game from a shelf instead of a video game and take it to the kitchen table. Turned out it was a board-and-card game.

"You playing?" Roxi questioned from where she set it up.

"This looks like—"

"Sam. You are more than welcome to play. Eric would love it if you joined in." She neared and put a hand on his arm, the strength and warmth of her touch like a shock to his system. "It's our way of staying close and not allowing technology to get in between us."

"You're playing, right, Sam?"

He caught Roxi's subtle flinch when Eric didn't use 'Mr' before his name and he quickly assured them both that Sam was just fine.

Eric's big brown eyes watched him expectantly. "So you'll play?"

"Yes."

The boy's answering grin was enough to banish any remaining uncertainty. Eric hurried to the table in his camo pants and brown shirt.

A warrior in the making. They played the game Sequence until Roxi called it a night.

"Night, Eric." She hugged and kissed him.

"Night, Aunt Roxi." Eric skidded to the edge of the kitchen. "Goodnight, Sam."

"Goodnight, Eric." Sam found Roxi grinning at him. "What?"

"I'd begun to wonder if you ever smiled. You do. You're good with kids." She gathered up the chips. "He likes you."

Sam moved towards her and reached around her to place the cards in the case. "What about you?"

She quivered beneath him. "Oh, I like you too."

His cock hardened to the point of almost being painful. Lord, he wanted to rip her clothes off and sink between her thighs, into her velvet heat. She called to him on so many different levels, he couldn't even begin to start explaining it.

Roxi rotated so they were face to face. So close. So tempting.

"Sam?"

He lowered his lids until he stared at her through his lashes. Her full, plump lips begged to be kissed. He longed to drag his tongue down her throat to the neckline of her shirt. And beyond. Expose the treasures she kept hidden.

"Roxi."

*Ding dong.* Disappointment flashed across her face and he knew it was echoed on his own. She reached up and cupped his cheek.

"That's going to be for you," she murmured.

"Me?"

"It's Laila." She slipped away from him and finished gathering the items from the table.

How she knew, he didn't know and couldn't explain. What he did know was he was upset with the interruption. He walked out only to re-enter the kitchen and kiss Roxi until her curves sank into him. If he'd thought his cock was hard before, it was nothing compared to right now. Roxi's gaze was glazed and he couldn't help the arrogant smirk he felt flash across his face. He headed for the door, untucking his shirt as he went. He opened it to find Roxi had been correct. It was Laila.

"Hey, Sam."

He ran his gaze over her. "Laila."

She stared at him before launching herself into his arms. He caught her instinctively and held her close. Backing up, he closed the door on the cold, rainy night. A sound from behind him had him turning his head. Roxi stood there watching the two of them before she disappeared down the hall.

*Damn it!*

Setting Laila away from him, he then led her to the sofa. She didn't give him any room, just clung to him crying. He was out of his league. Crying women weren't anything he'd had extensive experience with. But this was Laila. His sister in every way that mattered.

"Is it Dean?" he asked with trepidation.

She shook her head against his shoulder and relief swamped him. One thing off the list.

"Is it money?"

"No." Her single word was muffled by his chest.

"Laila. Tell me. I can't help you if you don't tell me what the problem is."

The woman in his arms hugged him tighter. He thought back to the first day they'd met. Laila burrowed closer.

"Do you remember the day we met? Dean brought me with him to your house. You and your mom had been baking all day." He drew back and smoothed her hair away from red, puffy, teary eyes. "Your hair was in pigtails and you had flour on your nose, as well as all over your apron."

As he'd hoped, she cracked a smile at the memory. "You were surly."

Surly was putting it mildly. Dean had picked him up from the home saying he had a surprise for him. They'd ended up at Laila's house. It was really Dean's birthday celebration but he'd made the day about the kids. Still, as the odd child who'd been tossed about so often, he hadn't been able to let down his guard. Terrance and Lenore Atkins had never seemed put off by his attitude and had welcomed him into their home with the same enthusiasm as they had Dean.

Their sole daughter had been another story entirely.

"You punched me in the nose," he reminded her.

"You laughed at me."

He nodded. "I did." A deep breath. "What's wrong, Laila?"

"Do you like Roxi?"

He wondered where this was going. "Yes. She's a very nice person." *And oh so responsive to me in bed.*

His cock twitched at the thought and he forced himself to remain focused on Laila.

"I see the way you watch her, Sam."

This time he did set her away from him. "What are you talking about, Laila?"

She played with her necklace and refused to meet his gaze. "You stare at her with hunger in your eyes. Have you slept with her?"

He shook his head. "Oh, no. I'm not having this conversation with you, Laila. I don't know what's bothering you, but you're not about to come over here and start that kind of stuff." Shifting so he faced her on the couch, he rested one arm along the back. "Roxi is a very beautiful woman, I'm not a blind man, Laila. I see her appeal."

"You like her." This time it wasn't a question.

"Let's say I do, Laila. So what?"

She chewed on her lower lip for a minute. "She told me to kick Dean and the others out of the house. That you're more my *family* that he is. I got so mad at her, I told her she couldn't possibly know what it was like to lose her parents and not have family."

He stiffened at the mention of Dean Jr but kept his mouth shut about him. "You know that wasn't nice, Laila. You have family. You know I'm always here for you, you know that, right? Now, you have Dean and his brothers as well. And Master Guns is gonna pull through."

"What if he doesn't?"

He swallowed hard. That wasn't an option he wanted to think on. "We have to think positive, Laila. He's a strong man, always has been."

Tears slipped down her brown face and he reached out to wipe them away with his knuckle.

"Bone cancer is not like a heart attack, Sam."

"I know. Doesn't change the fact he's still of strong constitution, Laila. We have to be strong for him, too." He lifted her chin with his fingers. "None of this tells me why she told you to tell Dean and his cousins to get out."

"I don't like them in my home. I don't feel welcome there anymore. And I don't feel welcome here now, after saying what I did to Roxi."

"So tell them to stay in a hotel." It felt odd saying those words, considering he hadn't had to go to one.

"After Thanksgiving. I can last a week." She tucked some hair behind her ear. "You are eating with us still, right? I've told Dean you are. He said he'd behave."

"So it will be you, me, Dean and his brothers, and Roxi along with Eric?"

She shook her head. "No."

He grew puzzled. "Roxi isn't here for the holiday?"

"Oh, she is, but she and Eric don't do a big thing for Thanksgiving. They go to a shelter and help out there, and usually eat there as well." A shrug. "She's done it for as long as I have known her. When she started keeping Eric for Ritchie, she naturally took him along."

He nodded. "Okay. I'll be there. You know I will." He touched her arm. "Laila, you need to apologise to her."

She began to pout and he shook his head.

"No, you know what you said was wrong and maybe you should think about why her words bothered you so much."

"Why are you taking her side?"

"I'm not taking sides, Laila." He pushed up from the couch. "Now, go home and get some sleep."

He could see her reluctance but he refused to cave. It was late and he knew she'd be working in the morning. She needed to rest.

She stood then threw her arms around him. "I love you,

71

Sam."

"Love you, too, Laila."

He walked her to the door then to her porch, dashing through the rain. Under the awning he waited until she opened the door before he sprinted back across the short distance to Roxi's house and let himself back inside. He slipped off his shoes by the door and walked in socked feet to double-check the sliding door in the kitchen before shutting off the lights and heading for his room.

At his door, he paused, glancing down the hall to where a sliver of warm light came from the opening of Roxi's room. He knew she slept with her door like that, habit from when she'd first started taking care of Eric, so she could hear him if he had a nightmare.

Like she'd done for him. *When you attacked her.* He shoved that unwanted memory away even as a spear of fear hit him. What if he did something like that to Eric? The mere thought soured his gut.

In his room, he swiftly changed into something dry then made his way to Roxi's door. He knocked softly but didn't receive any response. Sam pushed the door open and stepped in. She lay on her belly in the middle of her queen-sized bed, feet towards him and her head facing the wall. Repositioning the door to its original spot, he leaned against the wall beside it and stared at her.

She wore another camisole and pair of lounge pants, which looked cottony soft. The pants were a pale pink and the shirt white, which beautifully offset her darker skin tone.

"You just gonna stand there, Marine?" she asked in a soft voice, still flipping through the magazine which lay in front of her. "Or were you planning on coming over here?"

He couldn't stay away, so he joined her on the bed. The magazine was on boots. Different styles and types. Some of the pages had been dog-eared and he wondered if she were actually shopping or just browsing. She rested her head on his shoulder and his body immediately reacted. Like it hadn't with Laila.

"Get things straight with Laila?"

"Not sure," he replied honestly. "She isn't having a good time right now. This is hard on her."

Roxi stiffened. "It's hard on a lot of people, you can't be thinking it's a walk in the park, seeing Master Guns lying there, weak and sick. He was a father to you as well."

Resting his head on one hand, he lay on his side and used his other hand to swipe her hair off her shoulder, allowing him to see her face. Her eyes remained transfixed on the glossy pages before her. His fingers skimmed along the smooth skin of her neck.

"He is more of a father than I ever knew a man could be to a child."

She looked at him. "Tell me how you met him?"

He hesitated, his reaction instinctive to someone asking him about his past. But he was lost in her eyes, drowning in her compassion.

"Never mind. Tell me about some of the things you and Laila did growing up together."

So he did, took a deep breath and began to tell her of the times he'd spent with Laila and Dean. Those magical times when he hadn't had to be at a home where he didn't feel like he belonged and had been able to be with the people who meant more to him than he'd ever believed possible. Even Terrance and Lenore had been important to him. Those four had taught him what a family was supposed to be like. How it *should* be — filled with love and support.

Roxi pushed the magazine away and mimicked his position. She listened to his story with rapt attention without interrupting him. He could see her feelings on her face as he continued.

The room shrank to just the two of them on the bed. Nothing else mattered. Him and her. That was all there was.

"Can I ask you a question?"

He nodded.

"He didn't adopt you? All that time you spent with him

73

and he didn't try?"

"No. He left so often with the Corps, the state wouldn't allow it. He did try." He swallowed as he recalled the places he'd been sent. "He would always come visit, though. And he came to get me, so I could attend Laila's parents' funeral. I was in another part of the state by that time. Older and angry. But then he showed up and I wanted to be angry with him as well, but I just couldn't. Then he told me why he was there. I'd never felt hurt like that before." He smiled sadly. "Her parents were so wonderful, never treated me like an outside white boy who didn't belong. Lenore always smelt like some home-baked goods. And Terrance taught me about cars and how to fix them. Some visits, the three of us, Terrance, Dean and myself, would be out most of the day under the hood of a vehicle."

She trailed her index finger over his hand, now on the bed. In and out of each digit, over the knuckles — a soothing, sensual touch.

"You and Laila learned to get over your differences?"

He watched her touching him. "Yes. Eventually. We're both a bit headstrong." He lifted his shoulders in a laconic move. "She's my sister. We've always kept in touch."

"I see that. You're much different with her."

"How so?"

"More open. She sees the Sam you hide from the world."

"Does that bother you?"

"On some level, yes. But, I also know I'm not held in the same regard as Laila. You have every right to your secrets, Sam Hoch. We all have them."

Roxi was right about that. She wasn't held in the same regard as Laila. For in no way did he view this sexy woman before him in any sisterly fashion. And had no plans to do so. He captured her fingers with his and stroked them as he brought them to his mouth. Nipping the tip of her thumb, he then licked away the bite.

"You are a beautiful woman, Roxanne Mammon."

"You sure you're okay with Eric following you around?".

Her change of topic was abrupt and he wanted to draw her back to a more intimate one but let it go. "He's fine. Great kid."

"He is that. Ritchie will be here the Saturday after Thanksgiving. I don't know what Laila's plans are for her house guests but you are more than welcome to continue to crash here. I don't mind. I do go back to work that week but you have a garage door opener, so that shouldn't be a problem for you."

"Why aren't you working this week?"

"I always take off when Eric comes to see me. At least for the first week. If he's here longer, then other arrangements are made during the day while I'm working."

He kissed her middle finger before sucking it into his mouth. Her lids fluttered and she took a deep breath.

"You're an amazing woman."

"And you are trying to distract me."

He flashed a wicked grin. "Is it working?"

"Most definitely."

With a quick jerk, he dragged her to lie across his body. "Wonderful." Then he captured her mouth in a hungry kiss, explaining all of the emotions he'd not been able to vocalise when it came to this woman. Soon, the only noise in the room was that of skin on skin and Roxi's soft moans.

\* \* \* \*

Roxi smiled at the man across from her and served him some stuffing. "Happy Thanksgiving," she said.

With a nod, the man moved on and she cast her gaze askew to check on her nephew. He was a few people from her, serving the mashed potatoes. As if he felt her stare, he glanced at her and gave her a big grin.

Eric was so outgoing, the complete opposite of how she pictured Sam as a child. Being shuttled from home to home, tossed out on his ear in some of the coldest parts of winter. Hell, it was no wonder the man was withdrawn and very protective of his emotions and who he chose to share them with.

Since that night in her bedroom when he'd opened up to her, he'd fallen back into the man who barely said anything. Not that he was being snobbish, he just didn't speak unless what he had to say was truly worth it. Eric had taken a huge liking to him and it made her tear up to watch them together. No matter how he was with adults, Sam never kept things from Eric. He would help him with anything. There'd been a few times she'd overheard them laughing from the living room as they played a video game. Eric was as good for him as Sam was for Eric.

Sam. Just the thought of him made something warm unfurl in her belly. She wanted to climb as close as she could and wrap around him. Allow his powerful body to press against her, his scent in her nose, the feel of his skin beneath her hands.

Shaking off the thought, she continued serving the numerous people who stood in line to get a warm holiday meal. When it was time for her and Eric to eat, they took their plates and sat down at one of the tables, joining the members there.

After dinner, she and Eric helped clean up before they meandered out into the cold, windy night. She hugged him to her as they walked.

"I'm proud of you, Eric."

"For what?"

"Helping out today."

"It's our thing, Aunt Roxi. I like doing it. Especially with you."

Damn, he knew how to make the tears start. She nodded and surreptitiously wiped them away before they could fall. "You're one heck of a kid, Eric."

At the car, she started the engine and did a quick check to make sure Eric had fastened his seat belt. "Hungry for some dessert?"

"Yes," he said, grinning from ear to ear.

"Let's go home then."

They chatted easily and told jokes on the way there. When she parked in the garage, Eric was bouncing in his seat. She chuckled as he bounded from the vehicle and dashed for the door. After waiting for the garage door to shut behind her, she followed him in. The house was empty and she tried to ignore why it hurt her so much that Sam wasn't there and was still over with Laila.

Putting her things away, she returned to the kitchen to find Eric waiting for her. His large eyes were bright and hopeful. She winked at him and went to the fridge to withdraw the mint chocolate mousse pie she had made before they'd left this morning.

"Something hot to drink, or would you like milk?"

"Hot chocolate?"

"Hot chocolate and chocolate pie?" Her tone was full of teasing shock. He flashed a disarming grin and she shook her head. "Okay. You got it."

Soon they sat at the table eating and drinking. When they heard the garage door open, Eric grinned widely. "Sam's back," he said with obvious joy.

He slid from the table before hastening from the kitchen. She knew exactly where he was going. Same damn place she wanted to be, near Sam.

She exhaled on a long breath and prayed for strength. The strength to see him and not run into his arms, lift her lips for his kisses. They'd not been intimate since the first night Eric had arrived — not sexually, anyway. That first night had been pretty damn intimate in her opinion when she'd learnt more about him, but Sam had withdrawn since then.

Her life was spinning out of control and she wasn't completely honest she wanted it back to normal. Yes, she knew this hurtling down the mountain road wasn't the safest, smartest way to go about life, but she'd always been more of an impulsive person. The Corps had put structure and order in her life. But she was still the woman she'd been earlier, the one who would just jump in her car and go for a weekend, destination unknown. If it meant sleeping under the stars, then so be it.

Enter Sam Hoch. Every facet of his life was in order. It wasn't solely because he was a Marine—granted, that enhanced it quite a bit. She had him figured out. Sam didn't want to get hurt and kept an emotional distance from people. Except Laila, Dean, and Eric.

He didn't keep such a huge distance from her, she noticed it. She tried not to be hurt by it, but it wasn't easy. Especially when she heard him carry on a full conversation with Laila, however, only to reduce interaction with her to a sentence. The more it happened the harder it was to deal with.

She got it, truly she did, but, come on, surely she was entitled to a bit more. They'd shared their bodies on occasion. The man had gone after her when she'd tried to wake him from a nightmare. None of it mattered to her. She wanted the Sam who she knew honestly expected anyone he allowed close to leave him at a moment's notice.

Yes, Roxi knew he wasn't the type of man to just go out and sleep with people. So somewhere, she must have struck some kind of chord in him. If she could just find it and have it all the time.

She missed him at night. Missed his large strong body next to hers in bed. Sleeping with his arms around her, the beat of his heart identical to her own. She'd never felt as safe in another's arms. Not that she had been with lots of people, for she hadn't. But neither had she been a virgin when she'd met Sam.

*Hadn't been one of them in a long time.* Flipping a mental bird, she forced herself to remain seated. Eric would come back in soon, his pie wasn't finished nor his hot chocolate. And there was no reason for her to rush in the other room and see Sam.

*Are you sure about that?*

Damn unwanted questions from the subconscious. Tightening her fingers around the mug she held, she ignored the query and lifted the drink to her lips. The warm brew slipped into her mouth and she swallowed the hot water with lemon just as Sam walked in the room with Eric.

Their stares locked, his gaze full of hunger before it was masked. She gave him a short nod, maintaining the pretence she still drank, refusing to let him know how much he affected her. Damn, he looked good. He wore navy blue slacks and a silver-grey long-sleeved button-down shirt. The first few buttons were open and she stared at the expanse of tanned skin which peeked out at her.

"Have some pie, Sam. Aunt Roxi made it. It's mint chocolate mousse." Eric began pulling down a plate for him even as he spoke.

Sam stared at her and she back at him. Neither spoke, yet she could feel the line between them strengthen. She had shifted in her chair before she knew it and gave herself a strong mental reprimand when she realised she'd begun to move in his direction.

"Roxi," he finally said, his voice deep.

"Hello, Sam. Did you have a nice day with Laila and family?"

Terseness flashed like lightning across his face before it vanished. He gave her a nod and she lowered her cup— white with a black Marine logo—to the tabletop.

"Here you go, Sam." Eric handed him a plate.

"He may be full, Eric," she said gently.

He held her gaze for a moment before he gave Eric a small smile. "I'd love a piece." They went to the counter where it sat.

Rolling her lower lip in her teeth, she got up from her chair. "Can I get you something hot to drink, Sam?"

"Whatever you're having is fine." He glanced at her over his shoulder, blue gaze raking up and down her form.

She returned the gesture then faced the kettle and turned on the burner. While it heated, she ducked back in the fridge to grab another slice of lemon to put in the cup. She got him a mug and soon was joining them at the table, sliding the drink over to where Sam sat across from her.

He cut off a bite and ate, his gaze locked with hers. Her belly exploded like a flutter of butterflies taking off when disturbed. The deep blue of his eyes darkened as he withdrew the fork from his mouth. His tongue sneaked out and swiped at the corners of his mouth.

"Delicious."

She swallowed. Was he referring to the pie or memories of her? She wasn't sure. Her heart pounded and her nipples were tight, pressing against the fabric of her bra. She tried not to squirm under his observation but it wasn't easy to hold still. Her pussy pulsed and grew wet as she had a vision of him feasting on her the same way he'd seemed to enjoy that first bite of pie.

"Glad you like it." She willed Eric to speak up and distract him but her nephew was far too into the pie to notice anything amiss between the two adults in the room.

The corner of Sam's mouth turned up as if he knew precisely what she wished for. Something to break the spell between them. All he'd have to do was drop his gaze and she'd be okay. She hadn't the strength to shatter it. And damn if it didn't seem like he wanted her eyes on him. She sat and suffered through three more bites before he released her.

Insides a tumultuous mess, she dropped her gaze to the nearly empty cup before her. *Damn him!* Damn him for having such an effect on her. More to the point, damn her for not being stronger.

She took a slow, deep breath to centre herself. When she looked up he waited for her, his eyes drawing her back in until she was saved by the ringing of the phone. Pushing away from the table, she went to the cordless and lifted it to her ear.

"Hello?"

"Hey, sis."

Relief swarmed through her. No matter how often he was away overseas, hearing her brother's voice was such a reprieve.

"Hey, yourself. You okay?"

"Wonderful. Happy Thanksgiving. Is he still awake?"

"He sure is. Hang on." Turning back to the kitchen, she said, "Eric?"

"Yes?"

"It's your dad. He would love to talk to you."

Eric was at her side before she'd even finished talking. He took the phone and Roxi left as he was saying hello. She went back in the kitchen to allow him some privacy.

Sam wasn't at the table when she looked in but she sure found him once she stepped fully into the kitchen. He stood at the sink, rinsing off his plate before he placed it in the dishwasher. She licked her lips at the way his pants tightened around his ass, courtesy of him bending over.

He stood up and peered at her. Her heart hitched a bit before settling back into a comfortable rhythm. He had such long lashes, it just wasn't fair. Though there was no way his face would be considered feminine — he had too many angles and a masculine hardness to his features. *I could stare at him for hours.*

Silently, he strolled towards her. She didn't move. She *couldn't* move. Their gazes locked on one another as she waited for whatever he had planned. In the back of her mind she could hear Eric still talking to his father but she never took her attention from the man who made her kitchen seem a quarter of its size with how he filled it up.

The closer he got, the more her body craved his touch. She was such a shameless hussy. His stare flickered past her briefly before returning to her face. One hand lifted to touch her cheek and she inhaled sharply at the contact.

"Happy Thanksgiving, Roxi."

"Same to you, Sam. I hope you had a good day."

That look drifted down to her lips then back up. "It was. Yours?"

The smile on her face felt a bit forced. "Wonderful. I love helping out at the soup kitchen." How could one man make her feel so out of control? Damn it, all she wanted was to feel the press of his lips on hers. She dug her nails into her palm so she wouldn't reach for him.

"Good." He stepped back and even though it was just a simple touch he'd given her, she still felt the loss deep inside her soul.

Her legs trembled as she made her way to the table and sat back before her slice of pie. Only about three bites remained but she didn't feel much like eating anything. Oh, she was hungry, but not for anything on the plate. If it wasn't Sam Hoch, it wouldn't do.

Eric came back in and handed her the phone. She listened half-heartedly to her brother as he told her when to expect him on Sunday. After the farewell, she ended the call and placed the receiver beside her.

"Finish up your pie, Eric. It's getting late."

His eyes sparkled as he did as she'd told him. She knew he was extremely excited about his father coming home. Hell, she was as well.

Soon, Eric was in bed and she was brushing her teeth. Shutting off her light, she slid beneath the bedding. The sheets, they burned her, she was so hypersensitive in wanting Sam. Each shift she made was like flames licking at her skin. Her nipples, tight and pebbled, ached for something. No. Not something. Someone. Sam. His touch. Each breath she took rubbed the cotton sheet against her breasts, shooting sparks through her as she struggled with the need to cry out.

It didn't work—each time she moved a bit in an attempt to find a position which didn't make her almost crazy with lust, she enflamed the urge even more. She drifted her hand down, over her flat belly, the close-cropped hair at her pussy, and she slipped two fingers through into the moistness.

She captured her lower lip in her mouth and tried to contain her whimper. She was wet. She circled her clit and shuddered. So near already to her release. She closed her eyes and conjured up the image of Sam Hoch, which never seemed far away. Chiselled features, muscled body and those damn blue eyes. It was the eyes that got her every time. Faster and faster she stimulated herself as she struggled not to come so soon. She wanted it to last. Wanted the feeling to build, more and more until she could just not take it any longer.

*You want to feel like you do when in Sam's arms.*

That revelation disturbed the hell out of her and she gave in, allowing herself some respite. An easy flick of her fingers and she orgasmed, fragmenting as pleasure washed over her. But now it had a hollow feel to it. Like something was missing.

*Yeah, Sam's cock. Long and thick, filling you. Shoving you and the bed against the wall with each forward thrust. His hands on your breasts, tugging and flicking your nipples. Rolling them until there is just a hint of pain in with your pleasure. Or is it his fingers between your legs as he powers into you, over and over again giving you that extra little push to get over the edge as he plays with your clit?*

Frustration welled over and she swore as she rolled then punched her pillow. Hell, now she couldn't even get off without her brain adding in some damn comments. But that wasn't what truly bothered her, it was the fact they had been dead on. She wanted Sam. And in more than just the physical. Something deep inside her found peace when she was with him.

Her sleep, once she succumbed, was light and fitful. When the phone jarred her from it, she was more grateful than pissed off to be receiving a call at two-thirty in the morning. Reaching for handset, she pressed the talk button after she held the phone.

"Yes?"

"Ms Mammon, this is Chet Haskell from Security Protection Inspection and Enforcement Services. The silent alarm at your bank has been activated. The police are already en route, I called the bank manager, Jules King, and he asked that you be there in his stead, since he is out of the state."

The minute the caller had identified himself as being from SPIES, she'd been fully awake and already on the move. They were expecting a large shipment of diamonds to their safe deposit and vault area and she immediately wondered if that was the target. "I'll be on my way, thank you for the call, Chet." She hung up on him and finished throwing on her clothing.

At the door, she paused. Eric. Without thinking about the wisdom of her decision, she opened the door to Sam's room and approached the bed.

"Sam," she whispered, remembering at the last moment it may not be in her best interest to grab him while he was sleeping.

"Roxi?" His sleep-laden voice dragged along her skin like warmed velvet.

"I have to run to the bank. Can you keep an eye out on Eric for me? If I'm not back by the time he wakes, he knows how to get his own—"

"What's wrong?"

"The alarm's been activated."

His hand gripped her and held her as he stepped from the bed. In the dark of the room she couldn't see him, but she sure as hell could feel the heat from his body. Lord, she wanted to rub against him. Lick him. Bite him. Suck him.

"I've got Eric. Go."

He drew her in closer instead of releasing her, though. When his lips brushed hers lightly she held her breath, anticipating a kiss. She didn't get it.

"Be careful, Roxi."

"Thank you, Sam." She swallowed. "For...you know, keeping an eye on Eric."

"You'd better go."

Was it her or did his voice sound even more raspy? She stepped back and headed for the door, closing it almost all the way. Ignoring the pounding of her heart and the cry of her body which told her to hightail it back into that room

84

and join that man in bed, she hastened to her vehicle and headed off.

As she drove, she cursed the number of cars on the road. *Damn Black Friday shopping deals.* She wove in and out of traffic nearing her destination. She parked next to a large SUV with flashing lights and jumped out. Scanning the crowd, she spotted the man in charge.

She headed for him only to be stopped by another officer. "I'm sorry, ma'am, you need to stay back."

"I'm Roxanne Mammon, my boss sent me here. He's out of town. I'm part of security for the bank."

"Head of security?"

She shook her head. "I need to speak to the man in charge so I can get in there and let you know if anything was taken."

After he looked at her identification he led her to the man she'd come to see. His name turned out to be Eric as well. This man was tall, white and balding.

Together they went in the building and she immediately began her assessment. Yes, some money had been taken, but thankfully the robbers hadn't known about the diamonds, for they still remained where they'd been placed.

# Chapter Six

Sam woke earlier than normal. To be fair, he'd really only dozed since Roxi had come into his room and had woken him with her news of a bank break-in. He sat out in the living room, watching the news to see if he could catch any information on it.

He'd wanted desperately to go down there with her. *For what?* His brain posed the question. *The police were there and Roxi is capable of handling herself. She* was *a Marine after all.*

He knew that and logically he knew she didn't need him at her side. It didn't stop him from wishing, though. He heard Eric stir and got up, shutting off the television. In the kitchen he poured himself a cup of the coffee he'd brewed earlier.

Not much later, Eric walked in, still appearing a bit sleepy. "Morning, Sam," the boy said.

"Eric."

He studied the room. "Where's Aunt Roxi?"

"She got called to work early this morning."

A flash of emotion filled Eric's face. He knew the look. Concern.

"She said she'd be back as soon as she can. And that we're to start breakfast without her."

That seemed to be what Eric needed to hear for he nodded and smiled. "We usually do waffles the day after Thanksgiving. Can you make them? I know where the iron is."

Never had before, but he'd do his best. "Why waffles over pancakes?" He was curious.

Eric's grin lit up his entire face. "Aunt Roxi says they're

better because they have little pockets to hold your syrup and butter. She says pancakes just can't compare."

"Waffles it is then." Made sense why she'd made them before as opposed to pancakes.

Eric knew where everything was and soon Sam was holding a box of mix as his helper grabbed the bowl. It didn't take long and he had the batter whipped up. After first measuring the one out, he poured it on the heated iron. He closed the lid, watching as Eric set plates beside them then grabbed syrup from the fridge.

"This gets heated." He handed Sam the syrup.

"All right."

He made waffles for Roxi as well in case she made it back before lunch. The hot links he found in the fridge were cooked up as well and it didn't take long until he and Eric were sitting down and eating, like only hungry men could. The boy had orange juice before him along with a glass of milk. Sam had juice and coffee.

A funny shiver went down his spine and he peered up to see Roxi leaning against the doorway into the kitchen. She looked tired but beautiful. Her hair cascaded around her face, hiding the shadows under her eyes.

"Any left for me?" she asked, hope in her words.

"Aunt Roxi!" Eric said with a grin. "Sam made me waffles."

"I see that." Her warm brown eyes moved back to his face and she gave him the slightest of grins.

He got to his feet and fixed her a plate, heating the waffles then placing the food on the table, beside her nephew and again, across from him. It was fast becoming a favourite pastime of his, watching her. She was so expressive. His Roxi was such a strong woman, fiercely protective of those she cared for, and from what he could tell, she cared for a lot of people.

But there were a few times, usually when she watched her nephew, that she got this almost wistful look on her face. Everything about her softened and he couldn't see a Marine, a security officer, all he could see was woman. And it called to him, deep down. He wanted to protect her, gather her close, and fight all her battles for her.

"Thank you," she said.

He saw the tension in her shoulders as she sat down. She was wearing a white T-shirt and jeans. There was an image of Calvin and Hobbes on her top. He read the words and shook his head, amused.

She ate and offered to clean up. He sat in his chair and watched her after Eric left them alone. Sliding his chair back, he rose and joined her at the sink.

"You look tired."

"Yeah, I am. Thanks for fixing him breakfast. I know how much he loves his waffles."

He inhaled and allowed the tantalising scent of autumn to flow over him. "He tells me you're the one who prefers waffles to pancakes because of the pockets in them."

"He's right. I do. But thank you still, for keeping an eye on him."

"Not a problem." He couldn't resist anymore and reached out to tuck some of her hair behind her ear. When she moved away from his touch, he frowned. Did she suddenly not wish for him to touch her?

She glanced at him and said, "I'm sorry, Sam. I don't want Eric to make up or think there's anything between us."

He nodded and stepped back. His mind raced with the words she'd just spoken. *Make up or think*…what did that mean? He opened his mouth to ask but snapped it shut instead. This was neither the time nor the place for this conversation. He watched how stiffly she held herself and paid no heed to the unpleasant feeling which coursed through him at the knowledge this may just be a fling for her.

*You have no claim on her,* he told himself, gathering the rest of the items from the table. A denial from deep within his soul roared at him. It shocked him — why was he suddenly caring about a relationship? True, he didn't go out and fuck anything that moved, he had way more discretion than that, but never once had he allowed real emotions into the picture.

Until Roxi.

Something clenched around his heart and he recognised the foul caress and stench of fear. She scared him. This woman had the ability to get him to care deeply for her. That in turn meant she wielded the power to eviscerate him as well, leaving him a shell of a man again.

It was his turn to stiffen. He wasn't about to go out that way. He had to protect himself. This was why he couldn't afford attachments. He didn't trust anyone with that type of power over him.

Still, he couldn't help but be drawn to Roxi. There was this magnetic quality about her that pulled him. He wanted to know more about her. He wanted more, period. Another clench around his heart. With a deep breath, he told himself it was nothing more than two people enjoying one another. Nothing more personal than that.

*Like sleeping with another person, being intimate with them, isn't personal.*

Okay, so his brain and subconscious really needed to shut their traps and keep opinions to themselves. He didn't need to think about it that way. Sex could just be sex. And sex with Roxi was…well…oh so nice.

The scent of her skin, the feel of her curves against him. Her tight sheath around his shaft. Those silken walls inside her heated, velvet core.

"Sam?"

He bit back a groan as his cock rose swiftly to life. Roxi was beside him. No, not beside, partially in front of, and her gaze was directed at his lower anatomy. The heat in her brown eyes was such that it burned him. His cock jerked as he read the blatant desire on her face. He almost lost his meagre hold on his control when she licked her lips.

"Roxi." His voice was raspy and full of his own need for her.

Her gaze jumped to his and she gulped hard before blinking a few times. "Um, wanted to know if you would like to join Eric and I. We're going to the hospital to visit Master Guns."

It took him a few seconds to process what she'd said. His mind was firmly wrapped around his desire to take her up against the nearest wall. Thrusting hard and fast. Slow and deep. Until her nails dug into his back and she screamed his name as they came together in a fiery ball of passion.

But sink in it did. Hospital. Master Guns. "I'd like that, thanks. Let me just…go change."

Her stare drifted down to his crotch again and he watched her swallow. Hard. Dear Lord in heaven, she was going to kill him. All without a single touch. Sam left the room before he gave into his desires.

"You coming with us?" Eric asked as he went by.

"Sure am. Just going to shower quickly." He grabbed some clothes from his bag without paying much attention to them and headed for the bathroom. Stepping in the shower, he released a frustrated groan and rested balled fists on the walls. His breaths were deep and uneven.

Never before had he felt so out of control with his emotions. The sexual pull towards Roxi was powerful and he wasn't sure how much longer he could resist it, regardless of the boy being in the house. Surely they could be quiet.

He showered and got out after quickly jacking off to thoughts of how amazing it had been to be buried balls deep inside Roxi. His release had barely taken the edge off his raw need for her. Forcing himself to calm down, he dried off and dressed. After he'd shaved, he left to find Roxi and Eric waiting for him in the living room.

Roxi wore the same thing except she'd put her hair up off her neck. They both rose when he walked in.

"I'll drive," he said, opening the door to the garage.

He'd partially been expecting an argument from Roxi but none came. After Eric was in they backed out of the garage. He idled in the drive until the garage door lowered then he got on the way. The ride was silent and he knew that Roxi had dozed off so he kept quiet. Eric just looked out of the window.

At the hospital, he watched her come fully awake after he'd parked the large truck. Her eyes snapped around as she gauged the situation before she seemed to settle. He didn't remark on it, knowing full well he did the same thing. It told him a bit more about her – she'd seen combat while she'd served.

They walked in together and took the elevator up to the room. He knocked on the door and just before he opened it, stopped. Roxi had slipped her hand into his and gave it a quick but reassuring squeeze. As fast as she'd put her hand there she took it away. They entered the room.

Roxi let him go through first, she and Eric following behind. He approached the bed, staring down at the man who meant so much to him. His skin had paled considerably and he just looked so damn weak lying there, it tore at him.

Dean opened his eyes and a smile filled his wizened face. "Sam." The voice was but a fraction of what it used to be – however, it was still full of love.

"How are you today, Dean?"

"I'll be out by Christmas."

Lord, he hoped so. And not to be fitted for a pine box. "Up for some visitors?"

"Always."

Sam waved them closer. Roxi walked up beside him – not on the other side of the bed, no, she moved beside him – and pressed a kiss to Dean's cheek. "Good to see you awake, Master Guns."

"Roxanne. I'd begun to miss your beautiful face around here."

"I know, I'm sorry I haven't come by more."

Dean turned his head to where Eric stood. "Good to see you again, Eric."

"You too, sir."

"Are you still at the academy?"

91

"Yes, sir. Top of my class this year."

"Good for you, son. Good for you." Dean looked back at Sam. "How're things at Second Chances?"

Leave it to Dean to worry about things other than himself. "You concentrate on getting better."

"Sam," Dean warned.

"Everything is fine. We're almost finished with all the restorations. That large room will be all squared away for Christmas. I'm going to get a tree for them next week."

"So the painting's all been done?"

"Yes, sir. Roxi helped out and finished that while I fixed the bathrooms." He touched Dean's arm. "Please don't worry about that. You need to focus on getting better."

"How's Laila?"

*Shit.* He'd not even thought about her today. He licked his lips and took a breath. Roxi brushed against him and he met her gaze.

"We'll give you some time to talk and be back in a bit."

He didn't want her to go but somehow managed to nod. She reached between them and squeezed his hand again and immediately he felt better. Her strength had been added to his own. He'd faced death numerous times and had barely blinked, but to see Dean, his mentor, his father, lying so close to death, scared the hell out of him.

Roxi smiled at Dean and took his hand as well. "I'll be back to see you, Dean. Going to give you and Sam some time to talk. I think your room needs some flowers."

Just that like, she and Eric were gone.

"Sit down, Sam."

He sat. "Laila is fine. I spent Thanksgiving with her yesterday. And your son and his brothers."

"Sam Hoch, you listen to me and listen well."

He straightened in the chair automatically at the firm tone. Years of doing so had his response so quick and instinctive, it didn't matter that the man delivering the order lay swallowed up by a hospital bed.

"Yes, sir?"

"Look at me, son." The order no less present but the tone softer, somehow.

He did. Immediately he found the dark brown eyes belonging to a man he'd respected above all others watching him.

"You know I think of you as my son. Always have. Ever since that first night I helped you up from that puddle in Minnesota. That's never going to change, Sam. I don't care if a hundred boys come in claiming to be sons of mine. You, Sam, *you* are my firstborn. Always will be."

Their gazes were locked for a few moments but Sam felt the gravity of the words all the way down to the marrow of his bones.

"Yes, sir."

Dean nodded and closed his eyes briefly. "Now. Tell me what is going on between you and that lovely Ms Roxi."

His heart sped up at the mere mention of her. Still, he shook his head. "Nothing. She is letting me stay at her house."

"You're not staying with Laila?" Some concern leached into his question.

Thinking fast, Sam shook his head. "No. With Dean Jr, Chris and Tom all there we didn't want it to be such tight quarters. Roxi graciously volunteered her guest room."

"Always could tell when you were lying, Sam." A wry grin. "But this is okay. So what's going on with the two of you?"

"Me and Laila?"

That greyed eyebrow rose. "No. She's your sister, I've always known that, despite her childhood crush on you. I know you've never viewed her in any other light. You and Roxi."

"Nothing," he reiterated his first claim.

"Right. You know, son, if you want people to believe that, you should probably stop watching her so intently when she's in the room with you."

He'd been doing that?

93

"Sam, there is nothing wrong with it. Roxi is perfect for you." Dean reached out and grabbed his wrist. "You are allowed to find someone to settle down with. Allowed to realise that there is more out there than just a temporary home."

He didn't even try to deny it, he just shrugged. Dean was well aware of his fear of committing to anyone other than the Marine Corps.

"You know how I feel about that, Dean."

He'd been left so many times as a child, he felt it was better if he didn't make any long-term plans or hopes with others. Disappointment was bound to happen. As had been proven with his would-be fiancée.

"Son, you can't continue to go through life like that. I won't be around forever and I want to know you are with a woman who lights up your entire world. Hell, even some children would be good. Some grandkids for me to bounce on my knees." Dean took a deep breath. "I want to know you'll be taken care of."

"Someday," Sam hedged.

"I think 'someday' has arrived for you, Sam."

There was a knock on the door and Roxi entered with Eric. Dean glanced pointedly between them and Sam.

"Promise me you'll think about it. Give it a chance."

"How are we doing?" Roxi asked as she moved up to the bed, again on the same side as Sam, even though her gaze lingered on Dean.

"You light up the room with your cheer, Roxi."

"Dean, you're an old charmer. I see what the nurses meant now." She turned her head and met Sam's gaze. His heart fluttered as she bestowed her smile on him. "I brought you a coffee."

He took it, unable to ignore the spark which flared up as their fingertips grazed along one another. Swallowing, he focused back on Dean.

"Thank you." He dragged some chairs over for her and Eric to sit in before returning to his previous seat. As he listened to Roxi, Eric, and Dean chat he tried not to touch her thigh. Her leg pressed against his and he could feel her warmth through to his soul.

"You okay?" Her whisper had him looking up to find her gaze upon his face.

He tightened his hand around the base of his cup so he wouldn't grab her. "Yes."

It was a lie. He was far from okay. His life had suddenly begun to spin out of control and most of it was due to the woman sitting right beside him. Roxi, with her large, thickly lashed brown eyes, firm lips and a figure which would make a saint willing to sin. If a person managed to make it past the outside packaging then they were confronted by a woman who had a heart of spun gold.

She cocked her head slightly to the side, as if assessing the truth of his singular word. But she didn't press him for any more, only gave a nod and focused back on the interaction between Eric and Dean, occasionally chiming in with a comment of her own.

When the nurses came in, Roxi, Eric and Sam rose to leave. He hung back a bit while Roxi pressed a kiss to Dean's cheek and whispered something in his ear. Eric said farewell then he moved back as well. Stepping up to the bed, Sam stared down at the man lying there.

"I'll be back," he promised.

Dean nodded and gave an exhausted smile. "Thanks for visiting. Remember what I said, Sam."

"Yes, sir."

The trio left and once they were in the elevator he shoved his hands in the pockets of his jeans. "Up for lunch?" he asked.

"Yes please," Eric said. "I'm starving."

"You're always starving, Eric," Roxi teased.

"Roxi?"

"Sounds great." Her gaze was soft when she looked at him.

He herded them out of the hospital and into the parking

lot, not at all ready to stop spending time with either of them—especially Roxi. They climbed up in his truck and he peered over the seat and asked Eric where he wanted to eat. After making sure it was okay with Roxi, he drove them to the restaurant.

Lunch was full of laughs and teasing. Mostly between Eric and Roxi but he definitely enjoyed himself. Afterwards he took them home. Pausing in the driveway beside Roxi's vehicle which still sat out front, he thought about that—that he'd begun to think of her place as a home. It didn't matter that he'd only been living there a short time—not much more than a month.

Once he'd parked, everyone got out and headed inside. He hesitated when someone outside called his name. Hitting the button to open the garage again, he found Laila standing there. She was bundled up, her teeth chattering.

"Hey, Sam."

"Laila." He gestured at her. "What are you doing out here? Especially if you're so cold."

"I was looking for you."

He put his keys in his pocket and approached her. "For?"

"I thought you might want to have lunch."

"Sorry, we grabbed a bite to eat on the way back from the hospital."

Her expression fell. "Oh. Have some time to talk?"

"Of course." He pointed over his shoulder. "Come in?"

She shook her head. "No, I think it's better if we go to my house."

"All right." He walked towards her and together they headed over the short distance to her home. Hearing the garage door lower behind him, he glanced back but didn't see anyone. *Damn, I should have told her I was leaving.*

Entering Laila's house now was so different to when he'd first arrived there. There was the lingering scent of cigarettes and booze in the air. He frowned and looked at the woman beside him.

"Sorry about the mess," she said. "I'm still working on

getting the smell out."

"What happened?"

"Dean Jr and his brothers weren't exactly nice houseguests. I sent them to a hotel today and I've been cleaning since I got home from work, left early. Just can't seem to get the stench out."

He wrapped his arm around her. "You okay?"

She shook her head and sobbed, leaning into him. "I feel like everything is falling apart. They hate me, Roxi hates me and you're staying with her."

He furrowed his brow at her outburst. "Roxi doesn't hate you." At least, he didn't think so. He'd never got around to asking what *had* occurred between them. "And I was staying with her to make it easier on you."

She peered up at him. "You can stay now."

Trouble was, he didn't want to leave Roxi. "All right," he said, willing his jaw to unclench.

"I've cleaned the guest room and it has fresh sheets and all of that. It will still smell a bit like smoke, but it's much less now than it was."

Cigarette smoke was the least of his worries. He'd bedded down in places that smelt much worse than smoke. "That's fine." A deep breath. "Let me go get my things and truck."

She smiled up at him and he couldn't help but smile back. There were times when she was just so cute and innocent-looking.

"I'll be here."

Another deep breath and he walked out of the house and through the cloudy, cold afternoon back to Roxi's. He went in through the garage and waited out there until the door had shut completely and shrouded him in darkness. Torn. That was how he felt.

He entered the house and was amazed by the difference. He immediately felt warmed and comforted in her place.

"Roxi?" he called out.

"Back here," she replied.

He spun on booted heel and headed towards the back,

hoping her 'back here' was the laundry room because he honestly didn't know if he would be able to control himself if she was in her bedroom. She stood in the hallway, a basket under one arm. She'd changed out of her jeans into a pair of cobalt-blue, cotton workout pants. And he still wanted her just as badly.

"Need me to do any laundry for you?" she asked.

He shook his head. Lord, she was beautiful. She'd removed her ponytail so her hair fell freely along the gentle curvature of her face to grace her shoulders.

"What's up?"

"Laila…" He swallowed.

Roxi brushed by him. "Laila wants you back over with her."

"Yes." How did she know?

"Okay. Just leave your garage door opener on the table." She walked into the small laundry room and set the basket down on the top of the washer.

*Wait. That was it?* He stole a glance up the hall and saw Eric's leg from where he sat in the chair playing a video game. Then he stepped into the tiny space after her, spun her around, and blocked her in with his arms and body.

Her expression was cool when she met his. "Yes?" she questioned with an arch of her brow.

"That's it? That's all you have to say to me?"

He lowered his face to hers, eyes locked, breath coming faster and sharper.

Roxi couldn't breathe without being engulfed by the masculine scent which screamed *Sam!* to her body. Her legs trembled at the fierceness in his features. All those angles she wanted to touch with her fingertips, trace with her tongue.

"What else is there to say?"

She couldn't ignore the throbbing of her clit as he drew closer. All he'd have to do would be crook his finger and she'd follow him anywhere. If he'd just promise to soothe

the unending and seemingly increasing ache within her.

"You tell me."

*Focus, Roxi. This isn't about how damn good he smells, how wonderful his hard body against yours feels. This is about...um, what the fuck were we talking about?* Her brain scrambled for her and thankfully found the answer she needed.

"Sam, I offered you a place to stay because there wasn't room at Laila's. If there's room now, then go. That's fine."

A deep rumble emerged from his chest and she knew he wasn't pleased. Why? She had no clue. She licked her lips and tasted him. Hell, the man hadn't even kissed her and she was so desperate for him her mind was conjuring up his taste on her lips.

"You stubborn woman."

She scoffed. "I'm stubborn?"

"Why don't you just say you want me to stay?"

"Why don't you tell me you want to?" she countered.

His face closed up and she knew he wouldn't. Or couldn't. Before she could contemplate that any further, he'd taken her mouth in a fierce, possessive kiss. Without thought, she arched into him, pressing herself as close as she could get without actually climbing up his body. *Although that idea has merit as well.*

He dominated her. Took what he wanted and once she'd surrendered that, he took even more. His tongue thrust deep, touching everywhere only to retreat and do it all over again. She shivered and rubbed against him. Her moan was eaten up by his mouth.

Deep strokes. Feathery strokes. All kinds with one purpose. To drive her out of her mind with desire and lust. It worked.

Her pussy was wet and her breasts swollen with need. The need for his touch. His caresses. Him. She could feel his thick erection digging into her belly and it only made her crave more. She knew how it felt to have his length deep inside her. Thrusting. Powering forward. Driving into her until her body exploded and she screamed his name. She whimpered and rubbed along it, inviting him to take her.

He didn't. Damn him, he lowered his hands and held her hips still, refusing to let her grind on him. Then the kiss ended. Her heart hammered and she looked up at him. His blue eyes swirled with dangerous passion.

"I'll see you later, Roxi." It was a promise when it fell from his lips.

He spun on his heel and left her alone there, horny and aroused, in the laundry room. She didn't move until after she'd heard him enter and leave his sleeping quarters, talk to Eric — whom honestly, she'd forgotten had been there during their passionate exchange — then leave through the garage.

She shoved her clothes in the washer then set it — she was on auto pilot — before leaving the small space. She forced herself up to the living room, knowing full well if she went to hers, she'd end up getting herself off and it would feel as hollow as it had before.

Eric sat on the overstuffed chair he loved to occupy when he was with her. He looked up. "Sam went to stay with Laila."

"I know, he told me." She ignored how hurtful that was to say and hear.

"But he said he'd come back over and play this game with me once he got settled."

Her smile was forced this time, she knew it. "How nice of him. I'm going to get his room cleaned up, so yell if you need me."

She spun on her heel and went to the one Sam had used. Pushing in, she sighed as she looked around. No trace of him ever having been there. Rolling her eyes at her sappiness, she got to work stripping the bed. The pillowcases held a faint hint of his scent — she held them tightly and inhaled. He smelt so damn good.

"I can give you a shirt, if you'd like one."

She jumped, whirling, to find him leaning against the door. Arms crossed and a slightly amused, still predatory and hungry look on his face. She had no comeback. There was no way to deny it, she'd been caught sniffing his pillowcases, for crying out loud.

"What are you doing back?"

His eyes narrowed slightly. "Eric?" he called out.

"Yes, Sam?"

"I need to have a private chat with your aunt. Stay up there until we come back."

"Okay. Then we'll play?"

"You got it." He stepped fully into the room and kicked the door shut with the heel of his shoe.

She gulped, fingers clenching the bedding she still held. "What are you doing?"

Christ, it was warm all of a sudden. He prowled towards her and she saw the fluidity and strength that made him good at his job. There was an untamed wildness in him. He didn't stop until she was back in his arms. No soft, gentle words passed between them. No. This was raw, hot and challenging.

He demanded and she gave. His kiss sapped her strength and she sank into him as he continued to sweep through her mouth with his tongue. One hand was wrapped in her hair and he pulled it back, angling her head how he wanted it. She dug her nails into his upper arms as she gave herself willingly and completely over to him.

Leaving her mouth, he worked his way down her chin, over her throat to the hollow of her neck. His teeth grazed her skin and she shivered with each pass. He lowered her back to the jumbled sheets on the bed, his body covering hers, and lifted his head to stare at her. She shuddered at the pure, undiluted possession in his heated gaze.

She began to shake her head but his hand gripped her tighter, holding her still. He reached for her waistband and removed her cotton pants. Kicking one leg free, she arched when that same touch trailed over her panties. He didn't linger, just drew them down as well.

His eyes never left hers as he freed himself. She reached

out and closed her fingers around his length. Velvet over steel. She purred in pleasure as her hand stroked him. Her thumb swiped across the tip and she smeared the droplets of pre-cum which lingered on the broad head.

He pressed a condom into her hand and she made short work of opening it and sheathing him. Her knees were off the bed and he wedged his way between her spread legs, pushing them wider. Eyes locked on hers, he slammed home in a single thrust. The bed squeaked and he froze before gathering her along with the sheets up in his arms and placed them on the floor.

"No noise," he muttered against her lips as he began to move.

Hard, fast strokes had her flying high in no time. Sam still had one hand locked in her hair while he kissed her. His tongue matched the thrusts of his shaft deep inside her. Her body slid along the soft sheets with each forward piston of his hips. He dragged her to him as he pulled almost all the way out then they went all over again. She pressed her mouth tighter against his to ensure she didn't scream.

Back and forth.

In and out.

Harder and harder.

"Lock your legs around me," he muttered into her mouth, never slowing his strokes.

She followed his guttural command and whimpered at the increased angle of penetration he acquired. So thick, so long, he filled her unlike any one had before. Made for her.

She couldn't hold out any further and nipped his skin as she fragmented around him. Her internal walls gripped and milked his cock. Faster he moved, refusing to give her even a moment's rest until she felt him stiffen and come inside her. She experienced his pulse even through the barrier provided by the condom. Hell, she'd been so far gone she wouldn't have insisted on using one. She was grateful he'd had the presence of mind to use protection, for she sure as hell hadn't—she did recall unrolling it over his shaft, however.

He lifted his mouth from hers and stared at her. His face was set in harsh lines of pleasure and sweat dotted his brow. Lord help her, she wanted to go all over again. From the hardness inside her, she realised he was of a similar mind.

Slowly he withdrew from her and as he did, she was hit full force with how exposed she was like this. Pants and panties gone, having been kicked free during their escapade. Clad only in shirt and socks, sprawled before him like a feast. Her body responded when his gaze drifted down to linger at the apex of her spread thighs before moving back up again.

Silently, he got to his feet and removed the condom before tying it off and dropping it in the trash. He put himself away then returned his attention to her. She'd yet to move. Roxi watched him as he crouched down beside her and reached out to touch her face.

She pulled back and awkwardly sat up, trying to hide her naked lower body. Eventually she gave up attempting to use her shirt that way and just tugged some of the sheet over her. He was fast at camouflaging his emotions but not quick enough to keep her from witnessing the flash of pain.

"That can't happen again," she said, even though her body disagreed with her decision. Her heart wanted more. That was the problem, though. She didn't think he could give her his heart. And as much as she loved being physically intimate with him, she wanted more.

"I'll leave you to dress." He stood and left the room, taking the trash with him.

"Shit!" she whispered to the empty room.

Out of her league. That was how she felt right about now. On trembling legs, she got up and redressed before grabbing the sheets and heading to the laundry room to place them on the floor. She'd do them next. Once she'd ducked into her bathroom, she cleaned herself up and splashed some ice-cold water on her face.

Staring in the mirror she scoffed. "What the hell are you

doing?" she demanded of her reflection.

*Enjoying the man.*

"No, we're getting in too deep. It's a good thing he's leaving to stay with Laila."

Yeah, right. Not even she bought that load of crap. She didn't want him to go. She wanted him to stay here. With her. Hold her at night in bed. Love her until the morning.

"Cripes, Roxi, what is this, fantasy? He made his decision. Suck it up and move on."

Reaching for a towel, she dried off her face then made her way to the living room where Eric and Sam played. A shiver overtook her as Sam's blue eyes raked over her. Dangerous. Seriously fucking dangerous.

She walked into the kitchen and stood there, gripping the edge of a counter while her gaze transfixed on something in the backyard. Nothing of importance, just a spot as she tried to get Sam Hoch out of her mind, body, heart and — damn it — her soul.

Roxi managed to maintain her distance from him while he was in the house. She kept to her bedroom, door open in case Eric called for her, but otherwise hung out in her room. The distance was needed or else she would lose what little of her cool she had left.

"Bye, Roxi," Sam said from the doorway.

Her fingers tightened briefly around the spine of the book she was reading before she looked up to see him lounging there.

"Bye."

"I'll see you."

*And I'll see you every fucking night in my dreams.* Damn it! He had her cursing much more than usual. She hated such displays of vulgar behaviour and now here she was, reduced to doing it as well.

"Right." She focused back on her book.

Too late she realised he'd not left. Of course not. He came closer and yanked the book from her hands. Snapping her head up, she glared at him. He rotated his wrist so he could

104

see the cover and stared at her.

"*The Amber Room*?"

"Yes. It's a very good book. Do you mind?" Steve Berry was a favourite author of hers.

He handed it back to her. "Nope." One last intensely dominant look—which made her wonder if there wasn't now a stamp of proprietary ownership on her body from him—and he left.

Her hand trembled slightly as she lowered the book to her lap. How was it possible for one person to affect another so powerfully? Unfurling her legs, she rose and padded in socked feet to the living room, where Eric still played.

"Want to play, Aunt Roxi?"

Bookmarking her page, she placed it on an end table. "Sure." It might be just the thing she needed to try to keep her thoughts of Sam Hoch at bay.

\* \* \* \*

She and Eric had a nice meal at the house that night and when he was in bed she paused in locking up to glance out of the front window. Another bout of rain had arrived and for a moment she debated whether to get her vehicle and put it in the garage. Flipping the deadbolt into the locked position, she shook her head and turned off the lights.

It would be fine until morning. She made her way back to her room, took a long hot shower, then slid beneath the blankets. Sleep didn't come easily and when it did, her dreams were full of Sam. She woke—again—to his name on her lips and her fingers deep inside her wet slit. *Nowhere as good as the real thing.*

Frustrated, she slipped from bed and cleaned up before dressing. The rain had ceased and she opened the door to Eric's room to see him still asleep. She backed out and headed to the garage. Opening the door, she smiled slightly as the dove-grey morning pierced the darkness. Shoving her hands into her pockets to get her gloves, she glanced around before locating what she wanted.

Bag in hand, she walked to her car and began cleaning it out. It had been a while and there were some things which definitely could afford to be removed. She put in an ear bud for her iPod and turned on some music, leaving one out so she could hear Eric if he called for her.

She cleaned, dusted and straightened up her Tribeca until it was back to her standards. Vacuuming would come later, once more people woke up in the subdivision—it was still early. Walking to her trash bin, she rolled her shoulders then disposed of what she'd collected and lifted her head when headlights came around the corner. A taxi.

Roxi went back into her garage and grabbed the broom to sweep it out. She paused when the yellow car stopped by the end of her driveway. After placing the broom against the wall, she went to the end of the garage and watched as the driver got out and the back door opened.

Joy filled her to bursting when she recognised the man who unfolded his body, climbing out. Ritchie. She removed her ear bud and shoved it in her pocket as she ran down the short drive.

"Ritchie!"

A grin split his dark face and he opened his arms. She threw herself into them and wrapped her own around his neck. He whirled her in a circle.

"Roxi, look at you. It's so good to see you."

She kissed his bearded cheek. "You too. Oh my goodness, I thought you weren't coming until tomorrow."

"I got an earlier flight." He set her down. "Is that a problem?"

"Of course not," she replied with a grin.

While he paid the driver, she grabbed one of his bags then together they headed up into the garage.

"Eric up yet?"

"Not when I came outside. We had a late night last night." She glanced at her brother. "You look tired. Guest bed is ready for you." Because Sam was no longer there.

"I just want to check on him."

She understood. "I'll put your bag in the room."

Soon she stood with her brother in the guest room. "Are you okay, really?"

His sigh spoke of his exhaustion. "I will be. It was a rough outing this time. We lost Hendricks."

She reached out for his hand and squeezed. He'd spoken often and fondly of that man. Sometimes people forgot that while he wasn't in the military, they still lost men when they were overseas. Just because one was a civilian didn't give them a free pass in a war-torn country. "I'm sorry."

"Thanks."

"You sleep. I'll begin breakfast in a bit. Do you want me to wake you when Eric gets up? Or just let you sleep?"

"Wake me, please."

"You got it."

She pressed another kiss to his cheek then left the room, closing the door behind her. Resting against the wall, she smiled. Her world was right again. Her brother was home safe and her nephew was here too.

*Almost perfect.*

Sam's face appeared before her and she bit back her groan as she headed out to the garage again. Deep in her gut, she knew he would be the one who could make the *almost* disappear. Shaking off the unwanted and honestly, not very helpful, thoughts of him, she picked up her broom and finished sweeping. At the driver's door, she paused when climbing in and peered over to the next house. Laila's. Where Sam was.

Her imagination had nothing on the real thing, for there he stood. Sam leaned against her porch railing and stared at her. He wore a sweatshirt and pants. Despite the distance — and it wasn't that great — she could feel the intensity of his stare.

Turning her back on him after a brief — she was determined to still be nice to him even when it hurt her to see him with Laila — wave, she climbed in her car and drove it inside the garage. For a moment she remained in the vehicle, gripping the wheel as she berated herself. *He's not* with *Laila, he's with her because she's like family to him.* Then she shut the door and went inside. Washing her hands, she began to make breakfast and soon Eric came up the hall to the kitchen.

"Is Sam coming for breakfast?"

"Sam? I don't think so, why?"

"You have three plates down."

She blinked. "Oh, guess I do. I'll be right back, Eric."

She woke her brother then went back to the kitchen. She poured juice as Eric fixed himself a plate. He was eating when she saw Ritchie step into the kitchen. "Eric?" she said.

"Yes?"

The gesture she made with her chin had her nephew turning. The squeal that followed made tears come to her eyes as Eric flew from the chair with a loud, "Dad!"

She waited patiently until their reunion was over. Eric talked a hundred miles a minute as she placed a plate of food before her brother. She ate while they talked. *It's so much different with Ritchie here.* The constant sound of his deep adult voice such a change from rarely hearing Sam talk.

"Who's Sam?"

She blinked and refocused on her brother. "I'm sorry?" Maybe she'd imagined his question.

Ritchie pointed at her with his fork. "Sam. Who's this Sam that Eric said stayed here?"

Shit. It hadn't been her imagination. "A friend of Laila's," she said, hoping he'd leave it alone.

The sparkle in his eyes told her she wouldn't be that lucky. Putting his attention on his son, Ritchie asked him. The description from her nephew had her brother looking back at her with heavy amusement.

"A friend of Laila's?" He shook his head. "I'm not sure I believe you, sis."

"And this is any of your business, why?"

"I'm your brother."

And that was why and when she knew this interrogation wasn't over. The doorbell chimed and she used the distraction to make her escape. She opened the door and found herself looking into those killer blue eyes.

"Sam, I presume?" Ritchie's question had her looking over her shoulder to see her brother leaning between the kitchen and living room, watching with avid fascination.

# Chapter Seven

Sam stood there in the doorway, his gaze flashing from Roxi to the new man in her kitchen. It had killed him to see her jump into his arms. He knew she'd not known he was outside. He'd been seated on the porch trying to calm the raging heat in his body from waking up with his hand around a rock-hard erection and Roxi's name on his lips. Once he'd taken care of that issue, he had dressed and come outside.

When Roxi had appeared in the meagre light of yet another grey morning, he'd stayed in his seat. He'd watched her clean out her car, somewhat singing along with the music in her ear. Then the taxi had arrived and it had been a roundhouse to the gut when she'd flown into his arms.

Yes, he'd heard the name, Ritchie, and wasn't an idiot. He knew that was her brother's name. Didn't make her display of affection any easier for him to watch. On two levels jealousy popped up again. One, let's be real, it was seeing Roxi and another man. Not good. Two, just another reminder of what he'd missed growing up.

Unable to stay away from her, he'd headed over to her house after she'd driven her SUV into the garage. He'd waited a bit before he went over and knocked. The shock on Roxi's face had him wanting to kiss it away. *Okay, not true. It wasn't the shock on her face. I just want to kiss her.*

She gave an almost resigned sigh and stepped back, allowing him entrance. He inhaled deeply as he moved by her. Instantly the scent of autumn filled his nose. Close on its heels was the smell of the breakfast in the house.

"Morning, Sam," she said.

"Roxi," he replied in the same low tone.

"Sam!" Eric called and waved. "Did you come to eat with us? This is my dad."

"Hi, Eric."

He put his attention on the grown man beside the boy who'd found his way into his heart. Ritchie Mammon wasn't a small man. He was tall, broad shouldered and in good shape. It was common for Sam to study the people around him. The man had a close-cut beard and short hair. His skin was dark yet Sam could still see a hint of tattoo peeking up from the collar of his shirt to linger around his neck.

One thick brow lifted as he crossed beefy arms over his chest. They held gazes for a moment before Ritchie grinned, something which changed his entire expression from one that bordered on menacing to relaxed. He pushed from the wall and walked towards them, Eric at his side.

"Nice to meet you, Sam. Eric's told me a lot about you. Ritchie Mammon." He held out a hand which Sam accepted and shook.

"Sam Hoch."

"Care to join us for breakfast, Sam?" Ritchie offered.

He could feel Roxi stiffen a bit beside him. "Sounds wonderful."

"Sam, can I have a word with you, *please*?" Roxi sounded strained.

"Sure. We'll be right in."

Ritchie nodded, draped an arm around his son's shoulders and the two of them went back into the kitchen. Once they were out of sight, he focused on the woman beside him.

"Roxi."

"What are you doing, Sam?"

"About to eat and talk to your brother. But first, kissing you."

He did just as he'd said. Swept her in close and kissed her. Teased her lips before slipping his tongue deep into her mouth. He captured her moan and settled a hand upon the

111

curve of her ass, pressing her tight to him, rubbing against her so she was sure to feel his hardness and know what she did to him.

When she began to sink into him, he drew back. Her gaze was soft and full of desire. He ran his thumb along her plump lower lip. "Morning, beautiful." He released her.

"You know my brother is going to grill you, right?"

A smile quirked up his lips. Odd how easy he found it to smile around her. He didn't much mind doing so, either.

"Are you concerned for me?"

She was. He saw it in her eyes. She never admitted it, of course not, not his Roxi. No, instead she huffed.

"Don't be foolish, Marine."

A warm shiver tingled up his spine when she called him that. He placed his thumb and index finger under her chin and lifted it a bit. Gazing at her, he gave what he hoped was a reassuring smile.

"I'll be fine. I can handle your brother." *It's you I'm not sure about.*

Sam walked off and after a mutter of something he was sure she'd not want him to comment on, her body materialised by his and they walked to the kitchen together. Side by side, not touching.

He sat down at the open seat, which just happened to be beside Roxi's place. Not that he minded. His gaze focused on Ritchie, even though he knew she was walking around, fixing him a plate of food.

"So, Sam, how do you and Roxi know each other?"

"I'm a friend of Laila's and she offered me a place to stay."

"A friend of Laila's?" A sharp glint appeared in Ritchie's eyes.

Interesting. He nodded. "We grew up together. I came out when they told me Dean was in the hospital."

"I was sorry to hear about his hospitalisation. So why didn't you stay with Laila?"

"Ritchie!" Roxi's admonishment came.

"No, it's okay, Roxi. She had Dean's son and his half-siblings staying there." A quick look at Eric before adding, "It would have made a stressful situation even more so." He leant back in his chair. "Roxi was there and offered me her guest room here."

"So where are you staying now?"

"Back with Laila. The other three have left so it's just the two of us."

Those brown eyes went darker again. *Ritchie likes Laila.* He filed the bit of information away for later.

Roxi set a plate before him and he tried to make eye contact but she refused to allow it. Instead, she went back to her seat and sat. He turned his head slightly and stared at her. She didn't look any happier than her brother did with his announcement.

"And you're here for how long?"

"Until Christmas."

Ritchie ate some more before talking again. "How'd you swing that? Isn't it hard to get so much time off?"

He nodded. "I put in a special request. Hadn't vacationed in a while so have quite a bit of time on the books. Plus, Master Guns is well respected so they cut me some slack." He left out that his attention span had greatly suffered after the news had come in. Luckily for him, his current CO knew of his close relationship with Master Guns and had pulled some strings to get the time allotted.

"Until Christmas." Another bite of food. "Over with Laila."

"Yes, sir." Sam glanced at Roxi who shrugged at his questioning look.

Ritchie's fingers clenched around his fork before he appeared to force himself to relax. "And what are you doing during the day while Laila works?"

"I'm filling in for Dean. Right now, at Second Chances." He shifted in his chair. "Today, I'm putting up Laila's lights and going to get a tree for her."

"Oh, a tree," Roxi broke in. "I have to get one, too."

He slid his gaze to Roxi and gave her a private smile. "I

113

can pick one up for you as well. Or you could come with me, if you wanted to."

"I'd like that." Her eyes widened as she spoke the words and he knew she'd been about to refuse him.

"Can we decorate today, Aunt Roxi?" Eric asked.

"I think that can be arranged. We have to let your dad sleep some more, though."

"But you'll make cookies? We can't decorate without cookies."

"Of course we can't." The smile she gave Eric touched Sam's heart.

Eric rose, took his plate to the sink and left the room with Roxi. Ritchie put his gaze back on him.

"How well do you know my sister, Sam?"

"About as well as you know mine."

"Your sister?"

"Laila. She's like a sister to me."

He could see Ritchie still wasn't convinced. "So you know about her parents?"

"I held her hand when Terrance and Lenore were lowered into the ground. I know you like her. That's fine. She's a grown woman but if you hurt her, trust me when I say there won't be anywhere you can hide. Not even going back overseas will protect you. I'm well acquainted with the Middle East. Just know that I love her and will protect her."

Ritchie nodded and finished the last bite on his plate. "Okay. That goes the same for my sister, you know. Don't hurt her."

He didn't speak, just ate the final bite of his own food. Sam had no wish to hurt her but he couldn't promise Roxi anything he wasn't ready to give. She had forever stamped all over her and he didn't know if he believed in it. He wanted to, especially with her, but he was unable to dislodge that demon of doubt and betrayal that had taken up a position on his shoulder whenever it came to trusting someone with his heart.

"Good to meet you, Sam." Ritchie left the room.

Roxi came back in as he cleaned the plates from the table. She stood there watching him, her hip propped against the countertop.

He lifted his gaze to hers, pleased by the flare of heat in her eyes, and lifted a shoulder in silent question.

"I don't believe I've ever heard you talk so much."

"I don't."

"Not to me, anyway," she muttered.

Setting down the dishes in his hand, he then moved to her and slid her out of the view of the living room, trapping her between his body and the counter. "Does it bother you?" He stared straight at her. "That I don't talk much?"

"Oh, you talk. You talk fine to my brother, and of course to Laila." She couldn't hide the hurt in her voice.

"Is that what you want, Roxi? Someone to blab about nothing just so you can hear him talk?"

"So talking to me would be nothing?" Her eyes flashed dangerously.

"That's not what I said and you know it. I'm a man of few words, Roxi. You know this. Laila's my sister. I'm not nervous around her. And your brother, well, he wanted to try and put me in an uncomfortable situation for staying here with you. And Laila. I wasn't about to let that happen."

She blinked a few times. "You're nervous around me?"

Shit. Hadn't meant to advertise that bit of information. "Yes."

"Why?"

*Because you embody everything I've wanted in my life and I'm scared you will take it all away, leaving me with nothing but memories.*

"I just am."

"I'm not that scary of a person, Sam," she said in a soft voice. "And I don't bite. Well, unless you want me to, that is." She touched his chest. "But then, you already know that."

She slipped by him and walked away even as he struggled

to find a breath. His cock threatened to punch free of his jeans. *Evil temptress.* Somehow, he managed to drag his lust—kicking and screaming—back under control.

He helped her clean up and went with her to the living room where Eric and Ritchie sat together on the couch, talking softly amongst themselves. After telling Roxi he'd be back in a bit to take her Christmas tree shopping, he said farewell and left the warm house, heading back to Laila's.

She'd just left her room and was buttoning up her blazer when he walked in. She looked at him and smiled.

"Sorry, I don't have time to make you anything. Just grab what you want, make yourself at home. And thanks for going to get me a tree."

He poured her a cup of coffee he'd made earlier. "Not a problem. I've eaten."

"Really?" She glanced around her kitchen, mug in hand. "You cleaned up after yourself? Thanks."

"No, I ate over at Roxi's."

Pain flashed through her eyes. "Oh. I see."

"I met her brother."

Her head snapped up and she froze. "Ritchie's back?"

There was a breathless quality to her voice. "Yes, got back this morning from what I understand."

She worked her lower lip between her teeth. "I'll swing by later and see him. I left the decorations in the living room. I'll help you later tonight. Lights are in the garage. Thanks for doing this, Sam."

He brushed a kiss along her cheek. "Have a good day, Laila."

She headed for the door. "No Charlie Brown trees," she called out over her shoulder.

He waited until he heard her vehicle leave, then went to the garage and checked on her lights. After seeing which ones worked, he went back inside and grabbed his hat, jacket and keys. Then he walked across the frosty grass to Roxi's house and rang the doorbell.

Ritchie opened the door and waved him in. "Did Laila

already leave for work?"

"Yes. She left before I came back over here. Said she'd stop by later when she got home to see you." He removed his hat and held it in one hand.

"Okay." Whatever Ritchie was going to say next was halted as Roxi came over to them.

"Ready?" he asked her, eager to get her alone.

"Sure am." She slipped her purse on over her coat and pocketed her keys. "You know where my keys are to the Tribeca if you need them, Ritchie. We'll see you later. Bye, Eric."

"Bye, Sam, bye, Aunt Roxi!"

Together they walked out of the house and back across to where his truck sat, idling in the next drive. He'd pressed the automatic start on his way over to pick up his date for the excursion. Like a gentleman, he held the door for her. Unlike one, he thought all kinds of thoughts which involved things not fit for public eyes. Tearing his gaze from her perfection of an ass, he went to the driver's side and hopped up.

"Thanks for taking me with you," she said quietly.

"I'm glad you could come along." After he'd spoken the words he realised just how true they were.

He watched her in his periphery. She pressed close to the door, almost like she was willing it to suck her up. Or as if she couldn't wait to get away from him. Neither was a happy thought for him.

Roxi wore blue jeans and a light blue jacket. He knew below it lay a deep red, long-sleeved T-shirt. *And beneath that?* His brain taunted him with recollections of her naked body, spread out under his. Over his.

Christ, he had it bad.

Her hair was clasped at her neck with a simple barrette and she had black boots on. Simple. Sexy as all get-out. His woman. The truck swerved a bit as those words sank in.

*His woman?* When the hell had that thought settled into his head?

117

He sliced his gaze to the woman in his truck. If she noticed the motion she never said so. In fact, she stared out of the side window as he drove.

"Roxi?"

She glanced at him, brown eyes wide and gentle. "Yes?"

Shit! He just couldn't say it. He gave her a smile and turned back to the road. She kept her attention on him for a few moments, he could feel it. The sigh which left him was one of frustration. He didn't know what to do. He knew what he *wanted* to do, but didn't know *what* to do.

Pulling into the Christmas tree farm, he parked next to a minivan and another truck. The place was surprisingly busy this early. They climbed out and he locked up behind him. Waiting for her at the front of the truck, he had offered her his arm before he'd realised what he'd done. Thankfully, she took it. Slid her hand right into the crook of his arm and walked beside him, the leather of her glove on his jacket.

"Ideas?" he asked as they walked among the rows of conifer trees. He'd never had a tree before. He usually wasn't around for the holiday, and if he was, he just didn't celebrate. The farm was huge, boasting both pre-cut and those you could pick from and cut down yourself. Right now they were out in the back area where the live trees grew.

"Blue spruce? Those are always nice."

He paused and looked around, lost in the woodland of Christmas trees. "We're in the what…pine? Where the hell are we?"

She laughed and he glanced at her, brows raised in confusion. "It's just funny to me. Two Marines lost at a tree farm. I can see the headlines now."

Her joy was infectious and he laughed with her. She stepped away from him, shoulders still shaking, and looked at the nearest tree. Then she shook her head. "I have no clue. I'd say yes, we're in pine but I didn't get a map, did you?"

"Nope."

"So even if we are in pine, it still really doesn't help us at all, does it?"

She had a point there. "Well, we could always just walk back the way we came."

"And admit defeat? Never. We're Marines, damn it. We can do this."

"Do you want one of these?"

Roxi shook her head. "I want a spruce." She turned to the left. "Let's go that way."

"Lead on, Marine."

She glanced at him, eyes alight with humour. "Oh I see, send in the lower rank first."

He flashed a grin. "Yep. Get a move on."

"Damn Gunnies."

He heard the affection in her tone and shook his head as he set off after her. She moved with a fluid gait and he could easily picture her dressed in combat gear. The blue parka and jeans exchanged for camouflage and a helmet. Purse for an M-16.

"You're supposed to let me know if it's safe."

"I thought you were supposed to lead by example."

"I do. But then, my Marines don't have an ass like yours, so I have no need for them to be in front of me."

She froze mid-step and turned. "Is that why you wanted me taking point? So you could stare at my ass?"

He could lie about it. But he didn't.

"Yep."

She snorted, rolling her eyes. "At least you're honest."

The amusement in her eyes morphed into desire and she stepped closer to him. He groaned when the tip of her tongue peeked out and dampened her plump lips. She smoothed her hands up the leather of his jacket, to the top of his shoulders, and tugged. He couldn't ignore her any more than he could stop breathing and live. He allowed her to do what she wished.

"So am I," she whispered, a hairsbreadth away from his lips. "I want to kiss you."

Oh, he wanted that too. Desperately. "You're in control

here, Marine. You want a kiss, you have to take it."

"I plan on it." Her words were a promise. One he personally couldn't wait for her to make good on.

She slid a hand around the back of his neck, grazing his skin with the tips of her fingers, setting up goose bumps in their wake. Her other hand continued to hold his jacket. As if he'd be going anywhere. She rose up slightly and brushed her lips against his. He willed his limbs to remain still—hard to do when every inch of him demanded he take control and dominate. Somehow, he managed to do nothing.

Roxi nibbled along his lower lip before he felt her tongue begin to slip through the seam of his mouth. He opened for her and bit back his groan when she entered. Her tongue dipped and swept along his, coaxing it out to play.

She released his coat and wrapped her other arm around his neck too, then arched into him, pressing her full breasts along his chest. Her moan was almost his undoing. His cock went from hard to marble-hard.

"Let's try down this row, Daddy!" a young voice ripped through the bubble they'd made around one another.

Roxi stepped back and stared at him. Her eyes were smoky with passion, her lips parted as her air left her in short little pants. He watched her chest rise and fall with the breaths she struggled to take. Not that he was any better. Grateful his longer coat kept his erection hidden, he reached out and stroked a knuckle down the side of her face, even as he looked up to see a family of three coming around the corner.

Roxi couldn't stop the flutters in her belly. What had started as an innocent kiss had quickly changed into something more. Much more. She licked her lips to retain as much of his taste as she could then turned to see the people who had interrupted what surely would have been a heated exchange, with her being taken at a tree farm.

The parents gave them a nod and a brief hello before

continuing on after their yelling child. Neither of them spoke but Sam did wrap an arm around her and draw her close to him.

"Let's go," he said, urging her to continue in the same direction the family had gone.

They found a sign which read "Spruce" and he looked up the row then back at her. "Here?"

She nodded and followed him in. She took her time, appreciating her view. One which had nothing to do with the trees around them and everything to do with the man before her dressed in solid black. He wore his jeans so nicely it truly wasn't fair to others. He also had on this black mid-length leather jacket which—in her humble and horny opinion—went so well with the black jeans, gloves and boots. He also wore a black turtleneck. *Can we say yum?*

He swung back around and pinned her with those incredible blue eyes. "You coming?"

Just about. Crap, she'd been so close during the kiss, especially after all her unfulfilling dreams. So near to splintering apart beneath his touch. "Right behind you."

He waited for her and when she reached him, he captured her chin before he brushed their lips together and whispered, "We'll have to pick that up later."

His voice was like warm melted chocolate. It invited her to jump in and commit all kinds of sin. Ignoring the part of her heart that told her to keep him at a distance, she took his arm and rested against it before she continued on again.

They walked all through the tree farm not talking, but she didn't mind. She thought over his question this morning, did it bother her that he didn't talk so much with her? No. She loved this, just spending time with him, knowing he was there with her. What did bother her was the way he tried keeping his heart from her. She caught glimpses of it from time to time, but for the most part she couldn't help but see the big wall he had erected around it.

A wall she wanted to breach. She understood. He'd not had it easy, but surely it was time to give someone a shot at getting close. A deep breath. *Not the time to worry about that.*

"Well?" he asked.

"Well what?"

"Which one?"

"Oh, um, well I'm fine with a pre-cut." She grinned at him. "Would you believe I just wanted to walk around?"

"I'd believe it." A fast, hard kiss. "Let's get your tree, then."

They headed back the way they'd come, just not going up each row this time. Back at the main part they purchased some hot cocoa and drank it while taking a short break as their selected trees were placed in his truck. Again, this was done in silence but she still didn't mind.

Her phone rang and she pulled it from her pocket. "What's up, Ritchie?"

During her short call with her brother, she kept her sights on Sam. He watched her right back. Not hiding it, just staring at her. His eyes were full of emotion that made her belly tighten.

"Everything okay?" he asked when she'd hung up.

"Yes. He just needed to know where some decorations were."

Sam quirked his lips. "More like he wanted to make sure you weren't off fucking."

"That too." She grinned. "Joke's on him. I can still hold a conversation when doing that, so he wouldn't have stopped anything."

Sam's eyes narrowed. "Really?"

*Shit. More of the cussing, why can't I stop doing that?* "Well... yeah...I mean...you know...um..."

"Seems to me that if you're able to carry on a conversation with someone else while a man is in between your thighs, he's not doing it right. No, ma'am, not at all."

She felt a bit flushed. "Maybe I'm just good at multitasking."

The predatory gleam in his eyes told her he wasn't buying it. "Is this with every man you've been with?"

She didn't even get upset he had asked about other men. Roxi knew exactly what this referred to. Their time together.

"Roxi?"

"Huh? Oh, um, no?"

"Why are you asking me? I asked you."

"If I say not with you, will that make you happy?"

"Only if it's true."

"No one called while we were together." His eyes flashed dangerously and she knew she was flirting with trouble. And yet, she couldn't help herself. "But I'm pretty sure I wouldn't have been able to talk on the phone."

His jaw ticked. "Pretty sure?"

"Well, yes. I mean, come on, Sam. This is like someone saying they can fuck me until all I can do is sleep. It's an expression. Just like my comment was just a comment."

*Okay. Not the right thing to say.*

"You know you should really stop while you can," he warned.

She realised that, just couldn't quite get her mouth to shut up. "Life is full of expressions like that. Doesn't make the—"

"Roxi!"

That did it. Her mouth snapped shut. "Hmm?"

"I'm pretty laid back. But this…"

"Really? You seem a bit tense to me." She squeaked when he shoved to his feet, his empty cup crushed in his hand. True, it was paper but still, it hadn't taken much.

"I'm beginning to think you like trying to make me crazy." He moved around the table to her side and used his arms to block her in. Nose to nose he waited, poised to strike. Like a panther.

"Not really. It's nothing against you, Sam."

His eyes narrowed. "So you're telling me I'm one you *could* talk on the phone during. Okay, Roxi. I accept."

That sounded menacing. "Accept what?"

"Your challenge."

She shook her head. "I didn't challenge."

123

"Oh, I think you did. One, that you can actually hold a conversation while I'm fucking you and two, that I can't fuck you into exhaustion." That last word fell from his lips in a dark and decadent promise.

"You're...putting words into my mouth." *Cripes.* When had she begun to sweat so much? It wasn't far from Christmas but she was so hot she could be wearing a bikini and it would still be too much.

"Scared?" he purred.

Her belly was in knots. Gulping, she shook her head. He leant forward, brushing her cheek with his. The stubble on it was like an electrical pulse through her system.

"I think you are. I wonder how well you'll talk on the phone when my scruff is abrading the insides of your silken thighs." He whispered the words into her ear before standing up and taking both their empty cups to the trash.

Her womb clenched and she felt a shaft of longing spear her. Clit throbbing, she tried to control the racing of her heart. It was to no avail. He reappeared before her and reached out his hand.

"Trees are loaded," he said, as if he'd not just said what he had to her. "Let's go. I need to stop and pick up another string of lights for Laila. One of hers is dead."

Girding herself, she placed her hand in his. *Fuck!* It was as if neither of them wore gloves. She could feel his touch so clear, so intimately, she didn't know if her legs would hold her up on her way back to his truck. Somehow they did and she sighed in relief as she sank into the leather seat.

She had slightly more control when they stopped at a store for lights. They walked together, not touching, yet that did nothing to calm any of the storm within her. She kept replaying his words in her mind.

*Stop it. Cripes, I can't walk around with a river flowing from me. What is he doing to me?*

"What's between Ritchie and Laila?" Sam looked at icicle lights.

A shrug. "I'm not sure. I know they always try to see

one another when he comes but honestly, I thought it was just because she was always at the house so they'd become friends."

"They're more than friends."

"How do you know for sure?"

"He was mad when he learnt I was staying at Laila's. More so than the idea of me staying at your house."

She wasn't quite sure what to make of that so she left it alone for now. "They're both grown."

"As are we."

She clenched the finger she'd been using to trace along a box of lights into her fist. "Yes."

Sam put three boxes in the basket he held. "What?"

"What what?"

"Your expression says something is wrong. Is this about us?"

*Yes.* "Nope. I'm aware of what's between us, Sam. And I am not going to try to make more of it than there is."

He became very still. There was a storm in his eyes but he seemed oh so still. Like he'd spotted his target and was waiting for the right moment to make his move. "What's that?" The words were low and threaded with danger.

"Between us? I'm not a fool, Sam. I can see you don't do long-term entanglements. You're going with the moment. That's fine. I am, too. Like you said, we're both grown, same as Ritchie and Laila."

"How do you know what I 'do', Roxi?"

Really? He wanted to have this conversation here? Now? "I see glimpses of your heart, Sam. But I also see a lot of distance you keep me at. Like you're scared of me seeing the true Sam. You share it with Laila, but she's earned the right to have your trust. And I don't mean you trust me enough to sleep in my house. I'm talking more permanent. It scares you. That's fine. We've not known each other all that long. I'm not expecting talk of future or a ring from you. Let's just keep it simple."

A tic appeared in his jaw. "Kiss."

125

She took a deep breath. "Yes. KISS, keep it simple, Sam. I'd never call you stupid."

"No. Kiss. Kiss me. Right here, right now." He put the basket at his feet.

His gaze remained on her but she knew he was aware of their surroundings. The numerous people out shopping, all the noise, and he held her stare. She stepped up to him and placed her hands on the smooth, black leather of his jacket. On tiptoes she brushed her lips along his in a gentle, tender kiss.

"Not everyone will hurt you, Sam." Her words were whispered against his mouth before she stepped back. "Let's go," she said with more cheer than she felt. Almost everything she'd just said to him was a lie. She wanted a future with him—she'd already lost her heart to this quiet Marine who'd taken over her life.

She picked up the basket and continued on. Sam fell into step beside her and they crossed to the checkout in silence. Okay, maybe she had overstepped her bounds but to be fair to her, he had been the one asking.

Sam paid and slipped his arm around her as they trod to his truck. He held the door for her and soon he was behind the wheel.

"It's not that I don't trust you, Roxi," he began.

She bit the inside of her lip. "No, Sam. Don't. Like I said, I'm not expecting anything. Let's just keep this light and fun." It would be hard for her but she'd find a way to pull it off. She wouldn't ask anything from him he wasn't ready to give. And it was obvious he was in no way ready to give her what she wanted.

"Let me explain."

Roxi shifted on the seat so she could see him better. "It's not necessary, Sam. Truly it isn't." Then she faced forward and glanced out of the passenger window.

The silence remained until they got to the houses. She jumped out immediately and went to the back of the truck. Her brother stepped outside and she breathed a bit easier knowing he could help her.

"I'll get it for you," Sam said.

"No, it's okay, Ritchie is on his way." She touched his arm in a plea for him to look at her. Eventually he did. "Thank you, Sam. For taking me with you."

"Not a problem." His voice was gruff.

"Let me get that one for you, sis."

"Thanks, Ritchie." She gave him a smile. "Do you need any help, Sam?"

He shook his head. "Nope. I've got it."

"Okay" — she cleared her throat — "well, thanks again."

As she followed her brother inside the house, she was still thinking about Sam. "Ritchie," she said after he leaned the tree against a wall.

"Yeah?"

"Why don't you help Sam with the lights on Laila's house?"

"What about here?"

"I have to make some cookies first," she said, with a grin to Eric. "It would go much quicker if you helped him. Then you both could come over here and have something hot to drink and cookies."

His sharp gaze found hers. "Mean that much to you, sis?"
She nodded.

"All right then. Come on, Eric. Let's go put up lights with Sam."

Soon the door closed on them. Not even a minute later, she sank on wobbly knees to the nearest chair and put her head in her hands. Giving herself a moment, she took several deep breaths before pushing to her feet and heading to the kitchen. The smell of pine followed her every step.

She turned on some music as she washed up and got to work making some cookies. The familiarity of it soothed her wayward nerves and soon she felt better. When her countertops were full of cooling cookies, she began whipping up some frosting for them. Putting amounts in smaller bowls, she then added the food colouring to get the choices she wanted. Then she began to decorate them.

The front door opened and she peered over to see her three men walk in. Eric, Ritchie and Sam bringing up the rear. Her belly did a little flip at the sight of him. It hadn't been that long since she'd seen him but the reaction occurred nonetheless.

"Coffee's ready," she announced.

"What about me?" Eric asked with a grin. "Do I get coffee as well?"

"Take it up with your dad, little man." She shook her head at his question. He hated coffee, she'd given him some before and he'd almost spat it out.

"No thanks, I like hot chocolate."

"I'll have it ready for you in no time, Eric."

"You're the best, Aunt Roxi." He slipped from the kitchen, which left her and Sam alone.

She smiled and stared at the frosting on her finger. Before she could clean it off, she found it in Sam's mouth. Shit, her legs trembled as he swirled his tongue around her digit. He watched her as he sucked the frosting off her finger, eyes dark with desire. He slowly tugged on her wrist and removed her finger from the warmth of his lips before he licked his own.

"Delicious." He leant forward and kissed her briefly then moved to wash his hands. "Thanks for sending them over to help."

Still unsure her heart would ever calm, she joined him at the sink. "How do you know it was me?"

He merely looked at her and she shrugged as she washed her own hands. "Thank you, Roxi."

"Stop thanking me."

She left him there and went back to work decorating cookies. Soon her house was full of cheer as the men put up the tree in her living room and lights around, both inside and out. Later in the day, she went to her brother and whispered in his ear that Laila should be home. He slipped out and she stayed with Sam and Eric.

Hovering in the entranceway between the kitchen and the living room, she inhaled and smiled. Her house smelt like Christmas. Cookies, pine and cheer. She loved this time of year. Always had.

Laila joined them for dinner and when Roxi finally went to bed that night, she was exhausted. It seemed that sleep caught her immediately and she went willingly, knowing she had to get up early tomorrow and take Ritchie and Eric to the airport.

\* \* \* \*

It was Sunday morning and she'd just returned from the ferry ride back from Seattle. Making a cup of coffee, she curled up on her couch and enjoyed the quiet. Not that she minded having Ritchie or Eric with her, but most of the time she did live alone and so it wasn't always easy to have the noise.

*Ring. Ring.* She reached out with one hand and lifted the phone from its base. "Hello?"

"Hey, Roxi, it's Laila."

"Hey."

"Just thought you would like to know, Dean is getting out of the hospital on Tuesday."

She sighed heavily. "Oh, thank goodness. Yes, that's wonderful. Thanks for telling me."

"Sure." A moment of awkward silence before Laila said, "Just wanted to let you know. Bye."

"Bye, Laila."

She replaced the phone and shook her head. *I need to make up with her.* She missed her friend. Finishing her coffee, she got to her feet and placed the empty mug in the sink. Then she made her way back to the bedrooms. After stripping the beds, she put the sheets in the laundry and straightened up, although neither room really needed it.

Her Sunday morning was quiet. She didn't leave the house except for her run and she realised she missed seeing Sam. It bothered her to know how much she looked forward to being in his presence. She had to get a grip. He wasn't sticking around. Didn't matter to her heart, though.

*Ring. Ring.* She glanced at her phone with a sigh. Did she really want to answer it? She was slow to get up and lift the receiver.

"Hello?" She walked into the kitchen and turned on the kettle for tea.

"Hi, Roxi. It's Ariel."

She grinned. She and Ariel Greene had been in the Corps together. She'd got out after four years but the two had remained fast friends.

"Hey, woman. How the heck are you?" She paused, frowning. "Where are you?"

"I've just arrived in Texas, actually. Part of a security firm that's opening up a new office in San Antonio."

"Wow, congrats. So what's up? Fill me in."

Ariel began to talk about what she'd been doing and a whisper of feeling up her spine had Roxi turning from the stovetop to spy Sam standing there. Her heart beat thunderously and she covered the mouthpiece and said, "You scared me."

He didn't apologise. In fact, he didn't say anything, just stood there staring at her with those damn blue eyes that she couldn't escape from, not even in her dreams. She licked her lips and muttered a response to Ariel.

Sam stood there, clad in rinsed indigo-dye jeans, ones worn from age and use, not ones you purchased that way. These had to be a favourite pair. They hugged his strong legs and showed off the part of his anatomy which always made her weak in the knees. His shirt was long-sleeved, the hue of wrought-iron. It boasted a spread collar, wood-style buttons and a crosshatched pattern that looked good on him. It emphasised the power in his upper body. The shirt was untucked and hung over his lean hips. Lord help her, all she wanted to do was unbutton it and touch the man beneath.

"How long are you in Texas for then, Ariel? Are you staying permanently or do you move with the job?" Roxi didn't have a clue how she'd got the words out straight.

"I'll be here for a while. Then I'll go when we start up something else. I think we're heading to California next."

"You sound happy," she said.

Her breath caught when Sam moved towards her. Predatory steps. Determined steps. A fire burned in his gaze and she swallowed and dug her nails into her palm to keep from reaching for him.

"I am."

"How are your parents?"

Ariel began telling her and the second Sam touched her, her attention wavered. Nothing more than him reaching out and stroking a finger down her cheek. She arched a brow and gave him a questioning look. His smirk sent her spiralling down flashback road to the tree farm.

He wouldn't. Even as she shook her head no, he gave a wicked grin and dropped to his knees before her. *Shit.* He wasted no time, just drew down her sweats until they pooled around her socked feet.

His warm breath fanned her through the thin material of her panties and she grew wetter. He lapped at her, pressing the flat of his tongue against her. The friction through her panty material made her tremble.

"You okay, Roxi? You made a sound."

"I...I'm fine, Ariel. Just hit myself on the stove. I was making tea when you called."

"Okay." She got back to her story.

Sam pulled down her underwear with his teeth then went back and shoved his face between her legs. She trembled and almost dropped the phone. The feel of his stubble was like electrical shocks spearing her.

He sank his tongue in before withdrawing and doing it all over again. In seconds he had her on the edge of coming. Her legs shook and he didn't stop or slow. No, he put his hands on her thighs and spread them further, allowing himself to get deeper.

She barely contained the moan which threatened to escape. Her breaths were coming faster and faster and she struggled to follow along with Ariel's conversation. He took her to the edge only to back off and begin the build up all over again. With her free hand, she cupped the back of his head and tried to push him closer. He resisted. He hummed against her and she shuddered again. She very nearly screamed the roof off when he shoved two of his thick fingers inside her as he rolled her clit in his mouth. As it was, her breath left her in ragged puffs.

"What do you think, Roxi?"

Shit! She'd lost total track of the conversation. Scrambling to remember what she'd said, she snagged onto the first thing she could recall. A visitation.

"I would love to see you."

"Great. I'll get settled a bit more and we can plan something."

"Uh huh," she mumbled, fascinated by the naked man who stood before her, his cock erect and covered with a condom.

Flashing a glance up to his face, she was struck mute by the raw desire reflected there. He fisted his cock and stepped closer. Leaning nearer, he whispered in her ear, "Let's see how well you can carry on this conversation."

She whimpered in the back of her throat and did her best to focus on Ariel, who was telling her all about San Antonio and how much she enjoyed it there, despite the short time since she'd arrived.

Sam lifted her up onto the countertop and reached past her to turn off the kettle which had begun to whistle. Then he was back. The broad head of his shaft slid up and down her slit before he thrust home in a single flex of his hips.

"Ohh," she cried.

"Roxi?"

"Burnt myself on the kettle. I'm a klutz today," she lied.

Sam gave her a decadent grin and began to move. She

132

dropped her head back to rest against the cupboard door, the hand which held the phone shook as her body began to tune everything but the man between her thighs out.

He reached up lazily and cupped her breasts, rolling the nipples between his fingers as he continued his precision motions.

Back and forth.

In and out.

She was so fucked, she didn't know which way was up. Eyes rolling back from the pleasure awashing her body, she gave up.

"Ariel, I have to go, hon. Let me call you back."

"Okay. Great to talk to you."

"Uh-huh," she panted before hitting the button to end the call. She dropped the phone on the counter beside her leg and reached for Sam's broad shoulders.

"Damn you," she muttered as she dug her nails in and flexed her internal muscles about his thickness.

"I thought you could carry on a call when a man was between your legs," he rumbled around her nipple.

"I did," she insisted.

He chuckled and released her breast before staring at her face. "Mumbling isn't carrying on a conversation."

"I...I didn't mumble."

"You totally mumbled." He brushed their lips together. "That's one," he said in a tone that sounded remarkably like a promise.

"One?" Cripes, she could barely follow *this* conversation. She just wanted to give herself over to the pleasure.

"Now I get to fuck you into exhaustion." He punctuated each word with a slam of his shaft, as far in her as it could go.

She fragmented. When the lights stopped flickering around her eyes and she could open them to focus, she found he'd moved them to her bedroom. His length still deep inside her, he laid her back and began all over again.

Roxi stirred and rolled to her side, cracking open her eyes. Sam lay there like her, head propped up by his hand, watching her. The moment their eyes met an arrogant smirk filled his face, lifting those all too entirely kissable lips.

"Stop," she muttered.

"Why? I got two."

He sure as hell had. Every single muscle in her body was sore. Every one. Too tired to argue with him, she merely shrugged.

Sam reached out and smoothed back some of her hair, which was plastered to her head. They were both sweat-covered and naked. She touched his chest, trailing her nails down it until she got to his cock, which lay against his thigh. Curling her fingers around it, she grinned when it began to harden.

Stroking, she held his gaze until he became fully erect. Lowering her eyes, she licked her lips and moved her mouth to him. Casting a glance up, she saw the smirk had vanished only to be replaced by even more raw need.

When she succumbed to exhaustion once more she realised something—it wasn't so bad losing a challenge like that. Not at all. Although Sam was with her when she fell asleep, her bed only boasted one occupant when she woke the following day.

Cyber Monday came fast and she was at work early, aware that the day would be a busy one. Her body was still sore but it made her smile as she relived her time on Sunday with Sam. Jules King, her boss, had returned and was waiting for her outside her office.

"Morning, Roxi."

"Mr King." She nodded at him, taking in his suit. Impeccably dressed as always. He was a good man, married to his high-school sweetheart with three children,

134

one grandchild and another on the way.

He grinned. "Just can't bring yourself to call me Jules? A bit odd, don't you think? I call you Roxi and you call me Mr King." He waved a hand. "I'm just picking on you. I want to talk to you about the incident Thanksgiving night."

"Sure. Here? Or in your office?"

"Mine. Drop your things off and come on up."

"Be right there." She unlocked the door to her office and stepped in, turning on the lights. After she'd put her stuff away, she took another sip of her coffee and headed to meet her boss.

"Come in and sit down," he said when she knocked on his door.

She did as instructed then crossed her legs at the knees, waiting for him to speak.

"I wanted to commend you for taking charge when the call came."

"Doing my job, sir."

"It was Thanksgiving night and you shouldn't have had to be called. Do you know why you were?"

She shook her head. "I assumed it was because no one else was available."

"I've fired Mr Delf. That's why you were called. I want you to take over as the head of security."

She opened her mouth and he waved her off.

"I know what you're going to say, you don't have the seniority as some of the others here. True, you don't, at least not here in the bank. But you have more when we take into account your time in the Corps. You don't have to make a decision now. Please let me know by the end of the week at the latest." He opened his desk and withdrew a packet. "This is what we're offering you."

He stood and she followed suit, holding the packet in one hand. "Thank you, sir."

"No, thank you, Roxi. I'm glad I have someone like you on staff that I can trust so implicitly."

He walked her to the door and let her go with a gentle

squeeze of her shoulder. Back at her office, she debated looking at it now but knew she still had work to do, so she put it with her purse in the drawer and got to it.

At home that evening, she made a bowl of soup. She ate while reading the offer. By the time she climbed into bed, she knew she wouldn't take until the end of the week to give him her answer. It was a very generous package and she would be wise in accepting.

The next day, she was still in a good mood. The promotion offer and Dean would be home from hospital today. Lifting her cup for a drink of coffee, she paused when her phone rang.

"Yes?"

"Miss Mammon, this is Miss Whyte."

She knew who it was. From the front desk. "Yes, ma'am. What can I do for you?"

"I'm sorry to bother you, but you have a visitor. A Mr Hoch."

Her belly flipped and clenched. Whirling in her chair, she stared at the monitors and honed in on reception. Sure enough, Sam stood there. Straight and proud, not leaning on anything. That familiar reaction her body gave when he was around—or she thought about him—began again and she tried desperately to disregard the throbbing of her clit and the tightening of her nipples. To no avail. It was all too easy to recall the feel of Sam's touch on her body.

"Miss Mammon?"

She blinked a few times and took a deep breath. "I'll be right there."

"I'll let him know." She hung up.

Roxi stared at the screen for a few more moments. What could he want? Had something happened to Dean? No, that couldn't be it. Laila had the day off since Dean was coming home, and surely she would have called him had there been a change.

*Won't know until you get your ass up and go see.*

She got to her feet and headed for the door, doing her best

to ignore the butterflies in her stomach.

# Chapter Eight

Sam sat in the waiting area, legs crossed, leafing through a magazine as he waited for Roxi to appear. He'd missed her like hell. It had taken an amount of control he hadn't known he possessed to keep himself from remaining at her house. With her. In her bed. In her. Where he belonged.

On Sunday, he had watched her return from her run. Unable to stay away, he'd gone back over and slipped inside. Hearing her on the phone had brought back their conversation at the Christmas tree farm, so Sam continued in to prove that she couldn't carry on a discussion with someone while he was between her legs. Once that had been demonstrated, he'd moved on to the second bit. Where he'd got to fuck her into exhaustion. Was he arrogant? Hell yes, but he was good. And as he'd lain there beside her, watching over her as she slept like the dead, he couldn't help but feel smug.

She'd given as good as she'd got, though. The only reason he'd still been awake had been because he loved watching her as she slept. But he'd been tired. Then when she'd woken and had begun the blowjob, he'd known he was officially screwed. Hell, he would have given her anything she wanted so long as she'd continued doing what she was.

Roxi gave herself with such passion. There was no thinking it was all one-sided. She never hedged on her feelings or telling him what she liked. She didn't hide her sexuality behind a prudish mask. She knew what she wanted and had no problem taking it.

A tingle went up his spine and he glanced up from the magazine he'd not been paying attention to. She walked around the corner and immediately his groin tightened. Putting down the magazine, he got to his feet and watched her approach.

She wore a black pant suit with a single button closure on the long-sleeved jacket with its notched collar. There was studded detail at the waist, emphasising the nice tuck she had. He saw her black shirt beneath it. He dragged his gaze down her body again, noticing her pointy shoes with their tall heels as she strode confidently towards him. Her hair was drawn back in a severe bun and he growled low at that. He liked her hair loose and around her face. Where his hands could sink into it and hold her in place while he... *Okay, have to stop those thoughts.*

Her jewellery consisted of the Marine necklace, her usual grouping of earrings but the lowest pair matched—chain drop with a red stone in them—and some rings. When she stopped before him, he expected a cool reception given the way she'd walked across the room towards him—nothing but business.

A warm smile crossed her face and she softened. He, on the other hand, did not. Willing his unruly cock to behave, he returned her smile, aware of the people watching them.

"Hi, Sam. What's up? Everything okay?" She reached out and touched his arm.

"Yes. Sorry to bother you at work."

"No bother. What can I do for you?"

"Do you have a minute?"

"Of course." She glanced to the chairs. "Want to sit?"

He shook his head. "Dean comes home today."

Her grin brightened the fluorescently lit room as well as his world. "I know, it's great."

He nodded. "It is that."

She cocked her head to the side and looked at him. "You know you're always welcome, Sam. No need to ask. Just get the key from Laila."

"Are you sure?" he asked, even though he hated to give her an opportunity to say no.

"Of course I am. You know what, wait here for a minute."

She walked off without giving him a chance to say anything. It didn't take her long to return and he hadn't moved. Back before him, she held out a key. Her key. Her house key.

"Here you go, Sam. That way you can come and go as you please. The second garage opener is in the drawer in the kitchen. You know the one. Put that in your truck as well."

He closed his fingers around the key and stared at her. Guileless eyes watched him back. Damn, this woman amazed him. "I just—"

"Drop it, Sam. It's settled. You can stay. I get it. You need to give the room up for Dean but don't want to be too far from him. I understand. It's not a problem, really."

No. That wasn't all. She didn't get it. He could see it in her eyes, however, that was her truth and no matter what he said right now wouldn't change that.

"Thank you, Roxi."

She smiled again and his heart did that weird flipping thing. "Not a problem, Sam. I have to get back to work. I'll be home around eight."

"I should be as well. I'm on my way to Second Chances." He gave in to his urge to touch her, fingers caressing her upper arm. "Do you want me to bring dinner?"

"It's in the crockpot so it'll be ready by then." She reached up and pressed a kiss to his lips before walking away. "I'll see you tonight, Sam."

He'd bet she didn't even know what she'd done. Key in hand, he turned for the door and spied the tellers watching him. Laila would hear about it from them and she deserved to hear it from him. So he went to her house and walked in.

Laila was busy finishing up cleaning the living room.

"Hey."

"Hey, there. You gonna be okay getting Dean from the hospital? Or did you want me to come with?"

"We'll be okay, Sam. I know you're going to Second Chances."

"I can step aside for a while to help you if you need it."

"No, that's okay. I'm sorry about the couch for you. One of Dean's brothers used it while they were here."

"I won't need it."

He cleared his throat and she looked up at him from where she wrapped the vacuum cord around the machine. "What are you talking about?"

"I just got back from talking to Roxi. She's fine with me crashing at her place again. I won't be far if you need me and the place won't be crowded."

Laila crossed her arms and stared at him. "What's going on with you two?"

"Nothing." At the moment. Yet, he had plans to change that. "She did kiss me at the bank, but" — he rushed on when Laila shot up from the couch — "I don't think she meant it. She looked really preoccupied."

"Then why tell me?"

He pushed her back to a seated position. "Because it happened out in the lobby and I know the tellers saw it. I didn't want you to hear it from them and think I, or we, were keeping something from you."

Laila leant back and stretched her legs out. "You like her." It wasn't a question.

"Yes." He wasn't about to lie to her.

"Has anything happened between you two?"

"Anything happened between you and Ritchie?"

She flushed and looked away, which gave him his answer.

"It's not my business, Laila, so long as he treats you right."

She got up and walked to stand before him. "Same goes for me, Sam. Just keep in mind that Roxi is my friend, my *best* friend. Don't hurt her."

He drew her close and held her. "I love you, Laila."

"Love you, too, Sam. Please don't tell Roxi about me and Ritchie. She's still mad at me and I think this will only make it worse."

He chuckled and she pulled back to peer up at him.

"What's so funny?"

"Sweetie, she already knows. She's the one who told Ritchie to come over here."

"Really?"

He nodded. "Yes, really. But you two do need to talk and fix this thing between you. She's part of you and you her. This isn't doing either of you any good."

"So you're going to let her in?"

He stiffened and frowned at her. "What are you talking about?"

Laila led him to the couch and pushed him down. Once he was seated, she held his hand and sat cross-legged facing him. "Sam, I've known you for most of our lives. I know how you operate. You keep people at a distance. Not myself and not Dean. Other than that, you have this barrier erected to keep others out."

He didn't like the direction of this conversation. No, sir, he didn't.

"I know you don't want to hear this, but listen to me. Not everyone will abandon you. I look at you and I burst with pride. All you've accomplished, in the Corps and just in being who you are. But I still see the boy in there who was thrown away."

He clenched his jaw but forced himself to listen. "Is there a point to this?"

She sighed and squeezed his hand. "Yes. Roxi. She's the point to this. You're going to have to let her in if you want to keep her, Sam."

"Things are fine now."

"Not for Roxi. I know her. She won't push you into anything but there will come a time when she begins to withdraw from you, Sam. With Roxi it's kind of an all-or-nothing thing. When she loves, she does so with every fibre of her being. If she doesn't feel love from you in return she will pull back to protect herself."

"You think she could love me?"

"Of course." Laila actually sounded indignant. His expression must have shown his confusion. "You're my

142

brother, she'd be a fool not to see how awesome you are." She kissed his cheek. "And my Roxi is no fool."

He thought about her words and sobered. He'd tried giving his heart before. And that had just got him stomped on some more.

"I don't know if I can, Laila."

"She's not like Tracey."

He skimmed his teeth with his tongue. "I know that, logically."

"Look, Tracey was a bitch. Is a bitch. But she's not every woman out there." She nudged closer. "If you want, I'll tell Roxi about her and we can go kick her ass."

Laila sounded so hopeful he couldn't help but smile. "No. Roxi doesn't need to know and you two definitely don't need to be beating people up."

"Oh, it wouldn't be me. It'd be Roxi. She's good at things like that. We both know I can't fight my way out of a wet paper bag."

That was true. Laila was like a kid who closed her eyes and swung wildly.

"You're okay with me and Roxi?"

She rose up on her knees and captured his face in her hands. "I love you, Sam, and I love Roxi. So of course I'm good with the two of you together." Her expression demonstrated her worry. "But please don't forget what I said."

"I'm not looking for forever, Laila." The words didn't so much ring true when he spoke them.

"You may not be, Sam. But you're not the only one in the relationship." She jumped off the couch. "Come help me move the bed for Dean."

He followed more slowly, mulling over what Laila had said. Roxi. Even the thought of her made him think in long-term. And it scared the hell out of him. He'd been doing pretty damn good at being and remaining alone until he'd met the enigmatic Roxi Mammon.

After helping Laila he went to Roxi's with his things and

put them back in the spare room. He wasn't sure he'd be staying in that room but he didn't want to force himself into her space. Then he went to Second Chances and worked there, finishing up some more small projects.

"Sam, good to see you again," Father O'Toole said.

"Hello, Father."

"Do you have time to see if the Santa Claus suit fits?"

"Sure." He put down his hammer and climbed off the ladder from where he'd been fixing a loose frame.

After taking the offered clothing, he pulled it on. The woman who'd done the sewing, Reba, walked around him making small noncommittal noises as she checked the fit. "I think it'll be just fine. I need your boot size so we can get some that fit you. Then all will be set. We'll stuff you with padding so you fill it out but at least the sleeves and pants legs are the correct size."

He met Father O'Toole's amused gaze.

"You sure you're going to be okay doing this, son? You look a bit piqued."

"I'll be fine, sir. Just not used to dressing up like Santa Claus, is all." He glanced down at his red-clad body. "Anything special I'll have to do?"

"No. The kids will just want to see you and talk to you. Mrs Claus will be near as well, along with some elves."

"Gifts? Do I need to bring any gifts?"

"No, we have it all under control. If you want to make a donation we won't say no to that. But there's no need to buy gifts for everyone. We have more kids than are here for it. This is the gathering hall for them. It's a lot of fun and noise."

Fun and noise. Things he didn't do most of the time. But he wouldn't back out. "Very well. When is it?" He stripped off the costume and Reba took it from him.

"Christmas Eve. Is that a problem for you? Or rather, will it be one?"

They walked out to where the kids played and he'd been working.

"Not at all. I think Dean will be up for coming too, so he can see the kids."

A relieved smile filled Father O'Toole's face. "How wonderful." The man stepped forward and touched his arm. "Dean is so lucky to have you in his life."

"No, Father," Sam said. "I'm the lucky one. I was blessed the day Dean entered my life."

Father O'Toole nodded, his eyes full of wisdom.

"Were you like me?" a voice questioned from beside him.

Sam glanced down to find a child about seven standing there. His black face was open and trusting, unlike his own had been at that age.

"Hi, Derek," the priest said.

"I'm Derek," the boy added, which caused Father O'Toole to laugh.

"Yes, you are, son. I have some things to do, so I'll leave you here with Sam."

Sam didn't move as he walked away. The light touch on his hand had him looking back down. The boy still stood there, watching him with big brown eyes.

"Yes," he said. "I lived in places like this." Not really but he didn't see the need to tell that to the child.

"Did your parents not want you either?"

Christ. What did one say to a question like that? He crouched down by Derek and put a hand on his shoulder.

"Don't look at it like that, Derek. Look at it like Father O'Toole wanted you with him. And now you have all these brothers and sisters."

A childlike sigh. "I guess so. So you have lots of brothers and sisters?"

He thought about how lonely he'd been growing up in the different places. Licking his lips, he nodded. "I do." The Corps was his family now. And that was one large family.

"Will you be here later?"

"I'll be around for a while yet, yes. I'm here until Christmas."

His eyes sparkled. "I love Mr Dean. I miss him when he's

not here."

He understood the feeling. "He'll be back soon, Derek. Go play."

"Okay, bye." The lad scampered off.

Watching him, Sam sighed again and headed back to the ladder. Once he finished there, he left and went home. *There's that word again that doesn't sound so bad when I say it thinking about Roxi.* He parked and went over to Laila's to check on Dean.

"He's fine," Laila said beside him as he peered in on the sleeping man. "Made the trip home with no problem."

"Call me if you need me, Laila."

"I will."

He kissed her cheek and walked the short distance to Roxi's house and, using the key, he let himself in the front door. The Christmas lights were on and the house smelt like Brunswick stew.

"Hey."

He glanced up from closing the door in time to see Roxi leaving the hallway towards the kitchen.

"Hey, back."

She had changed out of her suit and now wore sweat pants and a T-shirt. Her hair was loose around her face, just how he liked it. He much preferred this laid-back Roxi to the other one. Not to say he'd not indulged in a few fantasies about her other style but this just hit him harder. She came across all soft and rumpled.

"How was Second Chances?"

"Good. Father O'Toole and I are going to get a tree for them tomorrow." He moved towards her. "Same place as we went, I guess there is a tree waiting for him."

She nodded. "Food is ready whenever you are." Then she walked away to enter the kitchen without a single look back.

He frowned. Not quite what he'd expected. He'd expected kisses, loss of clothing. But not this cold shoulder. Laila's words flashed again and he shoved them away with a

146

scowl. He went to his room and put down his keys before making a stop in the bathroom to wash up, then he joined her.

She stood at the counter beside the crockpot. Two bowls and spoons were there as well as a basket with piping-hot cornbread muffins. He hesitated before he figured 'the hell with it' and strode to her, grabbed her around the waist and kissed her.

Roxi went stiff for a moment and he kept up the pressure of his kiss, coaxing her to let him in. His cock throbbed when she opened and a little moan escaped. Sweeping his tongue through her mouth was heaven. He was addicted to her taste, her scent. The feel of her body against his. Reluctantly, he set her away from him and stared down at her smoky eyes.

"I've missed you," he whispered before setting her away from him.

She seemed like she wanted to say something back but the warmth faded from her eyes and she gave him a wobbly smile. "Grab some food." She turned from him and dished up some for herself.

He frowned and scooped up some for himself then joined her at the table. Her head was down and she focused on eating. He didn't like it. Yes, he didn't talk much but damn it, he liked hearing her talk to him.

"Is everything okay?" he asked.

Her head popped up. "Why shouldn't it be?" She took a deep breath. "I just have a lot on my mind."

"Anything I can help with?"

"Just an offer at work."

"Promotion?" He ate some of the rich stew and followed it with a bite of the muffin. So good.

"Yes. They want me to head up security."

"Wonderful." He gazed at her face and leant forward. "Is it not something you want?"

"I do, but there are others who've been there longer."

He understood that. "Obviously your boss thinks you are

the one for the job. If it's something you want, take it. I'm sure you going in and handling the issue after Thanksgiving helped solidify his decision."

She worried her lower lip and he shoved back the desire to kiss that lip and focused on her dilemma.

"Does this have something to do with Laila?"

"A bit. I just...she's worked there longer than I have."

"But not in security. She's a teller. Her progression up has nothing to do with you." He watched her weigh his words before nodding.

"True." He expected her to say something else, but she didn't. Never spoke again through the rest of the meal.

When it was over, she got to her feet and took her dishes to the sink.

"I have some cookies, or I believe there is a bit of pie left over if you'd like that."

His gaze locked on her figure as she stood by the sink. He could stare at her all day every day and never get tired of looking at her.

"Maybe later," he replied.

A nod was her only answer. He got up while she dug for a container and began to put in the extra stew. The table had been wiped off by the time she'd finished and had thrown away the bag which had lined the crockpot. Leaning against the counter, he watched her make a pot of coffee. Roxi was still distracted for she walked out only to return with a packet in her hand. He knew it was for her job when she spread it out before her and sank down with her lower lip in her teeth.

Although he didn't want to, he left her alone and went to the living room to remove his boots. The ring of a phone had him sitting up. Roxi answered it and he heard her soft voice but couldn't make out the words.

"Sam," she called out.

He hurried to the kitchen. "Yes?"

"Laila." She handed him the phone and went back to her papers.

148

"Hang on a sec, Laila." Sam reached for Roxi's face and tipped her head up to him. Before she could say anything one way or the other, he kissed her. A fast, hard kiss. Then he walked out of the room. "Go ahead, Laila."

Roxi exhaled sharply as Sam sauntered his fine ass out of the kitchen. Twice now he'd kissed her since he had got home. She didn't quite know what to make of it. Shaking her head, she got up then poured herself some coffee before retaking her seat. Pushing Sam from her mind, she read over all the papers Jules King had sent home with her.

When she'd finished, she rubbed her eyes and groaned. It had been a long day and she really just wanted to sleep. Looking up, she found Sam sitting across from her. His long fingers were curled around one of her Marine mugs and the pie was before him, a piece on each of the two plates.

"How long have you been there?" she asked.

He slid one piece towards her, shrugging. "Here."

She didn't argue, just accepted the plate and bit into the pie. It went down smoothly and she groaned in pleasure. She watched his eyes darken but he didn't move, though his fingers tightened almost imperceptibly around the cup.

"Everything okay with Laila?"

Sam nodded and began to eat. Soon their plates were empty, in the dishwasher, and they were on their way out of the kitchen.

"Did you make a decision?" he questioned.

"I did. I'll take it. I like what I do so why not, right? I mean, like you both said, he picked me. I guess I must be right for the job."

"Both of us?"

"You and Mr King."

"Who's Mr King?"

Was it her imagination or did she hear jealousy in his question? "My boss." She paused at his door and looked up at him. "Goodnight, Sam."

"Roxi."

149

She trudged to her room, half expecting him to grab her and kiss her again. Her control was so frayed all it would take would be one more touch and she'd be welcoming him into her bed. But the touch never came and neither did he. She closed her door behind her, ignoring the pull he had on her.

Once ready for bed, she roamed back through the house, double-checking it was all locked up tight. She paused by his door on her way back to her room before carrying on. Yes, casual sex was great but where Sam Hoch was concerned it had moved way past casual in her case. She'd fallen for him and she knew her feelings were only going to increase. Somehow she had to find the strength to not let him in her bed.

She climbed in and snorted as she drew the bedding up. Like she had any self-control around him. If she had, she wouldn't have slept with him to begin with.

Her sleep wasn't restful at all. When she woke the next morning, she was tired and cranky.

And horny. The hand which had been between her thighs had been inadequate and ineffective. She didn't want her touch. She wanted the touch of the man who slept in her house, down the hall from her. For him to caress her.

*Damn it!* She slapped the mattress and rolled out of bed. In the shower, she tried to calm herself down but nothing seemed to work. The water on her nipples only further aroused her.

Finally, she was dressed and in the kitchen, fixing herself a light breakfast consisting of half a bagel with honey-nut cream cheese and a bowl of yogurt with bananas and grapes.

She tensed at every sound she heard, thinking it was Sam. After she ate, she hurried out to her vehicle and drove off, well aware she was running away. Work wasn't open this early so she didn't *have* to be there, but she needed to get away from the temptation in her house. As sexually aroused as she was right now, all it would take would be her seeing him to jump on him.

In her office she did a walk-through. The diamonds were gone but they were expecting to get some more. It was unusual to have them so often, but she didn't think to question it. She was just in charge of protecting what was in the bank.

Her cell phone rang and she answered it without looking at the number. "Hello?"

"Why did you sneak out this morning?"

*Sam.*

She licked her lips and leant back in her chair. "Morning, Sam."

"Roxi." His voice was like a warm blanket she wanted to curl up in.

"What can I do for you?"

"Answer me."

"I didn't sneak out."

"Lying to me now, Roxi?"

"What do you want from me, Sam?"

"An answer."

"I just left a bit early. No real reason."

"Do you want me to get a hotel?"

She blew out an exasperated breath. "No, Sam. I don't. But if you want to, I can't stop you."

"You're angry."

No, she wasn't. Frustrated was more like it. "No, I'm not."

"Is this because of the kisses?"

Heat flushed her skin as her mind gave her an all-too-clear picture of what it had been like in his embrace. *Shit! I don't need to be aroused like this. Not here. Not now.*

"No."

A slight hesitation. "Okay. Laila told me to ask you if you'd like to have dinner with us and Dean tonight."

"Dinner? Sure. That's fine."

"I'll see you then."

"Right. Then."

"Bye, Roxi."

"Have a good day, Sam." She ended the call before she could say something like "come to my office so we can fuck on my desk." Or a similar phrase. Head to desk, she groaned. She really tried to avoid cursing but those words seemed to come easier and easier the more time she spent around Sam.

Not that she could blame him. It wasn't his fault she had no control over the words that were flying from her mouth. Or in her thoughts.

There was only one to blame. And it was her.

The day dragged by and she was extremely tense on her way home. There'd been a bit of an incident so she was behind, having had to stay back and put in her report. She'd told Mr King she'd be accepting his offer, so it was nice to know there would be more money coming in. Not that she spent a lot, but she was trying to save.

So she parked in the garage—beside the large, charcoal-grey truck she liked seeing there—and didn't even go inside, just walked next door, grateful for the brief spell in the rain, and knocked on the door.

Sam opened it and gave her a slight smile, at the same time moving his gaze up and down her body. "Hi," he said, eyes smouldering as he stepped back to let her in.

"Hey," she replied.

Past him, she viewed Dean sitting in a recliner and she brushed by Sam to approach him, doing her best not to pay all that much attention to how delicious Sam smelt.

"Good to see you out of the hospital, Master Guns." Her words were full of affection and she smiled bending to kiss his cheek.

"Good to be out, Roxi. Thanks for all the visits and the card."

She crouched by him, hand on his arm. "How are you feeling?"

"Like an old man with bone cancer." He touched her cheek. "Better than I was."

"That's because you're a fighter."

His smile couldn't hide how tired he was and in that moment, Roxi wondered if this would be his last Christmas. Master Guns had fought this for a long time now and it seemed was no longer up for it. She blinked back tears and stood when Laila came in the room.

"Roxi."

"Hi, Laila. Thanks for inviting me."

"No problem. We're ready to eat."

Sam appeared by her and helped Master Guns from the chair. Roxi watched him help his friend and mentor to the dining room table. There were times he seemed so gentle, it nearly broke her heart. She knew how much both Sam and Laila loved Dean. They weren't the only ones—he was a well-loved and respected man all over.

After dinner, she helped Laila clean up.

"Are we okay, Laila?" She snapped a lid on the leftovers.

"Of course we are. I was worried you were still mad at me."

"No. I'm sorry for overstepping."

"Don't, Roxi. You were right. The man is an asshole." She lowered her voice so she wouldn't be overheard. "I asked them to dinner tonight as well but they said they were busy."

Roxi propped a hip against the counter. "Master Guns knows what kind of man his son is, don't worry, Laila."

"I know, I just wanted..." She shrugged.

"Family."

Laila nodded. "I'm so scared I'm going to lose it when he goes. I'm not stupid, Roxi, I know he's not doing well. No matter how much he pretends. I don't know what I'll do without him."

Another container filled, she stacked it with the previous one. "You still have Sam."

"I don't know."

"What do you mean? He won't avoid you just because Master Guns is gone."

Laila's expression told her she believed otherwise.

"Really, Laila? You think Sam is only around because of Master Guns?"

"There've been years where I don't see him. Some days I wonder if he won't just leave and not come back, ever. Uncle Dean has been his rock for so long, when that's dislodged..." She shook her head. "I just don't know. I worry about how he'll take it."

"You two will have to be there for one another."

"He wouldn't come to me, Roxi. Not for himself. He feels the need to protect me. But he'd never let me in on his own emotions. That's just not—"

"You two okay in here?" Sam stuck his head in.

"Fine," Laila said. "Just finishing up."

Those blue eyes swung over to her and heated, making her think he envisioned what lay beneath them. And just like that he'd reduced her to a puddle. But he left without saying a word.

"Would you like some ice water?" Laila's question was teasing but it brought her back.

"What? No."

There was a smirk on her friend's face. "Are you sure, because you look a little bit parched there?"

"Stuff it, Laila."

"Not going to deny it?"

"Nothing to deny."

Laila rolled her eyes and put the food in the fridge. "Whatever. There's enough heat between the two of you, I could shut it off in the house and we'd still all be just fine."

"I'm just a temporary home for him, Laila."

Laughter faded from her eyes and she sobered. "I know it's none of my business, but I just have one thing to say."

"What's that?"

"He'd be well worth the fight." She gave her a sympathetic smile and left the kitchen to join the men in the other room.

Roxi hung back for a moment and stared at the trio gathered there. Another family. Father, brother, and sister. The sound of comfortable laughter reached her and she took a deep breath. *He'd be well worth the fight.*

As if he knew she was thinking about him, Sam lifted his head and met her gaze. One corner of his mouth lifted in a slight smile but it was the wink that got to her. Melted her wall further.

"Coming in, Roxi?" Laila asked.

She didn't answer, just walked over and paused while deciding where she wanted to sit. She headed towards an upright chair—she never made it. Sam gripped her wrist in his hand and tugged her to sit by him. Her instinct was to struggle but he gave her a look and she remained there. She slid to the end of the loveseat, trying to keep some distance between them. Damned if the man didn't move with her. His leg pressing up against hers, hips aligned.

Oh…what else had they done when pressed so close together like this. Slamming the door on that line of thought, she pasted a smile on her face and listened to Dean. It wasn't easy. Sam had a hand behind her and was drawing small circles on her lower back with his fingers. Nothing suggestive, but it didn't matter, it was nearly driving her insane.

"You're tense," he whispered in her ear when they had a moment alone, the other two having left the room.

"Really? I hadn't noticed."

His chuckle was positively decadent. "Another lie?"

"Can you stop touching me?"

"I'd rather touch you more. Remove your clothing a piece at a time. Lick your soft skin as it's revealed." The circles never stopped on her back and she felt on fire. "Lay you back on the bed and crawl between your bare legs. Spread them further and lower my mouth to—"

"Okay! I get it." Her voice was higher than normal.

"Let's go home."

She shook with the depth of her desire for him. A nod she could barely manage but Sam didn't need more than that.

He got to his feet and said, "I'm taking her home. She's barely keeping her eyes open."

Farewells passed in a blur and before she knew it, he'd put her coat around her shoulders and was leading her outside. They took a bit more time, keeping on the sidewalk given she still wore her work shoes but it didn't take long and he'd opened the door to the house, urging her inside.

The moment the door shut behind them, closing out the cold, blustery night, she was in his arms. Nose-to-nose, he shoved her coat off her shoulders then plastered his hands to her back, holding her close.

"Yes or no?" His question sounded gravelly and she felt an answering tug on her sex.

*Like I could say no.* "Yes, Sam."

He pressed his lips to hers and backed her into the wall in the hall. Ending the all-too-brief kiss, he went to work on her three-button, dark-blue blazer. After opening it, he slid it off then put her back against the wall. He moved to her white shirt next. One by one, he undid the pearl buttons, trailing his lips with tantalising slowness across her newly exposed skin.

"Beautiful," he mumbled as his mouth skimmed over her breasts.

Her nipples were visible through her lace bra and she shivered from the reactions his touch gave her. He sank to his knees and dragged his fingers along her waistband of her skirt. When he found the clasp he opened it with deftness before lowering the zipper. The pencil skirt slid down her legs and she fought for a breath at the feel of his callused fingertips on her thighs.

"No stockings?"

She shook her head. "No."

"I can see why. You don't need them." Up and down her legs he touched, catapulting her into an overload of sensations. "Your legs are like silk."

Each word he spoke blew a puff of warm air along her pussy and she rolled her lower lip in her teeth as she tried to contain her moans. She struggled to control her desire to flex her hips and initiate contact. Contact she desperately craved.

He lifted her left foot and caressed it before placing it back down. Looking up at her, he pressed a kiss to her bellybutton. Then another lower. And another. And another.

His tongue dragged up her panties, already damp, and he held her gaze. Slowly, he removed them, readjusting her feet one at a time to get them free. Then he leant forward and licked again.

She couldn't contain her moan anymore. "Sam."

He didn't say anything, just nudged her legs further apart and put his mouth on her slit again. Up and down he lapped at her, his tongue driving her crazy. He circled her clit prior to drawing it into his mouth, then he licked some more. She tossed her head back and forth against the wall and jerked when he slid one finger deep inside her.

"Sam!" The cry was louder this time.

His questioning "hmm" vibrated her sensitive nub and she shuddered at the feel of her impending orgasm. It raced upon her, fast and furious. She tried to stave it off but it would not be denied. One finger became two and he pumped them inside her as he continued to stimulate her. With his free hand, he draped her leg over his shoulder.

"I want to taste you, Roxi. I want your cream on my tongue. Come for me."

That did it. She couldn't hold it at bay anymore. She dug her nails into his head as she bowed her back and came with a scream of passion.

The tremors had barely stopped and he was on his feet, hauling her to him, slanting his mouth over hers. She tasted herself in his kiss and it only heightened her desire for the man. He removed her bra and she moaned as his chest hair rasped her taut nipples.

"Sam," she said, dropping her hands to reach for the button of his jeans.

He took the hint and freed himself then covered his stiff length. Their breathing was coming sharp and shallow. He lifted her then lowered her upon his shaft.

"Yes," she groaned as he slid into her in a fluid motion. This was what she needed. His thickness in her. His hands on her. Him.

"Legs around me, sweetheart. Tight."

She did.

"Yes, that's perfect."

Then he began to move. Nothing slow and romantic. He took. It was hard and fast. His cock was driving deep, each stroke felt like he hit her cervix. One hand was fisted in her hair and he kissed her neck, nipping and sucking on it. She cupped his head against her, wanting everything he offered and more. She scored his head with her nails as he powered within her. Nearing another release, her moans grew louder.

He flicked a finger over her clit and it sent her over. She came hard. Body bucking with the intensity of it. Muscles tightening around his length, she fell back again when he erupted within her.

Heart pounding, she held on as he carried them to her bedroom and laid her down. She watched him in the faint light from the hall. He made short work of stripping off his clothes and joining her. He gathered her close and trailed a hand down her side only to stop on her ass.

"More." His single word said it all.

She curved a hand along his cheek. "Yes." Roxi rolled him onto his back and rose up over him. Like it had before, a hiss of pleasure escaped as he filled her. He reached up and took her hair the rest of the way down—it fell around her shoulders and he tossed the clip off to the side. With her hands on his chest, she began to move.

# Chapter Nine

Sam walked beside Dean while they made their way through the grocery store. Christmas was two and a half weeks away and he was dreading leaving Roxi. He'd moved his stuff into her bedroom and they slept together every night. He was more than getting used to having her warm body beside him.

"How are things?" Dean asked as he paused his motorised cart by the cereal.

"Fine. Second Chances is all ready. The tree has been delivered and decorated. I'm going over tonight to help them start wrapping presents which were delivered there directly. The others will be delivered by the Marines."

"I meant with you and Roxi, but I'm glad to hear things are going well there, too."

"Me and Roxi?"

"Son, have you told her how you feel?"

"It's not like that with us."

Dean's expression was one of pure disbelief. He put in his cereal. "Is that what you're telling yourself? Because trust me, son, from where I'm sitting it's a whole different story." A shrug. "I told you, grandkids would be nice to have. And I want to know you're taken care of."

"I like her," he admitted. "A lot."

"Me too, son. I like her for you. Much better than Tracey."

He didn't want to talk about her. Not here. Not now. "I'm glad. How are things with you and Dean Jr?"

A fierce scowl crossed his face. "I'm beginning to see that boy is a lot like his mother. Selfish. Spoilt." He shook his head in disgust. "Concerned only with himself. Those two with him are the same."

"I'm sorry, sir."

He waved a veined hand. "Don't apologise for something not your fault. Maybe if I had been there he would have turned out differently." A disappointed sigh. "I'll never know now."

"Did he leave?"

"I suspect he will today. I told him yesterday I wasn't changing my will. Well, not in the way he wants me to." Dean fell silent as they made their way to the checkout line. After they'd paid and were back in his truck, Dean started again. "Have you picked up the things I want you to have from Laila yet?"

"I have them at Roxi's. I haven't looked at them yet." He didn't want to. Anything that reminded him that Master Guns was dying he tended to avoid.

"You know you and Laila are splitting my things."

"No. I can't take your things."

The laugh was almost reminiscent of the healthy man. "I wasn't asking your permission, son. I was telling you how it was going to be." Dean touched his arm. "Look, Sam, you are my son in every sense of the word. Let me do this. You and Laila are my family. No matter what. I wish I could have adopted you and made it official but that wasn't meant to be. None of it changes the fact that you are my son."

Tears pricked his eyes. He wasn't a man prone to showing emotions but he wanted to cry, hug him and cry some more.

"Just wanted you to know. I didn't want to leave this world without making sure you know that while your name is Sam Hoch, to me you're a Richardson. My son."

"Thank you."

Dean dropped the topic and they headed back to the house in silence. Sam put the items away, since Dean was tired and went to take a nap. Standing at a window, he stared across the space to Roxi's house. A knock sounded on the door and he opened it. Roxi stood there in jeans and a pink shirt, with a brown leather jacket and hiking boots.

"Hey," he said with a smile. "No work?"

"I have to work through the night so they sent me home. I saw your truck and came over to see how Dean was doing."

He arched a brow. "Just Dean?" Sam pulled her in and shoved the door shut behind her.

"Well, not just, but mostly." Her teasing grin was infectious and he felt himself responding.

"He's sleeping right now. We just got back from shopping."

"So." She placed her hands on his chest. "That leaves us with an empty house for the most part."

"You are a naughty woman." Her grin had him kissing her. "Trouble."

"Perhaps just a bit," she agreed. "So, want some company or should I go home?"

He helped her out of her jacket. "Stay."

She curled up beside him on the couch and he tucked her close. "Why are you working tonight?"

"We have a shipment arriving and since I just took over as head of security, I'm going to be there."

"All night?"

She nodded against his chest but didn't say a word. He knew she was tired. They'd stayed up until the wee hours making love. Brushing his lips over the top of her head, he didn't say anything else and soon, she fell asleep. Although reluctant to leave her, he slipped free and laid her down on the sofa before covering her with a quilt.

About an hour later, his cell rang. Father O'Toole.

"What can I do for you, Father?"

"Do you have time to come down here? We've got a broken window."

He stared at Roxi who slumbered on. "Do you need me to pick up a new one?"

"No, we have spares but I've just broken my wrist and can't do it. I got back from the hospital to find it busted."

"I'll be right there."

"Thank you, son."

He ended the call and crouched by the sofa. "Hey, wake up, Roxi."

She opened her eyes and stared at him. "What's wrong?"

"Can you keep an eye here on Dean until I get back? I have to go replace a window."

She pushed up and nodded. "Sure thing, I got it. Are there meds I need to know about?"

He checked his watch. "Nope. I just don't want him waking up and being all alone."

"Sam, go. I got this."

He gave her a quick kiss and got to his feet. "Thanks, Roxi."

"I know how important he is to you. We'll be fine. I just need a drink." She walked to the kitchen.

Sam followed for one more kiss then headed out before he did something crazy like tell her he loved her.

* * * *

He'd finished repairing the window and was adding the caulking along the frame when he started shivering from the wind that whipped around. The temperature had dropped drastically in the small amount of time he'd been here. He needed warmer clothing.

Once he'd completed his task and had cleaned up the area, he said his farewells and headed off to Naval Base Kitsap. He showed his ID at the gate and asked for directions to their exchange. Then he went in and shopped. As he walked by the jewellery section, he paused then swung in and started looking.

"Sam? Hoch, is that you?" a voice called from behind him.

He turned and spotted a guy he'd been stationed over in the Middle East with. Brent 'Killer' Agers.

"Killer. Good to see you."

"And you, man. And you." They shook hands and Brent stepped back to glance between him and the display case he stood before. "Getting married?"

162

"No." He could see the reason he had asked, though. When Brent had called his name, he'd been by the rings. *Is the thought of marrying Roxi really all that bad?* He ignored the question.

"Oh, so hanging out by rings is a common thing for you now? Looking to pick up a chick? I know some who hang out in hopes of snaring a man who will put a ring on their finger."

"Common when my name is called by them. I'm not getting married. What about you? Did you get married?" He paused. "To Sherri, wasn't it?"

Frustration filled Brent's expression. "No, that didn't work out. Apparently she had other ideas of being faithful while I was over there."

"I'm sorry to hear that."

A shrug. "Better I found out before I married her than after. I hope the bitch is happy now. I kicked her ass out when I got home. Not sure where she went or who she's with."

"And now you're here?"

"Yes. Not for long, though. This is just kind of a stop-over before we get back to Twentynine Stumps."

He nodded. That was the nickname Marines gave to Twentynine Palms base in California.

Brent seemed to size him up a minute before speaking. "Look, Hoch. I know you don't do a lot, but there are a few guys from our old group here. We're getting together tonight. It'd be great if you'd come along. If you have time."

He thought about it. Roxi had said she had to work tonight, all night. Why not hang out with some guys he'd served with a while back? "Sounds good. When and where?"

Surprise replaced the earlier frustration on Brent's face. "Cool. We're meeting around twenty-hundred at the bowling alley. You know where it is?"

"I can find it. I'll see you then."

"You got it, Gunny." Brent waved and walked off.

Sam turned back around and continued looking for

something. Fifteen minutes later, he walked out with a small box in the bag and headed for his truck.

He drove back to the house and parked in Laila's drive before hurrying inside.

It was quiet and for a moment there, he thought the worst. Then Roxi stepped into view from the kitchen and gave him a smile.

"Hey. How'd it go with the window?" she asked as she approached him.

Wrapping an arm around her waist and drawing her in for a brief kiss, he took a moment to relish the feel of her in his embrace. Lips pressed to her temple, he inhaled the intoxicating scent of autumn that surrounded her.

"Good. It went good. They're all fixed up. And here? How's Dean?"

"He's fine. Got up for a bit then went to lie back down. I told him to save his energy, he was going to need it when he went with you to the Christmas thing at Second Chances. And he agreed. So he's resting again."

"Are you coming?"

"No, I work that night."

Disappointment welled up in him. He'd wanted to celebrate Christmas Eve with her at his side. Or at least in the audience at his debut role as Santa.

"Maybe after."

"Maybe." She rested her head against his chest. "I have to go home and get some sleep or I'm not going to be worth spit tonight. I'll see you later."

"Thanks for watching him, Roxi."

"Not a problem. I'll see you." She stepped away and headed for the door. He watched her rub the back of her neck as she moved. He wanted to help her relax. But that wasn't all. He...slammed the doors on those thoughts.

"Roxi?"

"Hm?"

He shook his head. "Nothing. Get some sleep."

"On my way." With a slight wave over her shoulder, she

grabbed her jacket and swung it on as she walked out.

He waited for Laila to come home. "I'm going to drop some things off and I'll be back, Laila," he said after she'd changed from work clothing and had checked in on Dean.

"No problem."

It had started to rain when he left. Dashing to his truck, he unlocked it before he grabbed his bag of purchases then jogged to Roxi's front door, letting himself in. The house was quiet and her Christmas lights were on—but then she had them on a timer—offering the only light.

He made his way silently down the hall to her bedroom and hesitated with his hand on the doorknob. Waking her was the last thing he wanted to do. Well, not entirely true, he wanted her awake but he knew she needed to sleep. Once in the room, he put the bag down near the door and gazed over to the bed. All the curtains were drawn, shrouding the room in darkness.

Unable to stay away, he made his way there and waited for his eyes to adjust better to the lack of light. She lay there, on her side, wrapped around the pillow he'd been using. Resisting the powerful urge to touch her he made himself walk away and shut the door behind him. He could deal with his clothing after she woke.

Back over at Laila's, he sat on the couch and smiled as Laila and Dean played a game of chess. Dean had taught them both the game when they were younger. He had many memories of sitting outside at Laila's house, on the back porch, playing this in the late summer sun.

"What'd Laila think of you being Santa?" Dean asked, moving his pawn.

"What? You're playing Santa?" Laila's shock was evident.

"Just filling in for Dean this year."

Laila burst out laughing.

"What's so funny?"

"I can't imagine you as a jolly fat man who lets kids sit on his lap and tell him what they want for Christmas." She wiped her eyes. "Oh, this is priceless. I want to see this.

Hell, I want pictures of this for I doubt I'll still believe it even after seeing it."

He glared at her. She wasn't perturbed by it at all. He watched her move her bishop before putting her gaze back on him. "So who's Mrs Claus?"

"I don't know, why?"

"You get to kiss her."

He froze. "What?"

"Didn't you know? You get to kiss Mrs Claus after the last kid has been on your lap and has had his or her picture taken."

He jerked his gaze to Dean, who merely gave a sombre nod. The kids got pictures taken with him then the gifts were given out—which was where the things his fellow Marines dropped off came into play.

"No one told me that."

"It won't be bad, Sam. It's all for fun and for the children."

Dean nodded. "She's right. Plus this year I thought they said there would be Marines with more gifts than before. It's going to be a big thing this year. Bigger than most years."

He knew that, they'd already discussed the Marines being there. Sam didn't want to kiss anyone. Well, not other than Roxi, but he kept that to himself. He could kiss a woman for the kids to have a good holiday. Part of him wondered if they were yanking his chain but they seemed so serious about it. And there was the fact that Laila couldn't lie to save herself.

He thought about the women who worked there. Okay, a cheek kiss. This could work. "For the children, then," he said.

They had a nice dinner then he said goodnight and headed to the bowling lanes. Splashing through puddles, he ran to the door and slipped inside. He spied Brent and others he'd served with after searching the crowd and making his way over there. He was surprised at how glad he was to see them.

"Gunny!" Brent waved at him.

He gave a sharp nod and gestured for a beer from a passing waitress.

"You playing, Hoch?"

"Sure. Let me go get some shoes."

They split up into teams and had a great time reminiscing, talking and just bullshitting around.

"Where did you run into Hoch, Killer?" Josh 'Helter Skelter' Jones asked.

"The jewellery section. He was in front of the rings."

All heads turned to him. Both teams.

"You taking the plunge, Hoch?" another questioned.

Again, that unbidden image of Roxi filled his head. He could picture her in a wedding dress. All that white satin and lace against her dark skin. The lingerie she would wear beneath it. Garters, lace panties. His cock stirred and he shook off the vision.

"Nope. Just looking for a gift."

Five people watched him with disbelief.

He shook his head in mild amusement. "Just a gift," he reiterated.

"One that keeps on giving?"

He wasn't about to give them any information on Roxi. So he didn't say anything.

"Who's here for the toy drive?" he asked to change the subject.

"All of us. In fact, there's two more. Women."

He nodded. He didn't give a damn if it was men or women. The drive was the important thing. As they got back to bowling, he couldn't get the thought of one of those rings out of his mind. The minute he'd seen it, he thought *Roxi* and knew that would be the ring he proposed to her with.

Whoa! Wait a minute here. His hand trembled and he lowered it, grateful it wasn't his turn. When had those ideas begun to settle into his brain?

*From the moment you met her.*

*Yep. You knew she was different from the second your eyes*

*landed on her.* This from his subconscious.

Advice he didn't want from either.

"You're up, Hoch!"

Appreciating the distraction, he took another swig of his beer and got up to bowl his frame. The rest of the time passed quickly and he left after a few hours. The men were hanging out longer but they understood when he told them about Master Guns. They all knew of the man, even if they hadn't actually had the opportunity to meet him.

The rain still fell in torrents and he drove through it back to the house. Pressing the button for the garage door, he felt a stab of disappointment in his gut when he saw her vehicle wasn't in there, even though he wasn't expecting her home right now. He parked and headed inside.

He changed, after which he put his clothes in the laundry along with the ones he'd just purchased. While he waited for the load to finish, he picked up an album that sat above her television. A grin filled his face as he opened it and flipped through her childhood photographs. He took his time going through the expressive images.

The numerous pictures of her in various stages of growing up hit him low. She looked so happy. She and Ritchie both with their parents. Just another reminder of what he didn't have. He closed the cover, sighed, and replaced it.

He walked to the item he'd purchased today and opened the box. Staring down at the object inside he wondered what she would do when — if — he gave it to her.

Her phone rang and he almost answered it but held off at the last second. He went towards the laundry room to move clothing from the washer to dryer. The sound of a man's voice on the machine stopped him dead in his tracks.

"Hey, Roxi, it's me, Lance. I'm in town for a few days. I'd love to get together. You know my number. Hope to hear from you soon, babe." *Click.* The message ended.

Sam bristled. All over. Who the fuck was Lance and what the hell did he want with Roxi? And why did he care so damn much?

"Because I'm sleeping with her," he told the empty room. And he sure as hell had no intentions of sharing her.

*Roxi isn't yours.* More unwanted advice from the brain.

Unwanted? Perhaps. However, it was true. He had no claim over her. But he knew he wanted one.

*Have to get past your own insecurities if you want that to happen.*

Like he didn't know that already. He warred with that information and finished the trek to the washer to transfer the clothes to the dryer. Slamming his hands down on the top of the machine, he released a string of curses which would have had Dean looking at him in shock.

Did he? Did he have enough strength to defeat doubt and take a chance on Roxi? Sam wasn't sure but he knew he needed to find out.

Sleep didn't come that fast and he left early to run some errands with Dean. It was later in the following afternoon when he left Second Chances and was walking downtown looking for a gift for Laila when he froze. Roxi. He knew it was her. His body knew. He'd not seen her in the past two days. When she was home, he was gone and vice versa.

He'd missed her. Well, bully for him, now he got to see her. And she was with a tall, fit man. Jealously rose within him, tinting his world an ugly shade. The man had his arm around her shoulders and they were laughing and joking as they entered a small diner.

Why wasn't she sleeping? More importantly, why was she here and letting this other man touch her with such familiarity?

\* \* \* \*

"I was so glad you called, Lance. It's been far too long since I've seen you." Roxi gave the tall man a hug and kiss on the cheek.

"I know. We need to keep in better touch." He helped her with her coat and held her chair for her.

Pulling off her gloves, she nodded in agreement. "Coffee, please," she said when the waiter came to take their drink order. "We do. This once-a-year thing just doesn't cut it anymore."

"No, it doesn't. But, with me moving to Portland, we'll be much closer than when I was in Maine."

"Very true. Thank you," she said after the drinks arrived. Fixing hers the way she liked it, she stirred it a bit before leaning forward and resting her chin on laced fingers. "So. How are things?"

As Lance filled her in, she took in his shaggy, unkempt, dark-blond hair, piercing green eyes, and tanned skin. She couldn't help but appreciate how he looked. But it wasn't like that between them. Never had been. They were just very good friends. He travelled quite a bit and would call her whenever he got to town.

"Hey, I was thinking. We need to take a vacation."

She sipped some coffee. "Do tell."

"Remember when we went to Dubai?"

She sure did. She'd gone with him as his assistant but really just went for a free vacation. It had been a blast. "Oh yeah. That was a *lot* of fun."

"Well, I have a conference coming up in Sydney, if you'd like to go with me."

"Sydney? Oh, I haven't been there in forever." She shook her head. "I don't know, Lance. I just got the promotion, I should probably stick around for a while."

He waved it off. "It's not for a few months." He leant forward towards her. "Come on, Rox, it's Australia. And right now it's summer down there."

Oh, that sounded so tempting. Warm sun. Beaches.

"Come on, what do you say? Want to go to Australia with me?"

"Yes, Roxi, are you going to go to Australia with him?"

At the new voice she jerked and turned to find Sam there. No expression on his face but she could see the fury in his body language. Jealousy? From Sam?

170

"Sam? What are you doing here?" Her heart pounded. "Is everything okay with Dean?"

He never looked at her, just continued to stare at Lance. "Shopping for Laila."

Shortened sentences and a clipped tone. He wasn't happy. Lance cleared his throat and she tore her gaze from Sam and met Lance's.

"Oh, um, Sam Hoch meet Lance Noble. Lance, this is Sam. He's here because of Master Guns."

"Nice to meet you, Sam. I'm sorry to hear about Dean."

"You know Dean?"

She watched Sam stiffen. Seriously, could the man get any tenser?

"Yes. Roxi introduced me to him years ago. Wonderful man."

Now Sam looked at her and the emotions swirling in his eyes hit her in the gut like a sucker punch. "Nice to meet you. Sorry for interrupting." He spun on his heel and walked off.

Licking her lips, she shrugged. "I'm sorry, Lance. Excuse me, please. I'll be right back."

"Go, go. I'll order your food for you."

She dashed out after Sam. The cold bit into her but she didn't care. She spied him walking off down the sidewalk.

"Sam," she called out. "Sam!" Roxi ran after him and grabbed his arm to halt him. "Wait a minute. What the hell is going on here?"

He peered down at her and frowned. "Where's your jacket?"

"Inside." She waved his question off. "What the hell was that about?"

He took his off and placed it around her shoulders. Immediately she was swamped by his heady masculine scent and warmth.

"What about you, Sam?"

"I don't mind."

"Tell me what's wrong." She reached again for his arm

171

and touched it.

"Nothing. I didn't mean to interrupt."

She bit back her growl of frustration. Why couldn't he admit he felt something for her? "You weren't interrupting. Want to join us?"

"Join you and what? Listen to you make plans to go to Sydney with a man who took you with him to Dubai, *Rox*?"

"Is that what this is about? Him asking me to Sydney?"

"Your business is your business." The words were forced from behind clenched teeth.

Fine. If he didn't want to admit anything she wouldn't force him. "You're right." She removed his jacket and slapped it back at him, hitting him in the chest. "Have a good day, Sam."

She was angry. Her steps took her back to the diner where Lance waited. She wasn't sure if it was the cold or her fury at him making her shake so much. Her lunch companion lifted his brows and leant back in his chair.

"He's a hot one."

"Really, Lance, that's what you have to say?"

"Well, he is." Sitting forward, he tipped his head to the side. "You two going to be okay?"

"Why wouldn't we? Didn't you see how well that went?"

"Jealous boyfriend?"

"He's not my boyfriend. He's…"

A sly grin lifted Lance's mouth. "Oh, do tell, babe. You're just hittin' that?"

She groaned and dropped her head into her hands. "Think you could say it any louder? Or perhaps cruder?"

"Of course I can. So you and handsome there are just fucking—"

Her head jerked up. "Stop it!" Mortification spread along her face as the waiter stood there with the ordered food.

His wicked grin waited for her, well aware of what she would do. Nothing. "Well, you asked if I could. Just trying to help."

"I should hurt you. Really, *really* hurt you."

His green eyes sparkled. "Would you, please. You know what I like."

"You are such a pervert."

He blinked thick long lashes at her. "But I'm your pervert."

"I think I need to trade for another."

He just shook his head and laughed. "Okay, seriously. What's his deal?"

She released a long breath. "I really don't know, Lance. There are times when I think he's jealous but he won't ever say I mean anything."

"Have you told him you're in love with him?"

"What? I never said that."

"Didn't have to, babe. I know you well enough. And I have never, and I do mean *never*, seen you run out after a man. And I bet before this Sam Hoch you never have."

Okay, so that may very well be the truth. She'd not ever done that before. "Doesn't mean I love him."

"True. But that look on your face says otherwise." He took a drink of his coffee. "Look, I didn't mean to cause any friction between you two. I can talk to him and let him know I'm not a threat to your relationship and that our trips are purely platonic."

She shook her head. "No. I don't owe him any explanations. He's staying at my house because of Master Guns, but if he's not willing to say anything about how he feels then I don't have to say anything either."

Lance frowned. "Don't be so stubborn you lose him forever, Roxanne."

She didn't want to lose him. But damn it all, he had to face his fears and she knew he had them. She'd known that when this had started. *That was before I fell in love with him.*

"Enough about Sam. Tell me more about Sydney."

* * * *

She had a leisurely lunch with Lance then drove home. All the while, her mind lingered on Sam and their interaction

173

out in the cold. His truck sat in the drive—perhaps he was over at Laila's—and she parked next to it as she waited for the garage to open then pulled inside. If it started to rain again, she might as well use the garage. She had one after all.

The second she stepped through the door, she knew he was in the house. She heard him in the kitchen. Walking in the opposite direction, she made her way to her bedroom. Closing the door, she put down her things and sat on the chair to remove her boots.

She was tired and really wanted to sleep. But since she was going to be on days starting Monday, she needed to stay awake now and sleep at night. Dropping the second boot to the floor, she sighed and leant back.

No time to rest now, she still had to get her run in. Groaning, she pushed to her feet and went to grab some running clothes. She'd pulled on her sports bra when the door opened. Tugging her white, quarter-zip running shirt down over her chest, she turned and found him in the doorway.

He didn't speak, merely stared at her as she stood there in a shirt, socks and underwear. She arched a brow. "Yes?"

"Running?"

She shook out her black running pants then drew them on. "Yep." Grabbing her shoes, she sat down to tie them. She rolled her shoulders and pulled her hair up into a ponytail before going back to her closet for her jacket and gloves.

"Are you mad at me?"

She blew out a breath and stared at him. "Nope. We've been over this, Sam. This is just a 'now' kind of thing. Lance said he was sorry you didn't want to stay for lunch, but no, I'm not mad."

Well, that was a whopper of a lie. She was pissed off that he wouldn't tell her he was jealous of her being out with another man. Lance had it right, he wasn't a threat, and if Sam would ask her, she'd be more than happy to tell him just exactly what Lance was to her. But he didn't ask and she wasn't volunteering the information up.

"Mind some company?"

Part of her wanted to tell him to stay behind, but honestly, she liked him around. "Sure. I'll be up in the living room stretching." She sidled by him, careful not to touch him. That wasn't easy.

She waited while he changed and stretched as well, then they strolled outside. She readjusted her 180s earmuffs and watched Sam do the same. Then they took off and began running. He followed her stride and it seemed that they were pretty similarly matched speed wise.

As they ran, she thought about what had happened earlier and where she truly wanted to think of this going. Could she see long-term with Sam? Yes. But she wouldn't be in a relationship with a person who couldn't at least tell her how he felt. She wasn't going to do that. It wasn't fun when you had to fight for every single bit of emotion. To her, love shouldn't be like that.

It saddened her to think of no longer having him in her life. She may see him if he came to visit Laila but in all the years they'd been neighbours, she'd never seen Sam there. So perhaps when he left it would be for good. She gave herself a mental shake. *This is Christmas, Roxi. Think positive.*

She cut her gaze to the man running with fluid energy beside her. She had to get him a gift. What? She didn't know yet, but she'd find something for him. For some reason, giving him a good Christmas was important to her.

*Some reason my ass. I want to do it because I weep for the boy who never had a good one and cry for the man who is still unwilling to believe that people won't hurt him.*

She shook her head. He may have had a good Christmas at a foster home. Or perhaps with Laila and her family. But she wanted him to remember *her* and *this one* with fondness.

They didn't talk at all during the run and when they made it back to the house she was even more exhausted. But this was a good exhaustion — she loved how she felt after a run. They cooled down and showered — separately — before meeting in the living room.

"I'm making some coffee, would you like some?" she asked, hoping he shared her feeling that a truce had been called between them.

"Please."

"Tell me something about you, Sam," she blurted out as she added the grounds to the maker.

"What do you want to know?"

"If there was one thing you could have for Christmas, what would it be?"

"Dean healthy."

She nodded. "Okay, what else? If he was fine, Laila was fine. What would you want? Something for yourself."

He was silent for so long she turned her head to glance at him. A confused look was on his face. "I…I don't know."

"Something for your truck? Your apartment? You know, something other than an endless supply of porn," she joked, knowing some of the guys had kept a large supply of said materials while deployed.

He gave her a pointed gaze, which told her he knew what she was doing. "I really don't have any clue, Roxi, I'm not trying to blow you off, I just never gave it any thought before."

She grabbed some decorated sugar cookies and put them on a plate. "Well, think about it."

"What about you?"

"What would I want?"

He nodded, taking the plate from her and walking to the living room where he placed it on the coffee table. She followed him and sat on the sofa, curling up to face him at the other end.

"Let me think."

He ate a cookie and watched her. "Not so easy, is it?"

"No. I think another work of art like the one in the hall. If I could have anything. An oil painting of ships like that. I just love them. To see a clipper slicing through the water, they feel so real to me. Perhaps one of those. Of course, gift cards to sports stores are always good, too. That way I never worry about not having my running clothing."

"Running clothes?" he teased.

"Hey, I said a portrait as well." She gestured at him. "What have you come up with?"

"Besides the endless supply of porn?"

She laughed. "Right, of course. Beside that."

His blue eyes twinkled and her heart stuttered a bit before resuming a regular pace. He was teasing with her and she loved it. *Damn, there went that love word again.*

"Gift cards for music or books."

"Your porn thought was more exciting." She leant forward. "Come on, Sam. What do you want?"

His eyes heated and she felt the answering moisture between her thighs. "Not porn."

"I figured that."

He licked his lips and she watched him think. "I want a home."

"I thought Laila said you had a place. An apartment, right?"

"I have a house. I want a home."

*Okay, melting heart here.* She wanted to grab him and hold him close. "We all do, Sam."

As if he realised he'd imparted such information, he lifted a shoulder in a lazy move. "You know, filled —"

"With porn." They finished together.

She got up to get the coffee and give him a minute to get himself back together. Pouring the freshly brewed liquid, she shook her head. A home. Of course he did. How could she have not seen it?

# Chapter Ten

Sam rubbed a hand over his head as he exhaled. He hadn't expected to deliver anything like that to her. His own private wish, want, or desire. Didn't matter what you called it, a home was what he yearned for more than anything. But it was more than that now. Whenever he thought of a home, it had this woman, Roxi, in the picture with him.

He really didn't know how he was going to move on without her in his life. And he didn't want his relationship with Roxi to be as Laila's friends, not solely anyway. He rolled his lower lip between his teeth as he sat there, grateful for the moment of solitude she'd given him. He needed to recover.

*Should have stuck to porn.* He knew the stories—that being what filled a Marine's sea bag. It would have been much less personal and he wouldn't be sitting here feeling like he'd just opened up his heart for her to peer in and see his pain and wounds from childhood.

He watched her return from the kitchen with a tray holding their drinks. She placed it between them on the coffee table and gave him a smile as she picked her mug up. He searched for any sign of sympathy and found nothing. In fact, her face was devoid of almost anything other than her typical kindness.

"When did you decide you wanted to be a Marine, Sam?"

*Share with her. Don't push her away.* The words resonated within and he debated if he actually could or not. He'd try. The best way to explain this was to tell her of the man who had set him on that path, Staff Sergeant Dean Richardson, as he'd been then.

"I met Dean when I was seven." He reached for his drink and allowed the familiar scent to seep into him. "In Minnesota, around this time of year."

Sam almost expected her to say to him he didn't need to tell her if he didn't wish to, but Roxi sat forward, legs tucked under her and an eager light in her brown eyes. She *wanted* to know more about him. Unfortunately, Tracey had been the same way, or so he'd thought.

*Stop it! This woman is nothing like Tracey.*

"He took me to a shelter so I didn't have to spend the night out in the cold winter. He was wearing his blood stripes and I think that was the moment I wanted to be a Marine. He was so capable and to a young boy" — he shrugged — "especially to me, it was a pretty defining moment."

"Makes sense to me."

"What about you?"

"Me? Well, nothing quite so noble. I fell into a bad crowd my senior year in high school and when we got busted, the judge gave us the choice — jail or the military. So I joined the Marines. Never regretted it. Changed my life around and for the better. I can't imagine I'd not be in jail somewhere if not for that judge."

He was amazed. Never had he pegged Roxi for a troublemaker. She laughed and took a drink.

"Hey, don't look so shocked, it happens. We know this. I was one of the lucky ones who got their life straightened out and I have the Corps to thank for it. I'm not embarrassed or ashamed. I'm quite the opposite. I'm proud. Proof the Marines can change a person for the better."

"How'd you meet Master Guns?"

A grin crossed her face. "I met him in Italy. Laila had come to visit him and we met at the bar, hit it off becoming fast friends. So she introduced us."

He drew back and frowned, his eyebrows drawing together. "Laila was only in Italy once. I was there then." His heart pounded at the thought he could have met her sooner. Perhaps then he wouldn't have met Tracey.

"Were you? Well, too bad I didn't meet you then, Sam Hoch. I have a feeling that could have been a lot of fun."

He had that same belief. "Roxi," he said.

"You don't have to say anything, Sam. I know you're not into sharing much."

He *did* have to say something, though. She had to know how much she'd come to mean to him. But as much as he wanted to, he just couldn't push the words past his lips. The sadness that flashed in her gaze cut him to the core.

*Some Marine I am. Can't even tell her how I feel.*

He was disgusted with himself and his inability to do so. They passed the rest of the evening talking about places they'd served. It was nearly midnight when they finished the cookies and drinks. The coffee carafe now sat empty. He carried the tray back into the kitchen, Roxi on his heels. He watched her as she loaded the dishwasher. She looked tired and so he went around checking the doors. They met at the hallway and walked to her bedroom together.

They made slow love before he held her in his arms. As her deep breaths were the only sound in the room, he brushed a kiss along her temple and whispered, "I'm sorry about today, Roxi. I was jealous."

He slept fitfully that night and was awake when he felt her slide from the bed and walk away on silent feet. Moments later a door closed. When she stepped from the bathroom, he'd just sat up in bed and turned on the light.

"Morning," she said.

He watched her move in her robin's-egg-blue silk robe, skin scrubbed clean from her shower. The robe stopped at her thighs, leaving nothing to his imagination, since he knew exactly what lay below the material.

"Morning," he replied, desire moving through him.

"You going to be at Second Chances today?" She walked to her closet and opened the door, staring in at the clothing that hung there.

"Yes. Why?"

"Just swinging by with the presents from the bank."

"I'll be there. Come find me and I'll unload them for you."

He got up and ignored the stiff cock that wanted some attention from her. After drawing on his boxers, he pulled on some sweats then approached to stand behind her. He set his hands at her waist and nuzzled her neck, her tremor making him smile. He followed it with a light lick and graze of teeth.

"Stop, Sam," she said breathlessly. "I have to get ready for work."

He smoothed his hands down the silk of her robe and rocked into her. "Okay."

When she pressed back into him he almost lost it but stepped away. One final look in her direction, then progressed to the bathroom where he took his own shower. Dried and dressed, he went to the kitchen and found her eating a piece of toast, a mug of coffee beside her.

"That's all you're having?" he asked with a frown.

"Not that hungry this morning."

He paused and stared at her. She still looked a bit tired. Her hair was drawn back in a braid and her suit was black. Another pants suit which she wore the hell out of. Heeled boots today instead of shoes. All in all, he wanted to strip it off her and keep her in bed for the next few months. Maybe then he'd be assuaged of this clawing need to have her, over and over. She licked her lips and another jolt went from the action to his groin. *Then again, perhaps not.*

Roxi finished her breakfast and put the dishes in the sink. "Okay, I have to get going. I'll see you later on at the centre. Have a great day, Sam." She walked by him and brushed a light kiss to his lips before continuing.

He snagged her around the waist and drew her back. "What was that?"

"A kiss goodbye."

Fingers on her chin, he shook his head. "That wasn't a kiss."

"That so, Marine?" She ran her hands up his arms and looped them about his neck. Lord, she smelt so good.

"Try again."

She licked her lips and shifted her weight. Tipping her head from one side to the other she watched him. Just when he was about to growl at her, she grinned and did as he had wanted. Kissed him again. Properly. He was straining to control his desire when it ended. Roxi's lips were swollen and damp from their exchange.

"Catch you later, Marine," she said, trailing a hand down his face before stepping free and walking out of the kitchen.

He didn't move until he heard the door shut to the garage. He couldn't, well aware that if he had, she'd be naked in bed. After a quick breakfast, he cleaned up and went to finish getting ready. Not much later, he was on his way to Second Chances, after a stopover at Laila's to check on Dean.

Father O'Toole met him at the door when he arrived. "Good morning, son."

"Morning, Father." He removed his coat then hung it up, nodding at a few of the children running around. The day was frightfully frigid and a lot of the younger ones had to stay inside or limit their time out in the cold.

"A few of the Marines who will be delivering the toys for the party are here. They've come to help wrap items already here."

Past Father O'Toole, he spied Brent standing, wearing civvies, talking to some of the children. His friend looked up and waved at him with a smile.

"I see them."

"I'll leave you to it, then. Oh, before I forget, Reba got some boots for you, so try them on and make sure they fit."

"Yes, sir."

Walking off, he headed towards Brent.

"Morning, Gunny," the man said, smiling.

"Morning. I'll help you wrap after I finish fixing one final sink."

Ruffling the head of the child nearest him, Brent stood up tall. "I'll see you kids later. Have to go to work." He focused on him. "I can help out. I know a bit about plumbing."

"Great, it's one of the large sinks in the kitchen."

"Let's go."

"You come alone?" Sam asked.

"No. The women came as well. Corporals Blake and Weems."

Blake. He knew a Blake. Tracey Blake, but she'd been a sergeant, not a corporal. He nodded and led the way to the kitchen.

They worked in relative silence as they fixed the sink. He liked Brent, the man didn't talk for no reason. A man who weighed his words and chose them carefully. A tingle went up his spine and he turned his head from where he was under the sink and looked past Brent's legs where he stood holding up the sink, and would until they'd secured it to the wall. He saw a pair of black boots and pants. He knew that clothing.

Roxi.

"Hello, I'm looking for Sam. Have you seen him?"

He smiled at the sound of her voice.

"Under here," Brent replied.

"Oh." The boots moved closer and she crouched down by Brent's legs so she could see his face. "Hey."

"Roxi."

"I can see you're busy, let me just move the boxes in."

"No. I'll do it. Just give me five minutes to finish this up." He searched her gaze and waited for confirmation. When she nodded and rose, he released a sigh of relief he'd been unaware of holding.

He worked fast as he listened to her and Brent introduce themselves. "Let it down," he called out.

Brent did and they checked the stability before he tightened it further. Then he wriggled out of the back and got to his feet before cleaning up. Roxi waited with Brent and he took a deep breath when he approached.

"Sam," Brent said. "You didn't tell me you had met such a lovely woman."

183

Roxi laughed and shook her head. "I'm Laila's friend. That's it."

He growled low in his throat at her comment. It didn't appear Brent believed that either, for he cast a few glances between them. Before he could reach her, she turned and walked away.

"This the one you were looking at rings for?" Brent whispered.

"Wasn't looking at them."

"Keep telling yourself that, man."

"Come help me carry boxes of presents."

Brent fell into step with a chuckle. Roxi was already out of sight by the time they reached the back door. They pushed through and he saw her at her vehicle, the back open and four boxes of presents in the interior. And a few bags.

They made quick work of carrying in the boxes, placing them all into the large room under the Christmas tree. Roxi stood talking with Father O'Toole when Sam noticed someone move up next to him. A floral, musky smell hit him. A familiar scent.

"Hello, Sam."

He knew without even looking. But he still did. Turned his head and was met by a pair of baby blues. Shit. Tracey Blake stood there beside him.

Everything within him began closing up. "Tracey."

"Long time."

He nodded, not even speaking. Years. He kept his gaze across the way, on the woman who had this ability to make him feel invincible. Roxi laughed, her head tipping back, and he couldn't help but think how beautiful she was. She had one hand on Father O'Toole's arm and nodded at something else he said.

"Why so quiet, Sam? Nothing to say?"

"Like what? There's nothing for us to say to one another."

"Want to get together?"

"No."

Her huff of indignation made him peek at her again. "Are

184

you still upset by that? I thought you were cool about it."

"Cool about it? I thought we were a couple. I come back to find you in bed, the bed *we* shared, with another man. You really thought I would be okay with that?"

"I figured you were doing the same thing."

"How strange. I thought I was in a committed relationship."

"We had fun, Sam. And can have fun again."

"No."

Roxi walked away and headed for the door. That spurred him into action and he went after her, leaving Tracey there without a word.

"Roxi?" he called.

She paused, turning to face him. The smile on her face was only there for show, it definitely didn't reach her eyes.

"Thanks for helping me with the boxes."

"You're leaving?"

"You looked rather busy to me. Something you needed to say to me?"

*Yes. A hell of a lot.* He took a step only to stop when a hand curled around his arm. Roxi's face didn't change but he could feel the chill coming from her.

"Sam, you coming to wrap presents?"

"In a minute." He shook off her touch, disgusted by having it on him.

"And you are?" Tracey directed her question to Roxi.

"Roxi. You?"

"I'm Tracey. I see you know my Sam."

One brow lifted. "*Your* Sam?"

"Yes. We used to be an item and now that we've found each other again...well, you know how it is when things are all kinds of hot and heavy."

"Hot and heavy?" Roxi nodded and licked her lips. "Sounds lovely. If you'll excuse me, I should go wrap some presents before I have to get back to work."

"I'll walk with you. How well do you know Sam?"

"Pretty well."

"Where'd you meet him?" Tracey asked as the women walked off.

Rage built up within him and he wanted to scream and roar in anger. Brent draped an arm around his shoulders. "You and Tracey?"

"Ancient history."

"Did anyone tell her that?"

He swallowed back his curse and shook his head. "Let's go."

They neared the presents and he grabbed one before sitting across from Roxi. Her gaze met his.

"Hello, Sam. Tracey here was just telling me how *well* the two of you knew one another."

Her gaze was no longer bland and unemotional. A firestorm brewed in her eyes and he knew whatever information Tracey had imparted had pissed Roxi off. He refused to release her gaze.

"Did she also tell you it was over years ago?"

Roxi struggled to remain semi-calm and not rake her nails down that blonde's face and play tic-tac-toe on it afterwards. It grated on every last nerve she'd had to listen to this Tracey chick talk about how awesome Sam was in bed. Okay, so she knew that as well, first-hand, but that didn't mean she wanted to hear it from this one.

Sam held her gaze and she knew he knew she wasn't the least bit happy. Was it the fact he'd had a relationship with someone prior to meeting her? No. That wasn't it. Hell, she'd had ones as well. So that wasn't the reason.

It was the smug bitch who took such pride in telling her all about Sam. And not just about them, how they'd been so close. How she knew so much about him and his childhood. It bothered her to no end, especially when this woman had been allowed into his past and he tried to keep her out. Well, not tried. He did keep her out.

With a sniff, she looked at the present before her and quickly wrapped it. Taking a deep breath, she focused on the next one. "No, she didn't mention that."

"Well, it was." His decadent voice resonated through her.

"Oh." Lifting her gaze, she found him waiting for her. His blue eyes did things to her insides that no others could. She ignored the fluttering in her belly and took another deep breath.

"We were really close," Tracey added.

"How nice."

"Weren't you a sergeant when you knew Hoch?" Brent asked.

Tracey gazed at him. "Yes, what's your point?"

"What'd you do to be dropped to corporal?"

Brent sent her a wink and Roxi hid her smile. She liked him. Interesting, though, if she wanted to think about it.

Sam shoved his chair back, scraping it along the floor. She jerked her attention to him and gulped at the intensity in his eyes.

"Roxi, a word." He walked off and she knew he expected her to follow him.

Setting the toy down, she rose and walked around the long table, meandering after him. He opened a door that led to a small office and led the way in. She closed the door behind them and crossed her arms, waiting for him to say whatever it was he needed to get off his chest.

He spun and stared at her. Skimming his hand over his head, he sighed and crossed towards her. Her breath caught in her throat at the predatory way he sauntered.

"What was so important, Sam?"

"This...Tracey...we..."

"It's none of my business, Sam."

She could see he wanted to say something else. And she waited. But nothing came and her heart shattered.

"I get it. This woman is part of your past, I have a past. But don't expect me to stand around while the two of you relive your past. I have to get to work. I'll have your things in the guest room by the time you get home."

Without giving him a chance to respond, she jerked open

the door and walked off. "It was nice to meet all of you. I have to get back to work," she said, passing the group wrapping presents.

Jacket in hand, she went to the back, ignoring him calling her name. She shook on her way, her emotions ran so hard and strong within her. She swung by the house and did as she'd said—moved his things to the guest room. Back at the bank, she sat in the parking lot trying to get herself back under control.

Tall, blonde, fit and gorgeous. A perfect fit for Sam's darker colouring. And it rubbed her entirely the wrong way. Tracey Blake wasn't a woman she would ever like, for she'd been able to have one thing she wasn't allowed. Part of Sam he kept from her.

"Get it together, Roxi," she muttered, shutting off the engine.

Locking down her emotions, she climbed out and shivered against the wind. With quick steps, she hastened into the heated building. She waved at Laila as she went by and headed to her office. Not too much later a knock came on the door and she called out for whomever it was to answer.

Laila.

"Hey," she said, waving her in. "What's up?"

"I'm on lunch. Got a few?"

"Of course, sit down." She still had most of her time left since she didn't stay and help wrap as she'd planned to do. But let's face it, once she'd found out about Tracey she didn't want to be anywhere around them.

"How was the delivery?"

"Good. Everything is there and a few Marines are assisting with the wrapping. Nice people."

Laila narrowed her eyes. "Who is she?"

She blinked a few times. "Who is who?"

"Oh, please," Laila scoffed. "Don't play dense with me. Who's the woman that looked at Sam and has you in a foul mood?"

"I'm not in a foul mood." She denied it with a shake of

188

her head.

Thunder boomed and Laila arched a brow as she ate a bite of her sandwich.

"Don't say a word. Not a single word."

The sparkle in Laila's eyes told her all she needed to know. "Say what? I think God said it for me." She waved a hand. "I've known you long enough and you're damn near in a snit."

Roxi chewed on her lower lip and debated. She hated going behind his back and asking, but damn it all, she wanted to know. So she took the plunge.

"Tell me about Tracey."

A handful of different responses had been expected. She didn't expect the reaction she received. Laila, who didn't get mad all that often, put her unfinished Rueben on marbled rye down on the desk and demanded in a voice that was almost unrecognisable, it was so gravelly, "Why the fuck would you mention her?"

"I met her today."

"That bitch is here? With Sam?"

"Laila, calm down. Tell me about her."

A derisive snort. "What's to tell. He was going to marry her and came home early to propose only to find her in bed with another man."

Anger filled her. That woman could have very well been Mrs Sam Hoch. But instead she'd done something which kept Sam locked away from emotions. Swallowing, she leant back in her chair. "So…Sam let this woman in."

Laila seemed to have forgotten she was there and after a rap on the desk, she shook herself as if breaking free from the hold memories had on her. "What?"

"Sam and this woman. Come on, Laila."

"I told you, Roxi. He loved her, wanted to marry her, and she betrayed him. I don't think he'll ever ask another woman." Laila shook her head. "I can't believe that bitch has resurfaced."

Her friend continued to ramble on, but Roxi couldn't

focus on anything other than what Laila had said about him never asking another woman. So there was no future for the two of them. It wasn't fair. She'd gone and fallen in love with this man.

Perhaps it was best to begin to pull back from any deeper entanglements with him. *Yeah, good luck. He's already part of us,* her heart reminded her.

She would ignore it. She had to. There was no other way for her to get over him.

"He seemed a bit surprised to see her."

"I bet he did."

A sip of water did little to dislodge the dryness which had cropped up in her throat. Laila wasn't paying her any attention, she was muttering to herself as she picked apart her sandwich.

"What does that mean?" she tried again.

Laila shook her head. "I'm sorry, Roxi. That's Sam's to tell. All I can say is that I hated her from the day he brought her to meet us and it hasn't changed. She did one hell of a number on him."

"How long ago did they break up?"

"About two years ago."

Her phone vibrated on the desk, screen illuminating a single word. SAM. She hit ignore and twirled her water bottle in a small circle. Two years. Did he still care for her? Didn't appear so, but he could have been hiding his true emotions. Lord knew he kept them from her.

*Be reasonable.*

Trouble was, her sanity was reaching the edge of reason and she didn't have the energy or care to try to stop it from crossing that line. And it didn't make sense. Biting the inside of her cheek, she took several deep breaths.

"Roxi?"

"Huh?" She glanced to Laila who had this look of confusion on her face. "What, Laila?"

"Are you okay?"

"Yes, fine. Just thinking about a few things."

She balled up her sandwich wrapper and got to her feet. "Okay. Look, I hope I didn't scare you with what I said about Tracey. She's not a threat to you. I have to get going and clean up before getting back to work. Can you come for dinner tonight with the three of us?"

Not a threat. Roxi didn't believe that for an instant. "Um, no, sorry. I have a bunch of stuff I have to get caught up on. Maybe some other time. Give my love to Dean, though."

"Okay." She hurried to the door only to stop and turn back. Laila stared at her with a quizzical expression on her face. Several times she opened her mouth only to close it again. "Bye," she eventually said, before slipping out and shutting the door behind her.

"Fuck," she bit off, slamming her bottle on the desk. Roxi felt sick. And not lightly nauseous but something which she should go home and curl up in bed to get rid of. How could this Tracey person *not* be a threat to her? Whatever their past was, it had a serious effect on her future. A future she wanted with Sam.

"Who am I kidding. We don't have one. He's only here until Christmas and then he's gone anyway."

Her phone vibrated again with the same name there. As before, she ignored it. The phone on her desk rang and this time she answered. A call from the vault had her up and moving as she shoved all mental distress to the back of her mind.

The rest of the day was torture for her. She just needed to leave and work out until her body screamed with exhaustion. Then sleep and start over fresh tomorrow. What to do? Her answer came at closing. A familiar face waited for her out by her vehicle in the parking lot.

"Hey, there," she said with a smile. "I thought you were leaving? What brings you around?"

Lance hugged her and kissed her cheek. "In for another night. Want to get some dinner?"

"Yes," she said on a sigh. "I would love to."

"Everything okay?"

"Not even slightly. Where we going?"

"I'll ride with you."

They got in her vehicle and decided on a restaurant. Once there and they waited for their food, she filled Lance in on what had happened at Second Chances. He listened in silence then shrugged.

"So what's the problem if there's nothing between the two of them?"

She groaned. Sometimes he couldn't see the forest for the trees. "That's not the point, Lance. The point is this bitch may have ruined it for me."

"Ruined what?" he asked, glaring at her. "You're the one who's all set to push him away. That ain't that slut's fault." He looked around her, first one side then the other. "I don't see a gun to your head and someone ordering you to stay away from him." A shrug. "Unless they're invisible. Are they?"

"Stop with the mockery. Patronising me is not appreciated."

"Just not sure what you want from me, babe."

"Support, you jackass. You're supposed to be my friend."

"I am. Which is why I refuse to let you wallow in self-pity. You love this man, and don't bother arguing with me on it. We both know it's true. So don't let him go. Force him to face it. Christ, what, you want him to figure it all out on his own?"

"Yes! That would really be nice."

Lance grabbed her wrist and lifted it, pressing a kiss on the inside. "You want this man, babe. Fight for him. That is the best advice I can give you."

"Lance?" a male voice broke in.

Roxi cast a glance up and almost lost her breath. Cripes, he was gorgeous. Flicking her gaze between her friend and the newcomer, she smiled at the sight of admiration in Lance's gaze.

"Troy."

Lance laced their fingers and she arched a brow but held

her tongue. A distraction like this was what she needed.

"Who's this?" the man asked.

Disengaging her hand from Lance's, she held it out. "I'm Roxi. And you are?"

"Troy." The man shook her hand. Callused grip, strong and powerful.

"Nice to meet you, Troy. Would you care to join us? We've only just ordered."

She tried not to wince as Lance kicked her under the table.

"Wouldn't want to impose."

"Nonsense," she said with a wide grin. "Join us. I insist. Besides, when my boyfriend walked up the other day when Lance and I were eating, he said the same thing, so have a seat." She focused on Lance, whose gaze shot sparks, and gave him a sugary sweet smile.

Troy joined them and she spent the evening enjoying herself. As she and Lance walked out afterwards, she linked her arm in his.

"I should kill you," he growled.

"Now, now. I like him. Where did you meet a submariner?" She shook her head. "Never mind. I don't want to know."

"I didn't think so."

"So why didn't you want him to join us?"

"You really can just be all kinds of nosy, can't you?"

The food made her feel better. "Yep. Now, come on. Take me somewhere we can spar."

He muttered under his breath as she tossed him the keys and headed for the passenger door. Not too much later he took them into a gym and they sat in the lot, engine idling.

"You sure you want to do this?"

"Yes. I have a bit of excess energy."

He leaned in close. "We could always expend that another way."

She finished the distance until they were nose-to-nose. "We could, except for one thing. Your type left the table after we finished eating a while ago. And your type happens to be my type."

He cupped the back of her head bringing her closer still. "For you, I could make an exception."

"Like, your second choice? I don't do well as a second. You know this."

He kissed her quick and backed off. "Fine. Burst my big ole bubble. Come on, wench. Let's get in there."

They hurried through the increasing cold into the older building. When she finally made it home, she was tired and sore. Sam's truck sat in the spot she was used to seeing in the garage and she did her best to ignore the tug on her heartstrings. *I just don't need complication in my life.*

Chicken shit way out, perhaps, but she had to protect herself. And the words Laila had told her today had let her know that what she was beginning to hope for from Sam wouldn't ever happen. It was because of that bitch who was with him.

*The one you left him with.*

Not really words of encouragement, but her brain always had the worst timing and advice. Rolling her shoulders, she made her way inside. She didn't look around as she went to the kitchen to pour herself a drink.

"What the hell happened to you?"

She sniffed and opened the fridge to grab a beer. "Rough day." She didn't even glance over at him for she knew it would weaken her resolve to stay further away in an attempt to lessen the attachment she'd formed. Yes, she knew she looked like crap. That sparring session with Lance had wiped her out.

After removing the bottle top, she tipped it back and drank with a groan of relief. She wiped at her mouth with the back of her hand and walked out.

"Roxi?" he called after her.

She paused before her bedroom door and turned. *Shouldn't have looked at him.* He wore a red shirt and jeans. Her mouth went dry and she itched to touch him. Slide her hands up his torso, indulging in the muscles along the way. Wrap her arms around his neck, hold him close, and allow his masculine scent to sink deep into her nose and skin.

"What?"

"Can we talk about this?"

Fingers clenching around the neck of the bottle, she arched a brow. "Talk? I keep waiting for you to do so, Sam, and all you do is clam up further. I am understanding, but even I need something on occasion. I think it's better if this ends. I can't afford risking emotions when it's obvious you aren't going to ever let me in. I get this Tracey person did a number on you but we're not all her. Laila said you wouldn't let anyone else in since whatever happened with her and that's your decision, but it's also mine not to let myself get hurt. Goodnight, Sam."

"Wait, Laila said this to you?"

"Yes. I know I shouldn't have asked her, Sam, but it seems you're willing to talk to anyone but me. Even Tracey told me how you opened up to her and the two of you would spend nights talking after…well, you can imagine what she told me you did. So I asked Laila."

Shaking her head, she went into her room and shut the door behind her. The click sounded so final. She closed her eyes against the pain streaming through her. His expression she couldn't get out of her mind. *It's for the best.*

195

# Chapter Eleven

Sam swore a round of curses as he jumped from his truck. Four days from Christmas Eve and his life was just how he'd always expected it to be. He was lonely. And he hated it. Dean was doing better, that was marvellous. But there was a huge chasm between him and Roxi. That was what he despised.

He was still living in her place and she was nothing but nice to him. Yet he could tell she kept part of herself from him and it was tearing him up inside. He made his way into the house and smiled at the scent of cookies in the air. He'd gone to the bank first and they'd told him she wasn't there. They'd come to know him now and talked to him like family.

So he'd gone home, needing to talk to her. He'd parked out in the drive and had gone through the front door, not wanting to give her a heads-up he was back.

"Are you kidding me, Laila? Seriously? Do you really expect me to wear this?" Roxi's stressed voice reached him.

"Yes, I do. No, stop struggling. The kids need a Mrs Claus. And before you say you have to work, you don't. I talked to Mr King and explained how we needed you there for the kids. Then I told him how I was the elf and couldn't do that as well as Mrs Claus. He saw the thoughtfulness of what we're doing for the children and agreed you didn't need to work. So don't even try that as an excuse."

"Mrs Claus was a woman who didn't dress like...like *this*."

"She did last year and she does this year. And you're more of Santa's helper than Mrs Claus."

"Helper my ass, I'm more like Santa's slut in this. I can't wear this around children."

He frowned at the comments and entered fully. They weren't in the living room so he looked to the right, down the hall. Her door was open and he made his way to it. All the breath in his body left him in a whoosh as soon as he saw her. Roxi wore a costume for the holiday season and damn if he didn't want to unwrap her.

A plush, stretch red velvet mini, with a zipper front, large belt and powder-white faux fur trim. Her heeled boots had the same trim on them and the brilliance of it offset perfectly against her dark skin.

Blood thundered to his cock which stiffened and pressed against his jeans. He watched her turn slowly and a groan left him when he saw how the folds fell over her ass. Lord help him, he was thinking all kinds of naughty things.

"Hey, Sam." Laila's voice was full of amusement.

"Ladies." His, on the other hand, sounded more like a croak.

Roxi's head snapped up and their gazes locked. "Tell her, Sam, that Mrs Claus doesn't dress like this. Especially when there are kids around."

"I already told you, it's what she wore last year. Just... well, she wasn't as amply endowed as you, so, she didn't quite fill it out like you are."

"If she did it before why can't she do it again?" Roxi sounded distressed.

"Because she's eight months pregnant," Laila said. "Tell her how good she looks, Sam."

"No, tell Laila this is inappropriate."

He glanced between the two women, even as he moved nearer. Not sure it was good idea to do so, but damn he wanted a closer look, a *much* closer look. The front zipper was open, allowing him to see the firm globes of her breasts.

"Where are you wearing this?" he asked, allowing his gaze to move appreciatively over her. God, to have those heels digging in the small of his back as he powered deep into her...

"She's going to be your Mrs Claus," Laila informed him with an impish twinkle in her gaze.

His? His Mrs Claus? How the hell was he supposed to have kids on his lap if he was sporting an erection that could split wood?

"In that case, I think it's perfect."

Roxi's gaze narrowed on him and he chuckled.

"Seriously, Sam. We're talking kids here."

"They're going to get presents. You're Santa's." He crossed his arms. "And I must say, he is *most* appreciative of his present."

Heat flushed her face and he knew she felt it too.

"Give us a few, Laila," he ordered, not taking his gaze from Roxi's.

She chuckled. "Somehow I think this will be a bit more than a few. I'll be in the kitchen, with the music up loud. Don't ruin the costume." She left, drawing the door closed behind her.

"Don't, Sam," she said, her voice soft and sounding not all that sure.

"Don't what? I've not done anything yet." He prowled around her.

Roxi didn't move. He felt her stiffen the closer he got. Lord, she smelt so good. He wanted her all over him. Stopping in front of her, he reached out and tucked some hair behind her ear.

"What are you doing?"

"Spending some quality time with Mrs Claus."

"Sam," she whispered as he reached out to the zipper on the front of her outfit.

"Roxi."

"This isn't a good idea."

"You ignoring what's between us isn't a good one. This... this is a very good one." He trailed his finger along the collar of the dress and goose bumps popped up beneath his touch. "Your skin is like silk," he murmured.

198

She didn't move, just stared at him. Sam put his face to hers and kissed her lips. Lightly. Then he backed off. She gave a whimper and lunged at him, arms wrapping around his neck. Roxi pressed their mouths together, her tongue surging into his mouth as she stroked deep. Her passion inflamed his and he met her thrust for thrust.

His hands dropped down and cupped her ass beneath the skirt. A thong. The knowledge sent spikes of heat through his cock and it pulsed. With a low growl, he took control and backed them so she was against the wall.

"One chance," he rumbled, knowing he was close to losing his control. But if she said no, he'd find a way to stop. Somehow.

She fumbled with the button on his pants and he took that as her answer. He snapped her thong while she simultaneously freed him. His jeans were around his ankles then he spread her, lifted her and sank her down on his engorged shaft.

"Yes," she hissed, her muscles clamping down around him.

He couldn't speak. It seemed like forever since he'd been inside her velvet heat. Silken walls rippled around him and he knew she wouldn't last long either. He hooked her legs around his hips and grimaced slightly from the feel of the boot heels against his skin. Then she tightened around him and he forgot everything but her.

He thrust into her, driving her into the wall with each stroke. She dragged her nails over his skin, settling one hand on the back of his head. Guiding him to her breast, she arched into him and he took the hint. Popping it free of the tight constraint, he laved, nipped, and suckled on the nipple, and all the while Roxi writhed against him. Undulating to his thrusts.

His mind was shutting down everything except the woman in his arms. That was all he knew. Her touch, her scent, her feel. He noticed her moving her other hand between them and when it disappeared beneath the red of her skirt, he knew.

"Uh...uh...uh..." she mewled as her fingers played with her clit in time with his strokes.

He could feel the brush of her nails while he moved inside her only to withdraw and do it again. Over and over, he thrust. She kept up, asking for more and he gave it to her.

Skin flushed and sweaty, as she moved in tandem with him, the passion which had been ignored came to a heated culmination. He couldn't get enough. And he didn't think he ever would. Instead of soothing his hunger, it seemed each second increased it.

Releasing her breast, he stared at her. Her eyes were smoky with passion and she watched him from beneath half-lowered lids. Her lips were shiny and swollen, parted slightly with each panting breath she expelled.

Her lids began to close all the way and he tweaked her nipple. "Watch me, Roxi. Eyes on me."

She drew them back up to his and he bent to brush their lips together.

"Good girl. Come with me," he murmured.

She did. Her back bowed and she shattered around him. Her walls tightened on his cock, milking him, and he followed her into bliss. He erupted deep within her and he didn't stop pumping until his cock had finished shooting thick jets of his seed.

Roxi shuddered and he moved them to the bed. Laying her down, he covered her, not willing to separate yet. A light kiss and he lifted so he could look at her.

"For what it's worth, Santa likes the suit."

Her sated aura faded, leaving behind one of sadness. "Of course he does." She shook her head. "We can't keep doing this, Sam."

He knew her walls were snapping up into place and he hated it. Didn't know how to stop it, though. He kicked off his shoes and managed to get his pants and boxers off as well. Pulling out of her, he whipped his shirt off and tossed it to the side before going to work on her boots. Soon, she was just as naked as he was, her outfit hanging off the foot of the bed, and they were under the blankets with his arms around her.

"We're not done."

A sharp precursory knock came on the door before it cracked open. "Everyone decent in here?" Laila stuck her head in and shook her head.

Sam didn't release Roxi, nor did he allow her to bury her head. Beneath the blankets, he placed his hand over her stomach and drew small circles on her still-sweaty skin.

"Covered, at least," he said.

"Look at you two, how cute. Look, I'm off to go check on Dean. I see my outfit may be ruined after all," she said with a glare. "I'll bring the other one when I come back. I'll be back in thirty minutes. Please, please, *please* be dressed by then. I don't need to see my brother and his woman in bed."

"You're the one who came in," he reminded her.

"We were working, Sam, when you came and interrupted us," Laila growled back. "So I'm going. Get the rest of it out of your system and be dressed in thirty." She shook her head again and vanished.

Roxi made to move the second Laila closed the door behind her and he held her tight. "Where are you going?"

"Shower. And then getting dressed."

He took her hand and curved it around his stiffening length. "Roxi."

"Shit, I have no fucking willpower when it comes to you," she sighed, rolling over and lifting a leg to straddle him.

\* \* \* \*

He and Roxi had used up almost all of that thirty minutes Laila had given them right there in Roxi's bed. Despite the smile on his face, Sam was worried. He smacked her on the ass and said, "Come on. Let's shower."

She went with him to her master bathroom and soon they stood under the pulsing spray. He picked up the loofah and soaped it up when she gave him a wicked grin and dropped to her knees before him.

"Roxi," he groaned as she reached out and took his erection in her hands.

"Yes, Sam? Don't bother Mrs Claus."

She leaned in and licked around the crown of his cock before opening up her mouth and slipping him in. She stroked him with one hand and sucked and lapped at him as if his shaft was her favourite flavour of lollipop.

"Fuck," he muttered, trying to refrain from thrusting into her. Hard and fast.

Her teeth lightly scraped the head as her nails did the same thing to his balls. Faster her hand moved and harder she sucked until he sank his hands into her wet hair and held her there to power into the waiting recess of her mouth. Over and over until he came with a low roar. She watched him, her brown eyes content and satisfied. Pulling free of her mouth, he then lifted her and reached out to repay her.

She shook her head and said, "We have to get out. Laila will be arriving soon."

Damn it all, he wanted back inside her. Where those satiny velvet walls held him too tightly. Swallowing back his lust, he washed her, taking his time between her legs until she came around his fingers with a low moan of pleasure. Knowing that would have to hold him for a while, they finished up quickly and he had dressed and was out in the kitchen when Laila returned.

Once Roxi emerged she was a totally different person. It was as if what they'd done together hadn't even happened. She treated him as she had when he'd first arrived. Polite, but nothing really personal.

Now, as he drove to Second Chances, he couldn't help but be concerned. He wanted her and she seemed ready to relegate him to the past column, despite easily giving in to have sex with him. That wasn't okay to his mind. Then there was the fact he *again* hadn't used any protection. He'd come inside her numerous times but this time, the thought he may have got her pregnant didn't fill him to the brim with a mind-numbing fear.

"You're the reason," he told himself as he drove along through the rain. "Because you can't tell her what she means to you."

His cell rang and he answered it. "Hello, Laila."

"How'd you know it was me?" she asked.

"Hunch." He'd been expecting it. "What's up?"

"What the hell are you doing?" she thundered. "I warned you, I *warned* you about messing with her."

"What did you tell her about Tracey?" he countered.

"Nothing. I didn't say anything more than you broke up with her about two years ago. And wouldn't be asking another woman to marry you because of what that bitch did to you."

His heart sank and he swore. "What did you tell her that for?"

"It's what you told me," she defended her actions. "What's the big deal? You're the one who told me it wasn't serious between you and Roxi."

"I lied!" he shouted. "Damn it, Laila. You know she means something to me."

"Telling me ain't going to do a damn thing, Sam." Her voice gentled. "You need to tell her that. Not me." A moment of silence. "I warned you, Sam. I told you she would need more."

He rolled his shoulders, hating the tenseness in them. "I know, Laila. I need you to make sure she still will play Mrs Claus. I have a feeling she may try to skip out now."

"What are you going to do?"

"Deal with my past so I don't lose my future."

"Love you, Sam."

"Love you, too, Laila." He hung up and had the rest of the drive in silence. He flashed his ID and got on base. Parking at his destination, he climbed out and raced through the cold rain to the door.

He shook the rain off his ball cap and stepped into the

dry building. At the room he looked for, he pushed in and found a few of the Marines who would be at the children's home there.

"Hey, Hoch," Brent said.

"Guys." He gave a sharp nod of greeting.

"What brings you out here?"

"I need some help."

They all gathered around and he outlined what he needed them to do. Once they agreed he thanked them and headed back to the door.

"Sam, wait."

He turned and saw Tracey there. "What?"

He realised in that moment, he didn't hate her for what she'd done to him. No, if anything, he pitied her. She seemed so lost. When he'd talked to the guys, she'd not been there so she must have come in another door as he'd been getting ready to leave.

"What are you doing here? Do you have time to catch up?"

*Was she kidding?* "For what? You made your point perfectly clear. You wanted to sleep around. Or was it you just wanted to be in an 'open' relationship? Not sure. And I don't care."

She pouted. "But we were so good. We talked so much about everything."

And yet he knew less about her than the woman with whom he tried keeping at a distance. "And it meant nothing." He paused before he turned from her. "I expect you to be professional at this thing, Corporal."

"The woman from earlier?"

"None of your business." There was a silent order of *leave it alone* in his words and he expected her to follow them.

"For what it's worth, Sam, I'm sorry. And you're one hell of a catch. She'd be lucky to have you."

He ran his gaze dispassionately over her again before leaving. Tracey was wrong. He'd be lucky if Roxi would give him a chance. When he'd left the house this afternoon,

Roxi's face had been closed off as she'd stood talking to Laila.

Back in his truck, he placed another call. Once that one was over, he pulled out and drove off base. He stopped at a parking garage and climbed out. He had one more present to get.

\* \* \* \*

There was only one light on when he got back, other than the Christmas ones. Roxi was nowhere to be found and there was no note. He went to Laila's for dinner and sat playing chess with Dean after it was over.

"Ready, son?" Dean asked, moving a pawn.

"For what, sir?"

"The thing at Second Chances. You have your dress uniform ready too, right?"

"Dress uniform?"

"Yes. Your blood stripes. After the kids get their things, there is a party for the adults. It's a thank you from the staff. But, we dress up for it."

"No one said anything about it to me, but yes, I'm ready." He didn't usually like parties but hey, an opportunity to dance with Roxi. Grab her under the mistletoe. Any of it worked for him.

"And how are you and Roxi going?"

He slid his knight. "We're not going anywhere. She's going to be my Mrs Claus. I haven't seen her since this afternoon."

"I bet she is, son. I just bet she is."

"Pardon?" He looked up at Dean.

"You said she's going to be *your* Mrs Claus instead of just Mrs Claus. I was just agreeing with you."

Sam felt his heart pick up speed. He didn't try to correct Dean's understanding for he had no intention of letting her go. He grunted and repositioned another piece, capturing a pawn.

"Laila said Tracey is here."

"She is."

"And you've seen her."

"I have."

"Care to share anything else?"

"Nothing else to share, sir. She knows she needs to be nothing but professional at the kids' thing."

Dean harrumphed and moved his rook. "Very well."

Sam took a peek at Dean. He knew the old man just wanted to protect him. And he loved him for it, but he was fine. Didn't need it. Not anymore. Tracey didn't have any hold or power over him.

They finished the game while talking about other things. Dean reminisced and Sam enjoyed listening to him. As he ran through the rain to Roxi's house, he hoped to find her inside. It was almost ten at night.

Any colder than this and they would have snow for Christmas. He unlocked the door and pushed into the warmth. There were no more lights on than when he'd left to head over to Laila's. He peered out into the garage and saw her vehicle beside his truck and smiled. Only to frown seconds later.

Her door was shut. He went to his room and got ready for bed before padding back out into the living room where he sat on the couch with a book. After reading for an hour, he got the distinct impression she wasn't coming back out of her room. He went to knock on her door but stopped just shy of actually doing so.

Frustrated, he went to bed. He got up early the next day, determined to catch her before she went to work. He made her some breakfast and he knew she was surprised to see him when she walked into the kitchen. Again, she wore her typical attire of a dark suit. And again, all he wanted to do was strip it off her.

"Morning, Roxi," he said, sliding a plate with toast and eggs on it before an empty chair. "Sit. Eat."

"What are you doing?"

"Making you breakfast. Sit."

She did but he could see her hesitation in doing so. She picked up the fork and speared a bunch of scrambled eggs. "Thank you."

He fixed himself a plate and sat across from her. "No problem. You tend to leave so early, I wonder if you've been eating."

She wouldn't meet his gaze and he had his answer. She was trying to avoid him. He let it go, he deserved it—after all, he'd been the one keeping her at a distance. So if she wanted to create some of her own, he couldn't fault her. He may not like it—okay, he *didn't* like it—but he couldn't fault her.

"Are you joining us for dinner tonight?" he asked.

"I don't know. It's my late night."

"You still need to eat and you know Dean would love to see you."

She nodded. "Sure. I can swing by when I get done."

"Wonderful."

She gave him a slight grin and dug into her food. The moment she finished it, she pushed away from the table and took her things to the sink. "I'll take care of these later. Thanks for the food, Sam. Have a good day."

And she was gone. Nothing more personal and it grated him. He wanted a hug. A kiss. Both. Emotion.

*Still haven't told her anything, jackass.*

Like he needed it. His stomach was so knotted up, he wondered if he'd get an ulcer.

That was how it went between them for the final few days leading up to Christmas Eve. Roxi was as polite to him as ever but there was nothing emotional from her in his direction. He believed he saw lingering hints of it when he caught her staring at him on occasion.

* * * *

He stood in a backroom in his red suit, while Reba and

207

Father O'Toole helped pad him up. His gaze lingered upon the door, behind which he knew Roxi was getting dressed for her part. Her eyes had been alight with humour as she'd walked with Laila towards the room.

His breath hitched and Father O'Toole looked askance at him. "Everything okay, son?"

"Yes, sir. Just a bit warm in this. I shouldn't have worn such heavy clothing under it."

"Want to take a layer off?"

"No, sir. I'll be fine. No problem."

Reba buttoned up his suit and attached his belt, the smile on her face reminding him of Lenore's. "God bless you for doing this, Sam Hoch. The kids will appreciate it so much."

"There he is!" Dean said as he wheeled his way into the room.

"What do you think?" Sam asked.

Dean was all decked out and even had a jaunty Santa hat on. "You're going to be great."

The door he was focused on opened and he held his breath only to exhale when Laila exited. Alone. She looked at him and grinned. He couldn't help but return it — she was decked out like an elf. The curly shoes, striped tights, a green elf suit and a hat. She looked adorable.

Then behind her stepped Roxi. He forgot to breathe until Reba elbowed him in the side. Almost identical to what she'd worn earlier when he'd taken her against the wall, this one had a petticoat skirt and she had a hat on. The skirt was a bit longer but did nothing to quell the raging in his loins. This wasn't going to be easy.

Dean whistled. "Wow."

He couldn't have said it better himself. Come to think of it, he couldn't say anything, he was still trying to get air into his lungs. No stiletto-heeled boots this time, these were more modest. The white fur at the top still brought his attention to the hue of her skin.

She walked in silence to his side. Her gaze ran up and down him. "Ready?"

He adjusted his hat and accepted the glasses with attached moustache and beard. "Let's do this."

She tucked her arm through his and he swung the bag over his other shoulder. They went together to the door, Laila leading the way. She slipped through first and they heard the children scream in anticipation.

"You look great," she whispered.

"You, too." They shared a smile and he wanted to talk to her now. "Roxi."

"That's our cue," she murmured, tugging on him.

He'd not even heard it. With one more deep breath he went with her and stepped out into chaos.

Roxi stood to one side of the chair in which her temporary husband, Santa Claus, sat on as he listened to each child tell him what they wanted. The room was packed with children. She noticed the Marines who were by other piles of toys. Her gaze skipped over the one named Tracey. Now wasn't the time to get pissy.

Past the chair, she watched Laila as she joked and had a grand time with the children. She looked so cute in her little elf costume. *And what do I have to wear? This...whatever it is.* This one she'd agreed on, for it covered more than the previous one. And she wasn't about to look like Santa's naughty little helper for a bunch of kids. From the flare of heat in Sam's eyes, however, he liked this one just as much as the other.

She cut her gaze to the left again and smiled at the sight of a little girl sitting on his lap. He looked at her and winked before putting all his attention back on the girl. Her belly clenched and she wished she were anywhere but here.

Roxi had tried to get out of this, but Laila hadn't let her. She'd even gone so far as to play the 'what if' game with her. What if this were Dean's last Christmas? Surely she wouldn't want to miss that.

So she'd caved, much like she'd believed she would do anyway. And here she stood in this outfit. Then there was the adult party after. As a thank you to those who supported these places throughout the year. Child after child went to sit on Santa's lap, then she watched as some of the women began to make their way up.

She edged closer to the chair as the final few children scrambled up for their picture with him. Sam got to his feet and the kids fell silent as he adjusted his belt.

"The toys are split up based on ages. You'll see the signs by each Marine. Remember, no pushing. There are enough for all. So get your present and enjoy the cookies and drinks."

His voice was so deep she smiled. It wasn't like him at all. She was amazed he'd done so well at this.

"I'd like to thank my elf" — he gestured at Laila, who took a well-deserved bow — "and of course, my wife." He looked at her, beckoning her closer. "She stands by me through it all without fail, and never forgetting how much she means to me."

"Kiss her!" The cry rang out in a voice which registered as Laila's to her, only to be picked up by everyone else. It soon became a chant.

He glanced at her, his eyes twinkling. "Come here, Mrs Claus."

Her belly quivered even as her legs propelled her forward. She wanted to refuse, knowing each time he kissed or touched her, she fell deeper for him. He'd made it clear. She was good enough to sleep with but nothing else. And while it was fine for a while, that wasn't the type of woman she was. She was a long-haul kind of person. She needed a man to take home to her mom and dad. Raise children with. Have a future with. Not just a few weeks. No matter how amazing they had been.

"Mrs Claus is shy," he said, drawing her closer to him until they were belly to padding. Didn't stop the fissure of heat which exploded up throughout her at the contact. His callused hand skimmed lightly up her side *away* from the crowd while his other settled along her cheek.

He leaned in and she stood as still as possible, trying not

210

to even breathe for fear of embarrassing herself by doing something like…oh, jumping on him. His blue eyes held her prisoner as he lowered his mouth to hers. Light, feathery touches grazed along her lips and her lids fluttered shut. When she opened on a sigh, he pressed his advantage and slipped his tongue in.

It didn't take any more than that and her world had shrunk to just the two of them. He kept his touch and exploration gentle. The hand on her hip tightened and she shuddered, well aware of what he did to her body with something to simple as a caress. She held onto his arms as the kiss continued. Her whimper was eaten by him and when she didn't think she could stand it any longer, he drew back.

Slowly, all the cheers sank in and she realised what had just occurred. His eyes were dark and there was a wealth of heat in their blue depths. He turned his hand, which had been on her face, and stroked down her cheek with his knuckles.

No will power. That was what it was. Zero flipping will power. She took a deep breath before plastering a smile on her face and facing the room. *I need a moment to regain my senses.*

As if hearing her silent cry, Laila came and split the two of them, whirling her off to mingle with the children who were gathering their gifts and treats. So she walked among them, chatting and relaxing as the evening wound on. The kids finally left and those who lived there had gone to the other part of the building and headed for bed.

She stood with Laila in a small room, changing from her costume to her dress for their party. Sitting on a chair, she released a groan as she massaged the bottom of one foot.

"You all right over there?" Laila asked over her shoulder while she shimmied into her tight little sequined dress.

"Tired."

Laila faced her and tugged down the hem of her dress as she moved. "Let me do your hair." She went to her bag and withdrew a pair of hair sticks which took Roxi's breath away.

"Oh, Laila, those are beautiful."

They were bone, crafted into elegant twists and painted a satiny, pearlescent white, covered by a protective and glossy enamel. At the top were light Siam red crystals set in silver-plated filigree bead caps. They also boasted garnet-red beads and Siam crystals that dangled from three spots on a star-shaped, silver-plated filigree. They sparkled with each movement and she was truly touched by the gesture.

"I was going to give them to you as a present but when I saw your dress, I knew it would be perfect."

She sat still while Laila did her thing. It wasn't hard to figure out that Laila wanted to talk but gratefully she kept silent. When her friend had finished, Roxi got to her feet and moved to the mirror.

"Wow, Laila, that's...I don't know what to say." She reached up to almost touch the upstyle.

Her friend appeared beside her. "You look beautiful."

Roxi had to admit it, she did look pretty damn nice. She wore a red dress with silver strands shot through it, to make it shimmer when she glided. It was a deep V halter evening gown with a high leg slit and full, flowing skirt. The bodice had a beautiful centre detailed brooch. It screamed 'sex' without being a micro mini or having her breasts hanging out. She liked it. A lot. The elegant classical look made such a statement.

Laila had put her hair up in a loose bun, allowing for two sections to fall free around her face. Turning her head to the side, she could see the sticks and knew they were perfectly poised to gather all the light and add more of a sparkle to her walk.

"Thank you, Laila."

She brushed a kiss over her cheek. "Come on, let's get our shoes on and go mingle. I can't wait to dance with some of those handsome men I saw."

Roxi laughed as she put on her stilettos. She loved these shoes—they were silver and had clear rhinestones which wrapped all around her leg. She knew they would draw attention when she moved, given the slit in her dress. But more than that, these were *comfortable*.

"Let's go, you crazy, horny woman."

She watched her friend. Laila looked stunning in her dark green dress, long sleeves hugged her upper arms while being offset from her shoulders a bit. It stopped mid-thigh, showing off her nice, long legs. Laila put a Santa hat on and flipped the end over so it dangled over one bared shoulder.

"I think I'm ready."

Pushing to her feet, Roxi paused a few seconds then advanced to her side. They opened the door and were swamped by the sounds of the party. They were the only ones who'd had to change. Other than Sam. She shook off that thought, thinking of him naked or changing wasn't going to help her in any way, shape or form. She assumed he'd just shucked the Santa gear and was out there in a nice suit.

She paused at the edge of the room and just took a moment. Amazing how many people there seemed to be, even without the children. Laila hesitated briefly before she headed off into the crowd. Despite the smile on her face, Roxi hurt inside. She was saddened by the knowledge Sam would be leaving tomorrow.

The gift she'd got for him rested beneath the tree at her house. She'd give it to him either tonight when they got home or in the morning. *Home. Look at me thinking like it's his home as well.*

It was. No matter what else could be said, her place was part his. His soul and presence had settled into the walls and the very fabric of it. She would always feel him there.

"You played a pretty good Mrs Claus," a voice said from beside her.

She exhaled on a long sigh when she noticed who had spoken. Tracey stood in a dress instead of her Marine uniform. A black, slinky number which was ultra-low cut in the front, halter top, side slits, sequin detail beneath her breasts, and when Tracey walked from one side to the other of her, Roxi could see the low cut in the back that stopped right above her ass.

"Thank you. That's a lovely dress you're wearing." Small talk. She wasn't interested in trying to be polite with this woman but for the sake of the evening and the season, she would play along.

Her blinding white smile almost made her wince. "Thank you. It's Sam's favourite. It was the dress I wore our first night together" — she lowered her voice — "if you know what I mean by *together*."

She skimmed her teeth with her tongue and nodded. "I get the picture."

"So he didn't want me in uniform since then we would have to be a lot more professional."

Tracey kept right on rambling and Roxi gritted her teeth. Nearing the end of her patience, she gave a smile which was more of a grimace and said, "If you will excuse me, I see someone I need to say hi to." Roxi walked away without waiting for any kind of response.

Dean was making his way slowly along the edges of the crush and she stopped by him. "Master Guns."

"Roxi." He released a whistle. "Look at you. That man isn't going to know what hit him."

She leaned in to place a kiss on his cheek and ignored his other statement. This was the time to be reinforcing her walls, for she knew he would be here. And she had to not act like a fool.

"How are you feeling?"

"Good. It did me a lot of good being here."

She studied him and agreed. He did look really well. "Can I get you anything to drink?"

"Why are you here with me instead of out there, dancing with any number of cute men?"

She had no explanation so she shrugged. He wrapped a hand around her wrist and squeezed.

"Listen to me, Roxi. Don't give up on him."

214

"Nothing to give up on, Master Guns. He made his decision. Tracey did enough to him that no one else will have a shot at getting close. Or at least not now, not while I know him. Maybe later on in his life he'll be willing to do so."

"You have already gotten in close, Roxi."

"Not really. I needed more. It's okay, Master Guns, it wasn't meant to be." She ignored the shaft of pain which pierced her heart at that admission.

"I'm telling you, Roxi. You mean the world to that man."

"I've seen the way he stiffens up when he feels he's let me in too far. Besides, Laila said after Tracey he'd never let another woman in like that again. And I know that woman still affects him, I watched them together when I came here and dropped off the presents."

"That girl doesn't know how to mind her own business." He shook his head. "This isn't my place to say, all I know is I've never seen him so happy as when you came into his life. That boy and I have had lots of talks, Roxi. He's my son and I know him better than anyone. Yes, he's stubborn as all get-out, but he's a good man. And he loves you. Don't give up on him."

"I can't wait forever for him to figure out what it is that he wants, Master Guns. I just can't."

Although he nodded, she could see the sadness in his expression.

"I'll get us something to drink." Roxi waited for his nod of agreement then wove through the crowd to follow through on her word.

* * * *

As Roxi twirled around on the floor with one of the Marines, she laughed at what he said. He was a joy to be around. And he was a great dancer.

"Hey!" the shout carried over both music and conversation, gathering everyone's attention. "It's snowing!"

The room they were in had a large side door that someone had rolled open, allowing everyone the chance to see outside. Sure enough, large white flakes fell, fast and furious. The ground was already covered.

Laila appeared at her shoulder, in another's arms. "We're going to have a white Christmas after all, Roxi. Look at that."

Stepping away from her dance partner, she linked arms with her best friend. "I think it'll be a great Christmas this year."

"Laila Richardson!"

They both jumped slightly and turned at the sound of her full name. Ritchie stood there in a tuxedo.

"Ritchie," she whispered, even as Laila said it louder.

Her brother opened his arms and Laila flew into them. Without any hesitation. Roxi whistled and cheered right along with everyone else as they kissed. When they stopped, she moved up to give her brother a hug.

"What are you doing here?" she asked, doing her best to not be jealous at the look of pure contentment on both of their faces.

"It's Christmas. We didn't want to be away from you."

"But, Mom and Dad? And where's Eric?"

"At your house with your mother," another man spoke.

She turned to find her father there. "Daddy!" She hugged him hard and blinked back tears of joy.

"Hey, baby girl. You look gorgeous. Come dance."

She couldn't refuse and soon she moved with her father across the floor. At the end of their dance, he stopped and frowned at something behind her. She turned to see what he was looking at and her breath caught in her throat.

From where she stood, she could see out into the large back lot of Second Chances. A solitary figure strode towards the door. The tightening in her stomach told her who it was. Ramrod straight, this person moved with coiled precision and purpose.

Sam. Dressed not in a suit or tuxedo but in his blood

stripes. Snow dotted his uniform but he didn't seem to care. He paused right before he entered the building and removed his cover.

She stared, unable to move. His chest was full of ribbons and medals. Roxi barely noticed when Laila came and led her father away. Bit by bit, the room fell quieter until the music which played overshadowed what little din there remained from people.

His gaze locked on hers and her heart paused before thundering twice as hard. He came towards her, only he didn't make it. Tracey stepped into his path. When he lowered his head and stopped, her heart shattered. That was it. No more. She couldn't take it any longer. Whirling around, she slipped away into the crowd and made her way to the door.

# Chapter Twelve

The blonde woman wearing a slinky dress was the last person he wanted before him. Sam wasn't happy.

"Whatever it is, Tracey, it can wait," he bit off.

"Sam, don't you remember this dress? How much fun you had removing it that first night?"

"I don't. Get out of my way."

She placed her hand on his arm, nails digging in. "Come on, Sam."

He scanned the group and swore when Roxi was no longer visible. "Let go and step out of my way, Corporal."

She stiffened but did as he'd ordered. The second she did, he forgot about her. One thing and one thing only on his mind. Roxanne 'Roxi' Mammon.

"Marines!" he bellowed out.

"Yes, sir, Gunnery Sergeant!" came the hollered answer as one, easily identifiable over the noise the music had been making.

He moved deeper into the room. Talking again fell to a minimum and even the music had been turned down. His sharp gaze spotted his target on the other side of the room. She was trying to leave but thankfully his Marines had remembered what he'd asked of them. She was faced with Brent and he knew the man wouldn't let her go.

He almost grinned when she whirled around, frustration on her face. But it didn't come to fruition for he recognised the sadness there. She faltered the instant she spotted him. Not for long, but he noticed it.

Sam moved towards her, walking slow, taking his time and enjoying how beautiful she looked. He stopped with three feet or so between them.

"Hello, Roxi," he said.

Her gaze travelled up and down his uniform. "Sam." She couldn't hide the appreciation.

"Leaving already?"

Her brown eyes narrowed. "You know damn well I can't. Not until you call off your Marines."

"Will you stay and hear me out?"

She frowned and he shook his head.

"Then they remain."

"Not really fair to them, is it. I mean, this is a party...they should be able to party."

"They don't mind. It's for a good reason."

"And what's that? Making sure one person doesn't leave?"

"No. Making sure the woman I love doesn't leave before I get the chance to tell her."

The hope flashed in her eyes before she could mask it. "I think you already passed Tracey." Her tone was cold and clipped.

"Really?" he replied drolly. "You think I'd go through all of this for Tracey?" He stepped closer and dragged a knuckle down her cheek. "For her?"

"How the hell would I know? You don't let me in, and from what she's told me, you love that dress she's in. Had a *great* time that first night she wore it."

"Did you know your eyes sparkle when you're mad?" He tried to keep his mind on the matter at hand. "Are you jealous, Roxi?"

"No." The word was gritted out.

He arched a brow. "Really? Are you sure?"

"No."

Sam stepped closer yet. "Listen to me and listen well, Roxi. You have no reason to be jealous of her. She's my past. I'm looking at my future."

She shook her head and it was like she stood there, driving a knife into his chest, over and over. "I can't, Sam."

"Can't what?" *I will not panic and I will not run.*

"Can't deal with the zero letting me in. Physical is great and wonderful, but I need the emotional connection more than just rare glimpses."

"I know. I haven't let you in, Roxi. And that wasn't you, it was me. I wasn't able to reconcile my past and I almost ruined our future. I'm sorry. Give me another chance and you'll see I can do this." He eliminated the final step separating them. "I want to do this. I want it all with you."

She worried her lower lip between her teeth and he cupped her chin. "Listen to me, Roxi. You asked me what it was I wanted for Christmas. Do you remember what I said?"

She nodded.

"What did I say?" He saw her hesitation in airing his wishes to the public listening in. "Tell them, I don't care. What did I say?"

"You wanted a home."

He nodded. "Yes. But more than that, I wanted the home that you'd already given to me. From the moment I arrived here and you took me in, Roxi, you gave me the home I'd wanted all my life. You are my home. I love you, Roxi."

Her eyes shone like diamonds with her unshed tears. He drew her in close and put his forehead to hers.

"Sam," she whispered.

"Yes, Roxi?"

"I love you, too."

His sigh of relief was swallowed up by the kiss they shared. He groaned in delight as her taste seeped back onto his tongue, filling him with its heady flavour. The clearing of a throat had him reluctantly ending the kiss.

"It'll work," he vowed softly.

She reached up and brushed her fingers along his cheek. "I want you to meet my parents." Roxi peered around him and waved at someone. "Daddy, I want you to meet Sam."

"I've already met him" — Sam paused and amended — "met them."

Her gaze was wondrous as she glanced back up at him. "Already met them? When did you meet them?"

"I had to get in contact with them," Sam admitted.

He scanned the room and caught the gazes of each of the Marines by doors. They gave him a nod and stepped away, assured they didn't need to keep one Roxi Mammon in the room any longer. She seemed willing and content to be there.

"Laila?"

He nodded. "Yes, she gave me their number."

"Why?"

"You love Christmas, Roxi. That much is obvious. I wanted to give you the best one I could. Besides. I needed to ask your father's permission."

"For?"

He released her, moved back a single step, and dropped to one knee as he pulled a box out of his pocket. "To marry his daughter." Sam looked up at the vision in red and silver before him. He knew in his gut this was the right thing for him to do. There would never be another woman who was better for him than Roxi. No one who would give him more support, love him better, or make his life worth living even more.

"Sam," she said, capturing her lower lip between her teeth and reaching a shaky hand out to the box he offered.

The ring was platinum with a hand-crafted, sweeping design. There were two round diamonds set within the head and pavé diamonds along the ring. He'd also purchased the wedding band that went with it. Inscribed on the inside were two words which meant the world to him and he knew she'd understand the significance of them. *Semper Fidelis*. Always Faithful. For that was what he would be for her.

"Will you marry me, Roxi?"

The first tear leaked over and he had to force himself to remain where he was instead of standing so he could wipe away her tears. Her fingertips grazed along his.

"Yes."

His own hand shook a bit as he removed the ring from the box and slid it on her finger. Then he stood and gathered her close for a kiss, their hands linked between them.

"I love you," he murmured when he ended the kiss. "And you're killing me in that dress."

"Come dance with me."

He couldn't refuse her. So despite his own misgivings about his ability to dance, he followed her and began dancing with everyone else. During a break, he stood near Dean and enjoyed some drink.

"I'm proud of you, son." Dean laid a hand on his arm.

"Thank you, sir."

He couldn't begin to explain how Dean's words made him feel. Having this man proud of him was ultimate and meant everything to him. He never wanted to disappoint him. Raising his gaze, he found Roxi across the room. She stood with Laila and they were staring at her ring. His stomach flipped a few times when she lifted her head and looked at him.

Even though a room separated them, he could feel her gaze like a caress. It warmed him from the inside out. He hadn't a clue how it would all work out, but he knew it would. He knew he'd found more than a temporary home. One with the woman in the sexy-as-hell dress, who had been a Marine herself, and knew just what he needed in his life.

At the end of the party, she gave her keys to her dad to drive home, and Sam led the way to his truck. Laila and Ritchie were taking Dean back. The snow continued to fall and they walked slowly, his coat over her shoulders to keep her warm.

"What about tonight?" he asked after they were in the truck.

"What about it?" She buckled her belt.

"Your parents are at your house, as well as Eric and Ritchie."

"I'll remake the bed in the guest room. Mom and Dad can have that room and Ritchie and Eric can crash on the couches."

"And I'm with you?" He lifted her hand and kissed the tip of each finger.

"Better believe it, Marine."

He got them on their way and took his time, driving carefully on the snowy roads. Back at her house, he helped her make the bed and soon after everyone settled in for the rest of Christmas Eve night. He leaned against the door and watched her in that intoxicating dress as she made her way towards the bed.

"Wait," he said, moving to intercept.

He dropped to his knees before her and slowly unwrapped the rhinestone bands from around her lower calf then removed her shoes, massaging the bottoms of each foot before placing them on the floor.

"God, that feels good. These shoes are comfortable but I'm ready to not have any on whatsoever."

Sam dragged one hand up the silken length of her leg until he reached the high slit in her dress. Lord help him, he wanted to go higher until he reached the velvet core he knew waited. Swallowing back his lust, he took to his feet and turned her so he faced her spine. He undid the halter top and dragged his fingers to the zipper that kept the damn dress on. Ever so slowly he tugged it down, exposing inch after succulent inch of her dark skin.

His cock jumped when he tugged the red material over the globes of her ass. *Damn, she's wearing a thong.* Down and down he pushed it until the dress pooled around her ankles. Reaching for the sticks in her hair, he gently pulled them out and inhaled deeply as the strands cascaded around his hands. He wanted to grab it and rub it on his skin.

She turned to face him and his throat was dry. Her pert breasts and tight nipples—he wanted to lick them, suckle them, nip them. He lowered his gaze and saw the unadorned red G-string she wore.

Her hands settled upon the buttons of his uniform. "You're wearing too many clothes, Marine."

He got to work on it. Stripping off every article as quickly as possible. Roxi removed her final item and got on the bed. He faltered at the sight of her playing with herself. Her fingers lightly teasing her slit as she watched him, hunger flaring in her gaze.

The second his boxers were gone he was on the bed, replacing her fingers with his mouth.

"Ah, hell," she whimpered as her hips bucked under his touch.

He placed an arm over her belly, holding her immobile as he continued to lick and lave at her sex. The spiciness of her unique flavour flooded his tongue and his cock got even harder. He feasted until she coated his tongue with her thick cream.

Rising up, he covered her mouth with his own, sharing her taste. She moaned and writhed beneath him, making her desire clear. He wanted to go fast, sink hard and completely in her and yet, he wanted to go slow. To linger over the pleasure of making love to his fiancée.

She reached down and wrapped her hand around his shaft then began to stroke him. He groaned and thrust his hips into her touch. His fingers drifted down and lightly trailed through her moistness. She widened her legs on a soft sigh of pleasure.

He nuzzled the side of her neck. "I love you, Roxanne."

Her fingers tightened around his turgid length and she bucked her hips up, encouraging deeper contact from him. "Sam." The single word was barely intelligible but he heard it and understood.

"Not yet," he murmured. "I want you to burn for me."

"Al...already do."

He slipped two fingers inside her wet sheath, grinding his teeth as he struggled not to lose control right then and there. The feel of her snugness around him, along with the tight hold she had on his cock as she continued to fist him, was almost too much.

"Come first," he ordered.

Faster and faster his fingers moved inside her, one curved to stimulate her even more. Lowering his head, he captured a nipple in his mouth and grazed it with his teeth. She tightened around him as her grip increased. He did it again. And again. Until he had to cover her mouth with his to capture her scream of release as she shattered around his fingers, her desire slipping from her, over his hand and onto the bed.

"Sam," she panted, her body still sending out small tremors as he cleaned off her essence with his tongue.

He readjusted, sheathed himself with a condom and slid home in a single stroke, moaning as her heated walls gripped him with familiar possessiveness. So wet and so tight. She was his. And he hers. Nothing else mattered.

Lacing their fingers together, he stared at the ring on her finger, the diamond winking in the lone light shining in the room. He read her love in her expression. The amount of emotion in him stunned him for a moment but when she shifted and tightened her internal muscles, he focused solely on her.

He'd been so close to coming just with the firm touch of her hand, he knew it wouldn't take long now that he was in her. Back and forth he moved. Eyes locked on one another, neither of them said a word, just allowed emotions to be expressed in touches. He kept it slow and easy, creating a burn which threatened to engulf him. Faint mewls fell from her plump lips as she undulated beneath him. He knew she was close. So was he.

Rising up, he gripped her hips and angled them to allow deeper penetration. Her eyes burned with the need for release. He didn't want this to end and tried to prolong it even more. She wasn't having any of that. Her hands smoothed over her breasts and he felt a pull when she tugged on her nipples before moving her hands lower.

When she began to stimulate her clit, he growled low

in his chest at the response her pussy had. She tightened around him, rotating her hips. Passion flooded her eyes while she held his gaze. And he couldn't wait any longer. Gripping her hips, he increased his thrusts until the bed moved beneath them. Harder. Faster. Deeper. He was relentless and she kept up, her bottom lip caught between her teeth as she tried valiantly to keep her screams inside.

They came together in a powerful rush and floated back down slowly. Sam stayed buried inside her, just brushed a kiss along her lips, rolled to the side and wrapped her as close as he could. He buried his nose in her hair and the familiar scent of autumn flooded him. He couldn't believe he'd almost let fear take this from him. This was home. Here. Now. In Roxi's arms.

"I love you," he whispered as his heart began to slow its strong cadence.

She answered with a squeeze and a brush of breath against his chest. "I love you, too, Sam."

He disposed of the condom then returned to the bed. Reaching out to click off the light, he stared out of her window at the still-falling snow. A perfect end to his day. He had everything he could ever want. His friend and mentor was recovering and he had a woman who loved him and gave him the ability to turn any house into a home. There was also Eric, who'd come to mean so much to him and would hopefully continue to be a part of his life. As Sam drifted off to sleep, he knew the boy who'd been shuttled from temporary home to temporary home was content. There would be no more of that. He'd found his home. And he'd never let it go.

# Alone With You

## *Excerpt*

## Chapter One

Ariel Greene trudged up the steps to her fourth floor apartment after completing her early morning run. Fighting off a yawn, she dug for her key and unlocked the door. Once she'd showered and dressed in shorts and tank top, she went to her coffeemaker gratefully looking forward to that first cup.

There was none. No hot java brew set to make her a nice person and capable of facing her day.

"What? I thought I pre-programmed it." The moment she opened the filter's cover, she knew why the pot sat empty. Someone had forgotten to buy coffee upon their return. "Good job, Greene." Sure, it had been late when her plane landed, but to forget to swing by a twenty-four hour store and pick some up…egregious error on her part.

After swiping her favourite mug off the counter, she

headed for the door. Six-thirty in the morning. If one was to be awake, coffee—and never any of the decaffeinated type, which in her eyes was sinful and disgraceful—was a must.

Across the hall, she turned the knob and let herself into the apartment. The thick, aromatic scent of coffee greeted her like a familiar friend and she nearly groaned in orgasmic pleasure.

The man behind the island—who'd glanced up as she entered—gave her a smile. "Morning, Ariel."

"Hey, Steve." She hefted her cup, brushed some hair back from her eyes and yawned for what seemed to be the umpteenth time in two minutes. "Need coffee."

He tucked some blond hair behind his left ear. "Help yourself. I thought you might be by."

Steve Yost was a lean man. Sweet as the dickens and totally not her sexual type. Which was a pity, for she could use a friend with benefits—one who lived across the hall, even better. He was, however, a great neighbour and friend. His roommate, on the other hand, had her panties wet just by walking in the room.

She fixed her coffee then propped a hip against the platform where Steve worked and blessedly took that first life-giving drink. Hot or not, she couldn't function without this stuff. "How have you been?"

"Busy. Good, though. You?"

"Obviously not well enough to remember to bring coffee home after a trip so I have some in the apartment."

He smiled, a flash of straight white teeth against tanned skin. "How was Seattle?"

"Damn sight cooler than here, for one." She drank some more java and purred in contentment. Things were aligning right in her world. Today *could* be a good day now that she'd had some caffeine.

"And the wedding?"

She flexed her fingers about the mug. "Absolutely perfect. Roxi made such a beautiful bride." A grin. "Sam was pretty hot as well. So were the rest of the Marines standing up with him. And the ones in the audience."

Her friend, Roxi Mammon—now Roxi Hoch—had got married this past weekend. She and Roxi had served together in the Corps and Sam—her new husband—still did.

"Thanks for getting my mail," she said, falling silent when a leggy blonde strolled into view. One eyebrow rose and she knew exactly what room that woman had come from.

"This your girlfriend, Steve?" The question was asked with a thick Texas drawl.

"Nope. Our neighbour."

"Oh." Her smile came sugar-sweet. "I'm Daisy. Spent the night with Tuck."

*Daisy? Of course you are.* "Congratulations?" Ariel did her best to keep her emotions subdued. Hard to do when she longed to punch her in the nose. *I have no reason to be jealous. It's not like he's mine or anything.*

Before little Ms Daisy could say another word, the man himself ambled around the corner. Tuck Carter. Construction worker. Hot as sin. Not to mention the star player in many personal fantasies that had her reaching for the drawer that held a few toys.

Bronzed skin, jet black hair and brown eyes that could turn her to mush. He wore jeans—currently unbuttoned—that formed tight to his body, and nothing else. A smile split his bow-shaped lips when he spied her.

"Ariel. You're back." He poured himself some coffee and sat on a counter. "How was your trip?"

"Great. Looks like you're having fun."

His grin was intoxicating as usual and her panties dampened. Also, as usual.

"You know me."

"Not as well as some in this room," she tossed out casually.

"You have people just walk into your apartment?" Daisy asked, sidling up to Tuck and leaning against him, as if trying to put her claim on him.

"Ariel's not just anyone, she's our neighbour and yes,

229

she does," Tuck said without looking away from Ariel. "Jealous, Ariel?"

*Hell yeah!* She stood upright, lifted her mug and toasted him. "You wish." Attention on Steve, she gave him a smile. "Thanks for the elixir, hon. You saved my day. Catch ya later."

Then she walked out and back across the hall to her apartment where she sat on her couch and began opening her mail. The knock on her door wasn't all that unexpected. "It's open," she called out. An act she followed by taking a deep breath.

It was a good thing too, for in stepped Tuck. Still clad in only jeans, he filled her doorway with the width of his shoulders.

"You okay?" He sauntered in the apartment. In doing so, her pulse and core temperature skyrocketed.

"Why wouldn't I be? Got what I needed." She lifted her mug to show him.

He watched her intently before making himself comfortable on the love seat across from her. Lord, the man had muscles on muscles. A six pack was his abdomen and she had fantasies—numerous—about licking them. Licking stuff off them, trailing her tongue over the dips and swells.

# More books from
# Aliyah Burke

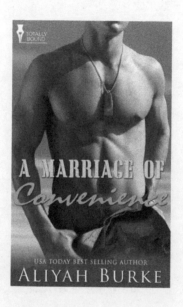

*A Naval pilot, a one night stand and years later a second chance, can they make it work this time?*

More books from
Aliyah Burke

USA TODAY BEST SELLING AUTHOR

IN AETERNUM

CASANOVA
IN
TRAINING

ALIYAH BURKE

Book one in the In Aeternum series

*A woman who is all about rules and a man who lives to break them.*

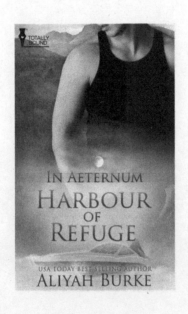

Book two in the In Aeternum series

*What happens in Monte Carlo stays…with you forever…
well, if you're one of the lucky ones.*

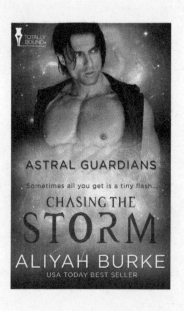

ASTRAL GUARDIANS

Sometimes all you get is a tiny flash...

CHASING THE
STORM

ALIYAH BURKE

USA TODAY BEST SELLER

Book one in the Astral Guardians series

*Sometimes all you get is a tiny flash…*

# About the Author

**Aliyah Burke**

Aliyah Burke is an avid reader and is never far from pen and paper (or the computer).

She is married to a career military man. They are owned by three Borzoi, and a DSH cat. She spends her days sharing time between work, writing, and dog training.

Aliyah Burke loves to hear from readers. You can find contact information, website details and an author profile page at https://www.totallybound.com/

Home of Erotic Romance